# STILL BEAUTY

*Cyrano Cayla*

www.cyranocayla.com

*Still Beauty* is a work of fiction.
The characters, incidents, and dialogues mentioned in this story are strictly fictional and the result of the author's imagination; however, most of the places where these incidents occur do exist in real life. All the factual information about the artists cited in the book has been obtained from renowned sources.
The opinions and actions depicted in the story do not necessarily reflect the author's.

Published in the United States of America by Goblet Press
6444 Longridge Rd, Mayfield Heights, OH 44124 - USA
Cover Design: Derek Murphy
ISBN: 0997543213
ISBN-13: 9780997543216
e-Book ISBN 978-0-9975432-0-9
Library of Congress Control Number: 2016908301
Goblet Press, Mayfield Heights, OH

# CHAPTERS

| | | |
|---|---|---|
| Chapter 1 | Minneapolis. Saturday, September 20, 2010 | 1 |
| Chapter 2 | Stockholm. Saturday, September 20, 2010 | 23 |
| Chapter 3 | Rome. Monday. | 37 |
| Chapter 4 | London. Tuesday. | 77 |
| Chapter 5 | Paris. Wednesday. | 123 |
| Chapter 6 | Liddell | 163 |
| Chapter 7 | Connie | 181 |
| Chapter 8 | Thursday, October 11, 2015 | 209 |

Epilogue 243
Author Biography 245

*Art is not what you see but what you make others see.*

**—Edgar Degas**

# CHAPTER 1
# MINNEAPOLIS. SATURDAY, SEPTEMBER 20, 2010

Connie stopped the car in the driveway, grabbed her cell phone from the passenger seat, and got out, leaving the key inside and the windows rolled down. She took slow, deep breaths as she walked to the front door of her house. The air smelled cool, crisp, and thin, with hints of pine and damp soil. She stopped to look at the flowerbeds in the front yard and then knelt down. Weeds were making their way through the dwindling brown mulch, encroaching on the rosebushes. She pulled them out one by one.

She had an assignment—write a three-hundred-word article for *Girls Now* magazine and e-mail it to Brenda, the editor in New York. The deadline kept getting closer, but there was always something sidetracking her. She made a pile of the weeds beside the flowerbed; she'd pick them up later. Brushing the dust off her hands, she walked to the mailbox and tugged out the thick pile of junk mail that packed it. Once inside the house, she threw the mishmash of brightly colored envelopes onto the kitchen counter without paying much attention. *What a waste.* As she washed her hands, the bright, clear sky painted blue the window over the kitchen's sink—a typical cool September morning in Minneapolis. The summer had been rainy, and the trees looked lush and green, gently rocking as the breeze combed their branches. The end of the sailing season was around the corner, and Lake Minnetonka remained busy with people enjoying the last days of warm weather—sailboats crisscrossed the ample blue surface while motorboats and Jet Skis buzzed from afar.

She sat on one of the wooden stools by the kitchen island and opened her laptop computer. "Pick a subject," she said out loud, "and break it down: introduction, main story, ending. Seventy-five words for the intro, a hundred and fifty for the main story, and seventy-five for the ending. Done!"

The hardest thing to do was find the subject. *Girls Now* was a teen magazine published in London and New York. *What will the kids want to read about?* She tapped her fingers on the countertop. What invariably frustrated Connie was that she was supposed to be "in tune," as Brenda the editor said, because she had two girls at home. Amanda and Stacey were sixteen and fourteen. *I don't know why I'm still doing this.* She rested her forehead on the back of her hand. With a dusty college degree in art history but no experience in the field, Connie still dreamed of writing for an art magazine. *But who'll hire a forty-seven-year-old housewife with zero background in the actual art world?*

She remembered her first attempts at poetry: longing and heartbreak—she was sixteen. It was not until her one and only trip to Europe, right after high school, that she realized that she could enjoy writing for a living.

The Europe Days, as she came to call that period, had been a golden age for her craft. With half-closed eyes, she smiled, treasuring the warm memories that came at their will. It was the first time she'd left the United States, and since she had made the trip with Deb, her only lifelong friend, it was the most memorable.

"Got it," Connie said out loud, back in the present. She would write about the six best things to do with friends on a Saturday. It would include breakfast at their favorite spot, window-shopping during the morning, squeezing in a light lunch before getting their nails done, trying on some shoes at the mall, and heading to the movies in the evening.

She felt proud of her ability to think fast and come up with what she needed at any given time. She started typing and didn't stop until she was done and satisfied with the article.

Connie e-mailed the file to Brenda and looked at the upper-right-hand corner of her computer: Saturday, 3:15 p.m. She smiled with satisfaction and closed her laptop.

Now it was time to relax. She turned the TV on and lay down on the squashy leather couch in the family room. The freelance, part-time writing job suited her and her schedule. And it made Nick, her husband, happy too. He always said that it was good that she had "something to do, whatever it is." After twenty-two years of marriage, they had managed to get to a "state of stillness," as Connie liked to think of it. It wasn't full of excitement but worked well enough for them to get things done and raise their children. *I can't complain.*

She zapped through the cable channels—volume muted—without much attention. Then a culinary channel featuring out-door cooking caught her eye.

The house was dead quiet. Amanda and Stacey were out with their church group and wouldn't be home until dinnertime, and as with any other Saturday when the weather allowed, Nick was drinking and golfing with friends.

She looked at her watch. *Four thirty. Where did the day go? Time to pick up Bryan.*

Once in the car, she glanced at her face in the rearview mir-ror. Time had added some gray and pale hues to her once-shiny brown hair. She still combed it with a part on the left side, letting it fall straight down to above her shoulders. A barrette clipped on the right side—an item that her mother, Amy, used to wear and Connie started using after Amy passed away—made Connie feel close to her. A snub nose; clear blue, almost gray eyes; and a shy smile were family features from her French mother's side of the family. Connie rarely laughed out loud; instead, her lips expanded sideways, never exposing her delicate teeth.

It was a short drive to her in-laws. Bryan came out of the house right after Connie gave two short honks, as if he and Nick's mother had been waiting for her arrival by the door. Pam quickly waved from behind the screen door and turned around, disappearing into the imposing three-story house. Bryan got into the car in silence and pulled his portable video game from his backpack.

"Hi, sweetie. Are you hungry?" Connie asked.

"Yeah…" said the twelve-year-old without taking his eyes off the little screen.

"Bryan. Look at me," she said.

Bryan lifted his blue eyes and met Connie's; she knew her smile was enough to bring him back to reality. She reached between the seats and poked his ribs.

"Stop! Please." He giggled among bursts of laughter.

They stopped at the grocery store on their way back home. Every time she was at the produce section, she thought of her French-born mother. *She was such a great cook.* Connie remembered going to the farmers' market with her; she recalled the excited state her mother used to get into. Connie could imagine her rapidly scanning all the bins, testing the firmness of the eggplants, and asking the vendors what day they had received the tomatoes. She used to smell the white peaches, and if they weren't ripened on the tree, she would toss them back in the bin with a hint of disdain. "They smell like nothing," she would say in her thick French accent. Even after all those years, every time Connie walked through the produce aisles at the supermarket, she felt that her mother walked with her, as though part of a subtle backdrop.

Connie picked out a few vegetables for a green salad and quickly headed to the cashier.

Back in the car her cell phone rang. She looked at the screen—Brenda, her editor. *Maybe there was something wrong with my submission?*

"Hi, Connie. Sorry for calling on a Saturday. Am I interrupting? Do you have a minute?"

"Yes, I mean, no, not interrupting. What can I do for you, Brenda?"

"Have you heard about *Life with Style*? It's a biweekly, focused on travel, art, spas, and whatnot." She didn't wait for Connie's answer. "It doesn't matter," Brenda continued, speaking really fast, her stress obvious. "We've decided to write an article series on four different pieces of art that people might know or have heard about, to be released in four installments. It will be called *Europe with Style*. The target is our average reader—not too artsy, but a fairly educated traveler. Four pages and around fifteen hundred words each."

"I see."

"The works of art are scattered across three different cities in Europe. The UK editor, who is also a photographer, and I were going to travel together to actually write it as we saw it—a bit about each city's background, some travel tips, and finally the review of the artworks themselves. You must be wondering what all this has to do with you, right?"

"A bit," Connie said with a calm voice. At least nothing was wrong with her article for *Girls Now*.

Brenda drew a long tired breath. "My husband and I broke up last night, after twenty-seven years of marriage. Twenty-seven."

"Brenda, I am so sorry to hear that." *Why would she tell me that?* Connie's thoughts rushed in different directions, as she didn't know what to expect next.

"As you can imagine, I am not in a position to appreciate any art right now. I need someone to fill in for me. I called a few people, but of course, they are all busy. Then I looked into your résumé. You have a degree in art history, and I like your writing style, so I wondered if you would be interested." She gave a loud sigh. "God, this is so unprofessional!"

"It's okay, Brenda. I…I'm not sure. Wow. I would have to ask Nick—oh, sorry. Nick is my husband." She regretted using the word *ask*. "I need to talk to him. I have three kids, after all. How long would it take? What cities?"

"You'd leave tomorrow, Sunday, for Rome. There, on Monday, you'd go to Galleria Borghese in the morning, where Bernini's *Rape of Proserpina* is, and then to Saint Peter's in the afternoon, for a look at Michelangelo's *Pietà*. Tuesday morning you'd fly to London to see Rodin's *The Kiss* at the Tate, and finally, Paris on Wednesday for Monet's *Water Lilies* at l'Orangerie museum. Your flight back is on Thursday, and you'd be home Thursday night. It's three days in Europe plus two travel days. Deadline for the articles is the following Friday. Pay will be double what you are getting for writing for *Girls Now* and all the trip expenses are covered—not to mention that you'll be exposed to adult readers. If the articles are good, you could get more work from us." Brenda paused, catching her breath. As the phone line remained quiet, Connie's heartbeats grew louder. Brenda finally continued. "I need to know now, or say, within the next half hour. I have a friend on standby who is a great writer. He preferred not to do it, but he'll reconsider if I can't find anybody.

"What do you think?" Brenda sounded exhausted; she clearly wanted this to be over and done with.

Connie's mind was a blank. She felt she needed more than half an hour. She needed days to think about it—time to discuss it with Nick and the kids, to organize things, buy things, prepare. But there was no time. This was her opportunity to go back to Europe. Old memories of images, sounds, and smells surfaced. They felt new and fresh as if they had been alive, just waiting for the right moment to come back: the smell of baked bread in the mornings as she walked past the doors of the small Parisian bakeries; the grand boulevards framed with mighty plane trees and thousands of chirping sparrows crisscrossing the air; girls and boys at the park, after school, laughing. She pictured herself sitting at a café, her notebook and pen resting on a small, round, marble-topped table. She could grasp the way she used to feel while she wrote poems—light, ethereal, luminous—and those never-ending afternoons as she sketched at the Louvre. Her heart was beating harder now. *What if Brenda calls this guy? He's probably waiting for her call. Maybe he is even packing. He'll do it for sure. And I will have missed going back to Europe.*

"I'm in." She heard her own voice, unfamiliar and distant, saying out loud. She closed her eyes, and for one second, she pretended that nothing had happened, that nothing had changed. Words were just that: words. For one second she thought that she could drive back home as if the phone had never rung: she would cook dinner, chitchat with Nick about his day, clear up the table after dinner, and watch TV before going to bed, just like any other Saturday. But she opened her eyes and realized she had committed herself. She had a made a single-handed decision on a whim, without thinking about anybody but herself. The blood rushed to her ears. Her right hand wrapped the steering wheel tightly as she looked for some physical support; all the while, arguments assaulted her in her mind, screaming why she should have not accepted.

"Oh, perfect," Brenda said with open relief. "I'll e-mail the details in a minute; call me if you need anything. Thank you so much, Connie, really."

"You are welcome," Connie said with a hint of uncertainty.

Connie dropped the phone on the passenger seat, her eyes staring straight ahead. *What did I just do?* All the reasons why she shouldn't have accepted took a real shape: Who would take care of Bryan while she was gone for almost the whole week? Pam and

Joe were lovely in-laws but not the kind of grandparents who would take care of a boy for more than a few hours. What about the girls? Stacey had a math test on Tuesday, and Connie was supposed to help her study; Amanda had the last soccer game of the season on Thursday, and Connie had volunteered to help at the after-game party. Nick had his night out with his friends every Wednesday, so who would stay at the house with the kids? *And the dentist appointment on Monday morning.*

"Oops, my passport!" Her eyes opened wide.

"What?" Bryan leaned forward, poking his head between the front seats.

"Ah, yes, it should still be good from the trip to Mexico; it was only two years ago."

"Where are you going, Mom?"

Connie turned to look at Bryan. "Back to Europe. I'm going back to Europe," she whispered with a quivering smile.

Back at home, Connie dimmed the lights and scattered a few scented candles around the room and on the table; her iPod played quiet instrumental music as she set the table with the Sunday plates and silverware. She placed her mother's cloth napkins with delicacy to the left of each plate, folding them in triangles. She made sure the water glasses were to the left of the wineglasses, which in turn she aligned with the knives. She placed the ice-water pitcher at one end of the table, walked two steps back, and glanced at the setup. It was ready.

Amanda dragged her feet as she crossed the dining room and sighed, letting her body slump into the chair, making no attempt to disguise her gloomy mood. Stacey ran down the stairs, rushing to her place; she looked excited about going to stay overnight at her friend's house after dinner. Bryan smiled as he lit the candles.

Connie carried in a large plate with the broiled sockeye salmon and placed it at the center of the table. Nick, looking over from the family room, turned off the TV and came into the dining room.

"Need help?" he said halfheartedly.

"Bring the salad, would you?"

Nick nodded, edged around the wide marble countertop, and came back with a large bowl. He pushed a few glasses around and put the salad of watercress, Parmesan shavings, and roasted almonds next to his plate. He looked at his phone, and without saying a word, went back to the kitchen to get the wine.

"Which one?" he called out to Connie, looking at the options in the fridge. "There is an Italian Pinot Grigio, some French stuff, and a Sauvignon Blanc."

"Bring the Sauvignon Blanc. It's a nice one, from New Zealand." Connie moved the salad bowl next to the basket of warm bread, and repositioned the glasses that Nick had moved. "How was your day, honey?" she asked Nick, trying to catch his eye.

"Uneventful," he said, returning to the dining room. He handed the bottle of wine to Connie and sat down at the far end of the table.

"Amanda, dear, can you bring me the corkscrew, please?" Connie asked.

Amanda moved slowly; she was somewhere else. Connie felt a tug of guilt; Amanda had a crush on a boy who didn't seem to care for her. *Another reason why I shouldn't go to Europe. I should stay with her.*

The wine was crisp, fresh, and lively, with the typical upfront tanginess and strong citrus scent of a Marlborough Sauvignon Blanc. "Delicious!" she said, looking at Nick. "What do you think?"

"It's fine."

Connie lowered her eyes; she put her glass back on the table and served the salmon. *Back when we met at college, he was nice to be around, and always smiling. He's the same Nick. He is just tired; he'll understand about the trip.*

"Stacey, what are your plans for tonight?" Nick asked as he munched a mouthful of bread.

"We're gonna watch three movies. Jenn got the Blu-rays today. Her dad remodeled the basement and turned it into a movie theater. It's pretty awesome!"

"I bet her dad bought that popcorn machine he was looking into. He likes to do things the right way," Nick added.

"Yeah, he bought a huge one! And there's gonna be a lot of us too: Jenn, me, Jenn's sister, her mom, and her three cousins."

"An all-girls night, that's exciting," Connie said and looked at Nick with an uneasy expression. *I'll talk to him after dropping Stacey off.*

⊨⊨

They left the house right after dinner. Connie drove slowly, she didn't like driving after drinking, not even one glass.

"Call me tomorrow when you want me to pick you up. No later than ten; we're going to mass in the morning."

"Yeah, Mom." Stacey closed the car door and jogged the short distance to her friend's front door.

⊨⊨

Back at home, Connie wandered through the kitchen; the lights were off except for the microwave's soft, yellow glow. The muted rumble of the dishwasher mixed with the sounds of the TV coming from the family room. She opened the fridge, pulled the open bottle of wine, and poured some into her glass. As she put the bottle back in the fridge, she noticed the neatly piled plastic containers with the dinner leftovers. That had been Amanda. *Nick probably didn't do anything.* She closed the fridge and headed for the family room. As she went past the sink, she saw Nick's glass in it, with the wine untouched, and two empty beer bottles standing next to it. *What a waste of wine. And he could have washed his glass.*

Nick and Bryan were on the couch, the big-screen TV flickering with cartoons and Nick's iPad reflecting on his face. Amanda was probably in her room. As Connie sat down next to Nick, Bryan moved to the floor and, without turning his eyes away from the TV, lay down on the carpet, elbows on the floor and his head cradled in his hands.

"Stacey was so excited; she'll call tomorrow around ten," Connie said, breaking the silence. Nick didn't answer. "Hey, honey, I need to tell you something." Her tone was quiet, expectant; she couldn't disguise a nervous smile as she spoke.

"Hmm," Nick mumbled while his finger moved up and down on his iPad.

"I had a call from Brenda; she needed a person to fill in for her on a trip to Europe and write a four-piece article about it." Connie was staring at Nick as she spoke, but his eyes were still on the small rectangular screen. "It's a five-day trip, and then another week for the writing time. I accepted. My flight is tomorrow afternoon at five."

"What?" Nick looked at Connie for what seemed to her the first time in days, maybe months. But his eyes were particularly distant, cold. "What do you mean tomorrow? What are you talking about?"

"Listen, honey, if I don't do it, I will regret it for the rest of my life. I had to accept, or she was going to call someone else!" Connie was unable to hide her childlike joy.

"What about talking to me before making a decision like that?" Nick raised his voice. "Damn. What the hell is wrong with you?" He threw his iPad across the couch. It made a loud thud as it hit the armrest. Bryan turned around to look. "Let's talk about this," Nick said. He pushed his fists down with contained anger, lifting himself up, and headed to their bedroom. Connie followed his heavy steps and closed the door behind her.

"This is really important to me. I'm feeling, I don't know, excited. Happy. You know how much I've always wanted to go back to Europe; I'll be home on Thursday. It's only five days. Come on, Nick."

She realized this was the first time in a long while that she'd spoken about the way she felt, about something that she really cared for. About herself. It felt like a mixture of guilt and pride, as if she were savoring an undeserved luxury.

Nick seemed to have pulled himself together, at least in appearance. "What if I did the same?" he asked rhetorically, moving his arms in wide circles. "What if I just decided to go out fishing with the guys for a week?" He paused, as if expecting an answer. "No. It doesn't work like that. You just don't do that, Connie. We are not kids anymore. I don't know what you were thinking, but you're gonna call Brenda and cancel. Let's pretend this never happened. Okay?" He produced a smug smile and dried his sweaty hands on his jeans.

Her mouth quivered. "I don't like the way you're talking to me. And as you said, we're not kids anymore. I have to pack. Excuse me." She walked past him toward the closet, yanked it open, and started pulling clothes out, making a small pile on the bed.

"You're crazy, like your father," he mumbled, shaking his head in disapproval. He slowly walked out of the room, but then he slammed the door behind him.

Connie couldn't keep her emotions in check any longer. She burst into tears, and covering her face with her hands, she tried to muffle the erupting sobs. Shortly after, she heard Nick slamming the guest-room door.

She closed her eyes tightly, forcing herself to stop crying—she decided at that very moment that she would not cry about anything that Nick said. Then she pulled a tissue from the box on the nightstand and quickly dried her eyes. Once she calmed down, Connie returned to her packing. *What does Dad have to do with this? He's under treatment; he's not crazy.*

Robert, Connie's father, had been diagnosed with post-traumatic stress disorder shortly after Aimée, Connie's mother, known in America as Amy, had unexpectedly died of a stroke in their bed nine years ago. Ever since then, Robert had cut off contact with friends and family, had neglected his personal appearance and the keeping of his house, which he rarely left, and had been particularly rude with Nick. During a fit of rage, Robert exclaimed that Nick was no more than an ignorant brute, whom he did not want to see ever again. Nick had not referred to Robert ever since—until this night.

As the only child, Connie had been alongside her father almost constantly since the first symptoms had appeared: trying to make him follow the doctors' instructions, cleaning up the house for him, making sure that he was taking the antidepressants, and sharing what now seemed to be his one and only interest—the life and work of Michelangelo, the Italian sculptor and painter. Connie had slowly learned to enjoy the endless conversations about art, although many times just monologues, that her father liked to indulge in. Her degree in art history had come in handy, if only to make sense of, and even somewhat enjoy, her father's long dissertations.

Piled on the bed were all the clothes she thought she'd need for the trip. Then she took a long, elegant, navy-blue dress from the closet, held it in front of her, and examined it carefully. *I can't believe I've never used it. Maybe on this trip.* She shrugged and laid it on the bed, covering the scattered patchwork of clothes ready to be packed.

She went down to the basement, where she kept the luggage, and looked around with half-closed eyes for her large suitcase. There, by the wine rack. As she picked up the empty hard-shell blue bag, a red-capped bottle resting at the bottom of the wine rack caught her eye; it was one of her mother's many favorite wines from her natal France. "Côtes du Rhône is my thinking friend," Connie remembered her mother saying. "It's gentle and unpretentious. It quietly accompanies me, and it helps me settle my troubled thoughts."

Connie dragged the big blue bag up the stairs with one hand while carrying the bottle of red wine with the other. *I never thought I'd ever use Mom's words.*

The alarm went off at 6:10 a.m., cutting the thick silence that filled her bedroom. Connie stretched her arm and pushed the clock buttons at random until it stopped; then she slowly opened her eyes and shifted around to the empty side of the bed, slapping the cold linens where Nick should have been. She peeled the sheets away with one swing and walked to the bathroom; a few minutes later she was out the front door in her running outfit, headed for the jogging trail.

The morning was cool, the sky looked like an expanding mass of azure, and the air felt fresh and young, like a new beginning. Connie was on the move. The trail, after gently meandering along the lakeshore, disappeared into the large wildlife reserve adjacent to it. Some parts were open and wide, while others, shady and narrow, pressed the tracks with trees and overgrown shrubs from both sides. Connie nodded at a slim older woman who slowly jogged in the opposite direction. Fall was coming early, and although it was only September, a few trees had already let go their brownish garment, covering the trail with random patches of fluffy fallen leaves.

She always chose the same path. But even though she had been running on that same trail since she was a teenager, she still got excited at the sight of a squirrel, a deer, or a bird. She always ran alone. It was her moment without any pressures from the external world, and once she was in motion, memories came to her mind with no apparent rhyme or reason, like a soft stream that she enjoyed letting flow.

She thought about the night before. Nick's sarcastic smile and preachy tone during their argument still annoyed her.

"I won't think about last night!" she said out loud, pushing that bitter taste away.

The idea of writing about art again brought her back to her college days. She saw herself sitting at her desk, writing her graduation thesis, surrounded by art books and her own notes on appreciation. "Art is another expression of life, and to understand it, we have to live through it. Art is not something static that you can read or be told about," were Professor Patterson's final words at the graduation speech. She liked him. Back then he was in his late sixties, a rather small-framed man with calm, bright eyes.

Connie's mother always made sure that the traditions from her homeland were respected in their house, creating in Connie a strong pull toward France, even though she had only been there once. She remembered when she and her friend Deb visited her mother's home village of Bandol in the south part of the country. They hiked the pebbly hills to take a look at the terraced vineyards that had been on those steep hills since Roman times, weathering the cold mistral, the baking heat, and the endless passing of time. Once up at the top of the hill, they turned around and gazed at the small valley patched with red-shingled houses threaded by zig-zagging pathways. They held their hands up together and laughed. *Nineteen years old. A beautiful and carefree trip. I still remember the wines we tasted that day.* The sun gave a particularly warm and intense light, bathing the vines and the workers alike. She wondered if Monsieur Gagolin, the most quintessentially French of the many winemakers she met along the way, was still alive. She recalled his thin, gray hair, slightly overgrown, combed back but always somewhat loose; his fiery small black eyes framed by a couple of hefty eyebrows; and his angular nose and thin lips. Monsieur Gagolin was an eccentric—and a man of few smiles—who spoke no English and made no effort to understand it. He was the son of an older era: a proud and inflexible perfectionist, especially with his excellent wines. A self-taught poet, when he recited a poem or a line from the classics, he held the wineglass from the base and moved it around as he spoke, catching the attention of his audience. *We all thought you were going to spill the wine all over the place!*

Gagolin was just one of Amy's many friends and acquaintances from her youth whom she didn't see again after she left for America. But Gagolin had been the only one who gave Connie a letter addressed to his long-lost friend.

Connie took the trail that ran along the shore, heading back to the house. She still had to arrange some help for the days she would be gone. The run, the brackish smell of water, and the sense of openness always uplifted her spirits.

She walked through the front door and across the family room. Nick was watching a recorded football game on the huge flat-screen TV.

"Hey," he said with a relaxed tone. "How was your run? Oh my God! I can't believe he missed that touchdown!"

"It was great. The lake is beautiful today," she said as she headed to the bathroom.

Stacey called at ten o'clock.

⇒⊹ ⊹⇐

The blond fourteen-year-old teenager dragged her feet into the minivan. "Looks like you haven't slept that much," Amanda said to her sleepy-eyed sister.

"Nah. I'll get twenty minutes while Dad drives to church," she said and closed her eyes.

The mass seemed longer than usual. Connie glanced at her watch. Eleven thirty—it would soon be over. She mentally checked that she had packed everything she needed for the trip. She gave Nick a hurried look, but he didn't look back at her.

Once the service was over, they went straight back to the car. Any other day they would have stayed around a little longer to chat

16

with friends, but not on that Sunday. Connie pulled her cell phone from her purse; Deb had texted.

"Sorted," Connie said as she slid into the minivan passenger seat. "Deb will stop by in the afternoons to make sure all is fine."

Nick didn't acknowledge Connie's words.

"Why? Where are you going, Mom?" Amanda interjected.

"Hey, kids," Connie said, shifting around to look at them in the backseat, "I have to travel to Europe for three days. It's for work. I found out last night. I leave this afternoon, and I will be back on Thursday night. Please be nice to one another, okay?" She tried to conceal her anxiety with a lighthearted tone.

"Okay," Stacey said nonchalantly.

"That's awesome!" Amanda added.

"I wish I could go with you." Bryan looked excited.

Connie turned her gaze to the road ahead with an uneasy smile. She had to tell her father about the trip, but she also wanted to be away from Nick. "Drop me off at Dad's house, please."

"As you wish," Nick said.

"Amanda, dear, would you take my car and come pick me up, please?"

"Yeah, sure."

They remained in silence for the rest of the short trip.

Robert had a well-kept front garden, with daisies on one side of the driveway and clumps of lavender on the opposite side. He cut the grass frequently, trimming the lawn's borders in precise lines. Amy had also planted rosebushes—which now look tired after a season's bloom—along the front of the house, under the wide dining-room windows.

"Hello, Dad! Pruning down the roses?" Connie said with a lively tone as she stepped out of the car. Her father's therapist advised her to always sound gently upbeat when talking to him.

"Connie! It's so good to see you!" Robert's eyes lit up. He put the pruning shears down, took off his gloves, and watched his daughter approaching him. "Look at you, my dear," he said softly with his arms open, palms facing the sky.

Nick and the kids got out of the car and followed Connie.

"Robert." Nick shook Robert's hand.

Bryan, Stacey, and Amanda took turns hugging him. "Grandpa, how've you been?" Amanda asked.

"What a nice surprise!" he said.

"We'd better get going; I have stuff to do," Nick said.

"Ah, yes, get going." Robert looked him in the eyes. "Connie, are you staying?" he said, turning his back on Nick.

"Yeah, Dad. I'll stay for a bit."

"I'll be back in a few minutes," Amanda said.

"I'll come with you," Bryan added.

"Fantastic!" Robert said, taking Connie's arm. "I have some coffee ready. You want some? Let's go inside."

Nick got back in the car. The kids followed him. The doors closed, and Nick pulled out of the driveway in a rush. Connie and Robert stepped inside the house.

Connie sat at the dining-room table where she and her parents had shared so many dinners together through the years. She slowly contemplated the austere room. Somehow she felt that she could recognize the scent of her mother but immediately realized that she was just remembering it.

Robert came out of the kitchen with two small cups of coffee on their saucers and gently placed them on the table. "I was just thinking about the Sistine ceiling. Do you remember the nudes in detail? Michelangelo went through appalling hardships while he painted it." He looked up and brought his palm close to his face. "After looking at the ceiling from this close for so long, he lost his sense of balance, and some of his sight too. To look at things, he had to bring them really, really close to his eyes, as close as the ceiling was to him while he painted." He sat down. "And the fresco technique is such a difficult one, the plaster has to have just the right humidity or the colors will not turn out as intended. Isn't it an enormous challenge for a single individual? Plus, he had to deal with the artistic side of it: the expression, the form, the color, and the essence of the story he was trying to tell." He had a sip of coffee while Connie looked at him with warm eyes. "*He* is not painted even once," Robert said, putting his cup back on the saucer.

"Who is *he?*"

"*He? Jesus!* But he did paint the ass of God!" He emitted a short laugh and continued. "What a great achievement. The painted God is turning around after creating the sun and the moon, but his robe was somewhat loose. Do you remember? It's toward the Jonah end of the chapel. I've always imagined Pope Julius's face when he saw it for the first time: God's butt." He shook his head, smiling. "Michelangelo—a sensitive man with such an enormous courage. Did I show you the poem I wrote for him? Well, in fact, it's a series of poems. The first one is dedicated to his Roman *Pietà*." His voice was low, and his bright eyes were shining with feeling.

"No, you didn't show me the poems. I would love to read them," Connie said with enthusiasm, as she did every time her father felt excited, which was not very often.

Robert sprang up off his chair and disappeared down the hall. A moment later he was back with a tattered brown folder.

"Here," he said, "gotta be one of these." His hands shuffled the papers around, and then he emptied the folder on the table, "Ha! I knew it." He pulled out a worn-out legal-size paper and handed it to Connie. "Read it, please, and then read this one," he said, picking another sheet from the pile. "This is also good."

She read the poems to herself, slowly, and as she did so, she felt transported to an imaginary world, where time stood still and form and meaning melded together.

Amanda entered the house while Connie was reading. Bryan trailed a few steps behind, playing a video game. "What are those?" Amanda asked, pointing at the pile of papers.

"Grandpa's poems. Want to read some?" Connie asked.

Amanda picked up one of the poems and sat down next to Connie. Robert came back from the kitchen with another cup of coffee and placed it in front of her.

Robert went on. "Even during his years painting the Sistine, he kept signing his letters as 'Michelangelo, Sculptor.' He thought that painting was a lesser art than sculpture. Can you believe it? But he took on the ceiling commission regardless. Why? Because the pope had asked. Well, I guess it wasn't that easy to say no to the pope, but still, what a pious man Michelangelo was. What a powerful faith he had. You know what, Connie? Sometimes I wish I had a stronger faith. I wish I could be as fervent a believer as Michelangelo was. He also wrote. His poems were so sublime—reflections of an exceptional soul."

Amanda put down the piece of paper she had in her hand. "I love the way you talk, Grandpa."

"Would you like some fig jam? I made the jam myself. It's delicious. You have to try it." Robert jumped out of his chair again and rushed to the kitchen. "Bryan! Come try my jam."

He came back with a jar, a plate with crackers, and a spoon.

"Dad, I am leaving for Europe tonight. A job came up. I'll be back on Thursday."

"Ah, a true blessing." Robert's face lit up. "You will have to tell me all about it when you come back. Do you like the jam?" he asked with a wide smile.

Nick stayed silent through the whole drive to the airport. Connie had preferred using a car service, but for some reason Nick insisted on taking her. She looked out the window with eyes lost on the passing buildings: *His stupid pride. But what if he is right, and this trip is a mistake? So be it. For once in my life I'll do something for myself. So be it.*

They stopped by the Delta Airlines terminal. Nick popped the trunk open from the inside, and they all got out of the minivan.

"I will miss you, baby," Connie said, kissing Bryan on both cheeks. "I love you."

"Me too, Mom."

Amanda and Stacey, in turn, hugged their mother in silence, tenderly. They had sensed the tension growing between their parents, and Connie realized that it was their way of staying out of the quarrel but quietly siding with her.

Nick pulled the big blue bag from the trunk and put it on the asphalt by the curbside. "Have fun," he mumbled, and got back in the minivan.

*He didn't even care to take off his sunglasses.*

Connie swung her purse over her shoulder, pulled the heavy bag onto the sidewalk, and headed to the airport's entrance without turning around. The large transparent glass door opened wide in front of her, and a fresh breeze came from the inside, caressing her face. She smiled and walked through the door.

"Small latte, please, and a chocolate-chip croissant," she said to the barista. Coffee in hand, she picked a spot at a nearby table and watched her surroundings. She saw a world on the move. A constant flow of families, businesspeople, and elderly travelers—men and women from all walks of life going somewhere. Regardless of their diversity, they all shared a certain sameness: the subtle rush as they walked through the terminal, and the slight sense of uncertainty while looking at the departure screens. They all shared a moment in time in a very crowded place that nobody belonged to. They were all in transit. They would all be gone in a matter of hours, maybe even minutes, and a new wave of people would replace them, restarting the ongoing cycle, over and over again, day after day.

She saw the light of excitement in the small kids' eyes, happy to be going somewhere; in the big families carrying an assortment of bags, backpacks, and strollers; but also in the lonely travelers searching for an experience, hungry for memories.

She felt content to be by herself. There was no one to talk to, and no one to attend to. No listening to complaints, no putting up with Nick's indifference. *Funny. All these people surround me, but I feel completely alone. It's so relaxing.*

Time passed by faster than she'd expected. Connie boarded the plane and sank low in the business-class seat. She felt nervous about the trip, but maybe more so about the way her departure had played out—a quarrel with Nick and a hurried explanation to the kids. It felt as if she had run away from them.

The plane took off, and the beverage service started. After a few glasses of Brunello de Montalcino, her mind and body relaxed; she turned in her seat, closed her eyes, and covered herself with the soft, thin blanket she had been given. The images of the day blurred and mixed with memories of her first visit to France, as the monotonous resonance of the cabin lulled her to sleep.

# CHAPTER 2
# STOCKHOLM. SATURDAY, SEPTEMBER 20, 2010

Liddell paddled as hard as he could. His kayak seemed to fly over the cold water. Sweat beaded on his skin beneath the neoprene suit, and his heart's violent beating pounded in his chest, resonating in his temples. He was far away from the shore, but he felt secure—water had always been his element. He was alone, as usual. The salted sea air filled his lungs, the sun's reflections on the water filled his eyes, and all the while scattered memories populated his mind.

With eyes lost on the horizon, he remembered sitting by Johanne, his grandmother, back in Cape Town, in the backyard of her small cottage by the sea. He used to go there every summer while she was alive. *So long ago, but still so present.* At dusk they would look at the shape of the clouds and the way the sun's rays cut through them. As it got darker, the dwindling light would turn the yellows into orange, then red and dark purple, until the deep gray tones arrived, announcing the inevitable darkness. "God is the greatest painter. Look at his canvas, right in front of us," she used to say. *I believed in your god too, Grandma.*

Liddell found solace at sea; something about the constant state of change of such an immense mass of a single unchanging element captivated him.

Born in South Africa, he was the only child of a Dutch mother and a Scottish father. His parents had moved from London when Sean, his father, got a position at the British embassy in Pretoria. Soon afterward, when his mother got pregnant, Johanne moved from Amsterdam to help her daughter with the baby, and she never left.

The shore was closer now. Two seagulls flew low above his head, under the clear and cold sky of Tyresö, a few miles south of Stockholm. Splashes of cold water spattered his face as he paddled through the breaking waves. Back at the shore, he propped himself out of the kayak and pulled his neoprene suit off.

"That was a relaxing run, wasn't it?" he commented out loud. He took his duffel bag from the Land Rover's trunk, put on dry clothes, and shoved the kayak up onto the car roof. He pulled a large-lens camera from the backseat and took several photos of the shore, the seagulls, and the sea.

The drive back home was all too familiar; after nine years of doing it at least once a week, he had memorized every turn on the road.

"Ah! Can't wait till Monday," he said, pressing the gas pedal harder. During his youth in South Africa, he became obsessed with traveling. That obsession had remained with him through the years, and every time a departure day approached, he got anxious. As he drove through the green hills of Tyresö, the yearning spirit of Vivaldi's Violin Concerto no. 222 in D Major harmonized with the winding landscape around him.

He looked at the clock; he would be home before noon. Sigrid and the kids would be busy cooking Saturday lunch, and given the long hours that she worked during the week—and his upcoming trip—it was an event he would not miss, at least not that day.

He approached his elegant, three-story, rationalist-style house. Decorated with large sections of pale-brown hardwood planks and thick-glass exterior finishes, it rested out of sight from the country road, standing at the end of a long driveway that meandered through a maze of pine trees—and had no neighbors. He parked the car in the garage and quietly entered the house through the kitchen door. Sigrid was by the stainless-steel impeccable stove, one hand stirring the contents of a cast-iron pot and the other holding her mobile phone. Rutger, just turned nine, was playing cards with Klas, Sigrid's twelve-year-old son from her first marriage.

"Dad!" The boys cried in unison, jumping out their chairs and running to Liddell's arms.

"You'll love the meatballs we made. Mum used an old recipe from a very, very old book," Klas said, pressing his head against Liddell's chest.

"Do you want to play cards with us?" Rutger asked.

"Of course!"

Sigrid put her phone down and poured a glass of Riesling for Liddell, leaving it on the counter next to him. "I'll take the boys to school on Monday. Elga will pick them up and stay with them until I get back from work. This trip of yours came at such a bad time."

"What are you playing?" Liddell asked Klas.

"Uno."

Sigrid went on, "I have a really busy week ahead, and you will be visiting museums in Europe trying to look interested. Nonsense."

Rutger and Klas looked at Liddell, waiting to see his reaction. "Uno, my favorite game. Give me a few minutes, boys."

Liddell left the kitchen and in silence walked down the long corridor that led to the main bathroom. He took a shower, dressed casually, and went to his studio at the back of the house. His large oak desk was covered with thick folders and prints of buildings plans. A calculator sat on a corner, next to his computer screen. Hundreds of books were meticulously arranged by theme on a floor-to-ceiling, double-deep bookcase covering the largest wall in the room. A big window behind his rolling leather chair overlooked the massive backyard.

The house was one of the many properties that Sigrid's family owned, their deep Swedish roots going back hundreds of years on both sides of her family.

Liddell opened his e-mail in-box. He was waiting to hear from his friend Will, UK editor for *Life with Style* magazine.

There it was, the travel and hotel information along with his itinerary. He looked through the e-mail and read the names of the hotels out loud, trying to remember if he had stayed at any of them before. There was a note from Will at the end.

Hey, mate. Ready for Monday?
Be aware that the American editor in chief
of the magazine will travel with you.
I'll let her know that you'll be going in my place.
If she asks why I didn't go, you don't know.
I don't think she'll care, anyway. Her name is
Brenda Greenberg, a very polite woman,
and very well versed in art indeed. She will guide
you through the works of art and most likely
advise you on their meaning. You won't need to do much
besides taking photos. Call me if you need to.
Cheers. Will.

*You told me an employee was coming, not the editor in chief.* He sighed, turned off the screen, and slowly walked back to the kitchen.

"Let's play. I'm feeling lucky today!" he said and sat next to the boys.

"Yay!" The kids laughed while Rutger's small hands wiped the table, gathering the cards in a big pile.

"Tomorrow, Sunday," Liddell said as Rutger drew the cards, "we'll go to a place you've never been before. It's a hidden spot I discovered today." Liddell took a sip of his wine.

"Where is it, Dad? Is it close to the shore?" Klas asked. His birth father had left when the boy was two years old. He never visited again, and Liddell had become his father ever since he moved into the house.

"I will give you a few clues. Let me see," he said, "this place is on the water, but it's not a boat; it has a roof, but nobody lives in there. What else? Oh yes, it has a door to the woods and a door to the sea. Can you guess what it is?"

"I know, I know!" Rutger said, raising his arm like he did in school. "It's a big, big tree that is right on the water, and it's the house for a family of birds, and it has a big hole in it so the birds can fly to the sea or to the woods."

"No, but that was a very good guess. Klas, what do you think?"

"I think it's the small pond by the rocks that goes under the cave. Do you remember, Dad? We discovered it when I was four, but we never went there again."

"Good memory, but no."

"What time is your flight on Monday?" Sigrid asked from the kitchen.

Liddell opened his eyes wide, exaggerating surprise, making the boys laugh. "Seven thirty in the morning. I have a car service to the airport arranged for five thirty. I land in Rome at midmorning."

"I don't know how Will gets away with it, but I don't like it. What if they found out?"

"Who knows? Maybe they'd fire him, or maybe nothing would happen. He has nobody to report to besides the general manager of the publishing group. They have thirty-two different magazines, and Will is a master at passing unnoticed." He had a sip of wine and continued, "The only thing I care about is that I get to travel for free to really nice places, and he does the writing."

"Whatever. The food is ready, guys. Clean up the table, please," Sigrid said and put the lid on the saucepan.

⚔ ⚔

They all dispersed after the short meal; the boys turned the TV on and sat on the couch. Sigrid turned on the dishwasher and took her purse.

"Are you leaving?" Liddell asked.

"I have a meeting. It's about the website," she replied, looking at her cell phone.

"On a Saturday afternoon?"

"The presale of the new apartments in Torsvik is around the corner, and we are running behind schedule on digital media. Besides—what's the problem?" Sigrid was the marketing director at her family's real-estate development company.

Liddell turned around and headed to the studio, closing the door behind him.

He had a lot of work to do before the trip. As a consultant engineer for two major timber companies, he was used to working long hours from home. *Advancing a week's work is just too much. One more reason to cancel the trip.* He sighed with resignation, sat on his leather rolling chair, and opened the folder in front of him. It was time to work.

⚔ ⚔

A gentle beeping sound came from his cell phone, announcing the start of his fifteen-minute break. He picked it up and turned the alarm off. Four hours were gone. He stood up and went over to the bookcase, where his eyes wandered among the books, scanning the titles. He stopped at one tiny volume, Cicero's *On the Good Life*. He gently pulled it from the shelf and caressed the worn-out hardbound cover. A birthday present from his father when he turned

28

twelve, it was the first adult book that he'd ever read, and the one that he always took with him on his early travels. Cicero's clear, exquisite style and ideas made a huge impression in him. Ever since, he had indulged in the classics with a passion. The book's simple but strong binding reminded him of the restrained and formal atmosphere in his house during his childhood.

The distant sound of the doorbell pulled him out of his reverie. Liddell left the studio and headed to the door, but Sigrid, who was back, had already opened it. His mother-in-law walked in, closing the door behind her.

"Hello, Mum," Sigrid said. "I just came back from a meeting and was about to make some tea."

"Oh, I'd love some, it got cold outside."

"Hello, Aina." Liddell walked into the kitchen and gave her two kisses.

"Liddell, dear, I haven't seen you in days! Sigrid says that you are working too much."

"Just the usual amount, Aina. I'm fine. What about you? How's the development going?"

"We finally got all the permits last week. Now we're waiting on the final agreement with the investors."

"You'll love the web page, Mum," Sigrid interjected. "I found this great designer, Harry. He's so creative. We are putting together this virtual-tour feature that lets you walk through the apartments."

"Harry? Has he been at the office?" Aina asked.

"No, we've been meeting at his place. But you know the cool thing about it? You can change the furniture, flooring, wall colors, lighting fixtures, and kitchen finishes. Everything! Do you remember when we had the printed catalogs? What a waste of time and paper!"

*Harry.* Liddell tossed a Redbush tea bag in his cup, poured boiling water over it, and quietly walked back to his studio.

He woke up at six fifteen, made a pot of coffee, and walked outside. The sky was overcast, and a mild breeze from the ocean carried the smells of the sea. It had rained the whole night; the trees and the driveway looked clean, dark, and fresh. He took a deep breath.

A strange memory came to him. He remembered his mother lying in bed, late in the morning. "I do not have energies today," she used to say. Sean, his father, would sit on the bed, next to her, and read Victorian fairy tales aloud. Her eyes seemed lost, but her hands squeezed her rosary's wooden beads with sickly impatience. "Mother needs to rest, Liddell. Go play outside."

Oblivious to his mother's depression, Liddell would ride his bicycle at full speed to his best friend's house. They would spend hours together, laughing about anything and everything. He smiled, uneasy. *I was too young to know what was going on.* He pressed his lips together and tried to erase a tug of guilt. *But I haven't laughed like that ever since.*

He sipped some coffee and went back inside.

Sigrid came into the kitchen and poured herself a cup of coffee. "Hi," she said softly.

"Good morning. I heard you get up after we all went to bed."

"Did you? The website project is monopolizing all of my energy, but it'll look fantastic. What time are you going to the sea with the boys?"

"As soon as we finish breakfast. You were on the phone."

"What?"

"I heard you talking on the phone last night."

"Ah, yeah, there were some details about the web page I had to work out," she said, looking him in the eye.

"Do you want to come with us?"

"No, I'm still a little behind schedule. Harry needs some more info from me."

"As you wish." Liddell pulled a pan from one of the cabinets and placed it on the stove. *Harry.*

The kids woke up. They all sat at the table for breakfast, and after a lively conversation about their trip to the sea, they packed up water bottles and snacks. Soon after, they were in the car, headed for the seashore.

Liddell parked the car under a large stand of poplars on one side of a narrow road. There was nobody around. The air was calm, and the trees were still. Only the birds moving in the foliage could be heard, making the leaves flutter and the branches tremble as they jumped from tree to tree.

"Come on, boys. Let's go!"

Their cheeks were rosy and their spirits high. They all picked up walking sticks and started their journey through the woods.

"The black tree! This way," Liddell said, turning toward a dead tree trunk. His steps through the dense tall grass grew longer and faster.

Liddell got excited about the same things as the kids did. He was particularly keen on small, insignificant details: a shiny red bird, a tree with a peculiar twist in its branches, or the light reflected on a brook as it tumbled down a rocky ravine—they all had something special about them that he liked to observe.

They walked through the thick, dark-green mass of trees for about fifteen minutes. There were no paths. An obscure plot of wilderness, the area looked like a forgotten piece of land, surrounded by many pockets of water, all of them ultimately linked to the sea. Finally, the forest opened up, and an imposing, stubborn blue sky reflected on a small patch of clear water, which—quiet and undisturbed—showed no human presence.

The three of them walked as close to the water as they could without getting their feet wet and stood there in awe for a few minutes. The deep silence created a reverential atmosphere; they looked at one another with sparkling eyes and open smiles.

Liddell pointed to a narrow tributary that joined the lake on one side. "That's the small stream I took when I found this place. It goes all the way back to the sea."

"There! The place you talked about!" Klas exclaimed.

What Klas had found was a small, empty, gable-roofed construction, with only one room inside. It was ten feet wide by ten feet deep. One half of the foundation was built on the land and the other half on a tightly packed array of log pilings dug into the water, so it effectively had one door facing the water and the other facing the woods. It also had a tiny deck from which to launch a kayak or a canoe. The place was well maintained; the paint looked fresh, and the roof was in good shape.

They all walked inside the small refuge, and after inspecting it for a little while, they sat next to each other on the small dock. They took their shoes off and submerged their feet in the water for a brief moment. It was cold. Rutger giggled and kept moving his feet in and out of the water, smiling at Liddell and Klas as he did so.

Liddell wished Sigrid were there with them, but he failed to identify the reason why. The idea of Sigrid and her new colleague, Harry, working together wedged in and interfered with every attempt he made to picture himself, Sigrid, and the boys as a family.

Liddell remembered happier times, when he and Sigrid first met, ten years before in the Philippines. Staying in the same hostel and traveling alone, they went out for a walk right after a short chat over a frugal breakfast. Sigrid had struck him with her audacious vivacity, her hunger for life, and her seemingly endless curiosity about places, food, music, and literature. He had never met such an intense person before. Sigrid's words and cadence, her English smeared with a sweet Swedish accent, soon became the most melodious music to him. During that long walk on the beach, he realized that he needed more and more of that melody. *We've changed so much since then. But we'll get back to what we used to be. This is just a rough patch.*

He shook the thought away and focused on the kids. As they chatted, the morning went by in a pleasant, slow-paced rhythm.

He knew that this moment was meant to become a comforting memory in the boys' lives as well as in his own. Satisfied, he pulled his camera from his backpack and took a few photos.

⇒ ⇐

It was shortly past noon when they returned home. Sigrid wasn't at the house, but her computer was on the dining-room table. Liddell called her cell phone. She didn't answer.

"Where is Mum?" Klas asked.

"She must be at the market. It's noisy there, and she probably can't hear the phone ring." *She is not at the market.* "I'll grill some chicken and make a salad."

Three pieces of chicken landed on the hot griddle, and a fast stream of white smoke curled up into the air. He turned the range hood on. *Maybe she's right, and actually this is a stupid trip. It may be a sign that she wants to mend our marriage too. But she was talking to Harry last night. Maybe she's holding on just for the kids. No, she still loves me, but she's feeling the same as I do: unable to open up to the person she's spent the most time with. Unable to break down the wall that daily life, with its chores and obligations, has built between us. Love doesn't have to be passionate all the time. It just can't be. What about Ma and Pa? There's no passion there, just companionship, duty, service. How could Pa have been passionately in love with Ma when she had such frequent bouts of depression? He just put up with it. He did what he was supposed to do and carried on with what he said he would do "in sickness or in health." And what about Ma? Did she ever love him? He's such a handful. Why did she get depressed all the time to begin with? Was it her way of saying that she was not in love anymore, but she had to put up with him?*

He heard Sigrid's car pulling in. She looked surprised to see them at the house. "I thought you were going to stay out until later. How was it?"

33

"We had a good time by the water. The kids liked it. Did you eat?"

"Yes, I had a snack at the market." She didn't have any bags with her. She rapidly walked to the family room and sat down with Klas and Rutger, who were watching TV.

Liddell and the boys ate a late lunch. Then Sigrid took the kids to the movies, and Liddell packed his bag.

Pulling up his laptop computer, he looked at the itinerary again, but his thoughts were still on Sigrid. *But she loves me still. Doesn't she? Rome on Monday, London on Tuesday, and Paris on Wednesday. I hope this woman Brenda is down to earth; I don't want to put up with a snobbish art connoisseur. I should cancel this trip and talk our issues through. I'm not putting enough effort into our marriage. Am I? Anyway, it's too late. The plane leaves in the morning. Damn it.*

He looked at his cell phone on his desk. On a whim, he picked it up and called Will.

He answered on the second ring. "You all right?" Will sounded curious.

"What if I told you I couldn't do it?" Liddell's voice was weak.

"What?"

"I need to stay. I have to sort things out at home. It'll do me no good to be gone for a week just now."

"You must be kidding me. Come on, Liddell, it's only three days. You'll be back on Thursday. You gave me your word!"

"I know, I know. But something came up, and I need to take care of it. Something personal."

There was a silence on the line, and then Will sighed. "I don't want to meddle in your private life, but I'll be in trouble if you don't go, and I mean big trouble, mate. I messed up in the last two issues of the magazine, nothing to do with you, but they warned me that if anything silly happens again, they'll sack me." Will's breathing got louder and faster. "And they will. I know they will. And if they sack me, I'm finished. I am up to my neck in debt. I can't afford to live one week without my salary. I'm a mess, mate, a real mess…but you do what you need to do."

When Sigrid and the boys came back from the movies, Liddell was waiting for them in the living room, a cup of Redbush tea in his hand.

"Rutger, Klas, come on and say good-bye to your dad. I leave tomorrow, early in the morning, but I'll be back on Thursday," he said, crouching down and opening his arms.

The boys sprinted forward, hugged him, and kissed him.

Liddell lay on the bed with eyes wide open, his gaze nailed to the ceiling. He had learned from a very early age how to be alone and quiet, and keep to himself. He had been a good pupil, but now he could not tell his wife how he felt. *How do I feel? Unnoticed. Insignificant. Forgotten.* He wished he was a different kind of man altogether—more open, expressive, and loving. If he could only twist the arm of his own flaws and release his emotions, then he'd be able to communicate freely with Sigrid, and everything would be just fine. But—how to do that?

Lost in small details of memories from his childhood, he finally fell asleep. He had no dreams, as usual.

He woke up a few minutes before his alarm went off, which was set for 5:00 a.m., and had a shower while the coffeemaker dripped. He got dressed in the dark bedroom, collected his cell phone, charger, and watch—all the rest had been packed the night before.

He filled half a paper cup with coffee and went outside, rolling his bag along as the car he had ordered parked by the sidewalk. "Good morning," he said to the driver. "I'll be back in a minute." The driver nodded.

Liddell went back in the house and entered the boys' bedroom. He gazed at each one of them for a few seconds as they slept, trying to memorize the way they looked. He smiled, turned around, and left the room, quietly closing the door behind him. He saw that the lights in his bedroom were on. He went inside, but Sigrid wasn't in bed anymore—the sound of the shower came timidly from the bathroom.

His heart beat harder. He wanted to tell her that he would promise to speak up from then on, if only they could talk thoroughly—full disclosure, then blank slate—and start their relationship all over again. He looked at his watch. It was getting late. *I have to go. There'll be time to talk when I get back.* He gave two gentle knocks on the bathroom door and ventured a whisper. "I'm leaving. I'll call you when I get to Rome."

"Have a nice trip," Sigrid replied.

# CHAPTER 3

# ROME. MONDAY.

Connie's plane taxied at Fiumicino Airport in Rome. The flight attendant made the usual safety announcements in English and then in Italian. *What a warm sound it has to it.* After a lengthy walk, she cleared immigration and was now waiting by the carousel to pick up her bags, where the chattering was noticeably loud. Children ran across the wide corridors, and words were flying from all corners. *The Italian way of life.* An easy smile appeared on her lips.

Right next to her, a woman who was on her same flight waved to a man and a small girl. As soon as they saw the woman, the girl ran toward her, and the man walked behind the little girl, smiling and waving at his wife. The lively girl hugged her mother, and the husband intertwined loud words in Italian with kisses and caresses. The woman, although not particularly pretty, and with a tired look after an overnight flight, looked radiant, fulfilled. Connie's smile turned uneasy, and she looked the other way. *What a contrast to me.*

She pulled her bag from the belt and went to the taxi queue outside the terminal. She had written down the hotel's address on a piece of paper, which she handed to the driver. The old man gave it a tired look, nodded, and loaded Connie's blue bag into the trunk.

Once inside the car, he slowly put the stick shift into first gear and crept through the terminal and onto the highway. Soon afterward they were stopped by a traffic jam. The driver turned the radio on and played some soft Italian music. *"Fa caldo, no?"* he calmly asked while looking at Connie in his rearview mirror. Connie nodded. *What is he saying?* He rolled the windows down and looked at the road in front of him without saying another word. *I guess he asked about the windows.* A few minutes later, they were back on the move. They picked up some speed, and as she looked through the open window, a warm breeze blew through her hair. *I like this.*

Liddell landed in Rome at 10:20 a.m. His flight, direct from Stockholm, had been on time, as almost all Scandinavian Airlines flights were. He pulled his roller bag through the terminal toward the exit, feeling fresh and confident. His brown hair was well groomed, and although his clothing was casual, he was stylishly dressed. He swept through the airport without even thinking about his surroundings—after a whole life of travel, airports had become commonplace, unexciting locations, with nothing for him to see. He got into a taxi and asked the driver, in decent Italian, to take him to the Aldrovandi Hotel.

The lobby had a luxurious nineteenth-century Italian atmosphere. Liddell looked at the multicolored, pristine marble floors that seemed solid enough to last a thousand years. Perfectly maintained carved wooden panels covered the walls, and paintings and vases with fresh flowers adorned the ample space. A hushed silence gave the lobby a sense of calm and timeless good taste. He walked toward the marble-topped front desk, where an elegantly dressed woman greeted him.

"Hello. I'm Liddell Lockheed. I have a reservation."

After a few seconds of clicking on her computer, she looked confused. "I'm sorry, Mr. Lockheed. I don't see your reservation. Is it possible your name was spelled incorrectly?"

"Possibly. But can you first check if you have a reservation under the name William Bale, please?"

"Let me see. Yes, here it is."

"I see. I'm traveling in his place. I guess he never changed the name on the reservation. Let me call him." He moved away from the front desk and called Will.

"Hello, mate. How's Rome?" Typical Will, he sounded like he was doing three other things while speaking on the phone.

"I'm fine, Will, but you didn't change the name on the reservation at the hotel. Can you give them a call?"

"Blimey! I totally forgot about that! Oh, I also forgot to tell Brenda you were going in my place! I'll call all the hotels now and Brenda too. No worries. Leave it to me, mate. I'm on it. Everything else all right?"

Liddell grinned. "Will, after all these years, you always manage to impress me. Let me know what Brenda says. I don't want her to get stressed."

"I'll keep you in the loop. Cheers, mate."

Still smiling, Liddell slowly walked back to the front desk. The woman was already on the phone with Will.

"Mr. Bale just called to change the names in the reservation," she told him. "It's all sorted now. Here is the key to your room, and please let me know if you need anything. I hope you enjoy your short stay here in Rome, Mr. Lockheed."

Liddell picked up a newspaper from the front desk and went up to his room. He wanted to give Will some time to clarify things with Brenda. *How could he forget the most important thing about this trip: that he was not coming? I wonder if he did it on purpose, and now he will make it sound like an emergency—yesterday was Sunday and he didn't want to call her, he is so sorry, Liddell is a great guy, blah blah blah.*

He laughed at his own imagined dialogue. He eased down on the bed and calmly turned the pages of the *Corriere della Sera*. After reading a few headlines, he put the paper aside and pulled out his computer, thinking Will had probably e-mailed him an update.

There it was—an e-mail from Will with the subject "All is clear." Before he could open it, the phone in his room rang. He looked at it and figured it was Brenda calling him after talking to Will. He set his computer aside and picked up the phone.

"Hello?"

"Good afternoon, Mr. Bale. This is Connie Stewart."

*Who is Connie Stewart?* "I am not Mr. Bale," he said dryly.

"Oh!"—the woman sounded surprised—"I am sorry. The person at the front desk told me that…never mind. I'm sorry. Have a good day."

"It's fine. I'm here in his"—he started, but the woman hung up the phone—"place," he finished as he put the handset back on the base. He reached for his computer and opened the e-mail from Will.

> This is funny, L.
>
> Brenda did not go either, got very sick. A woman by the name of Connie Stewart is there instead. She is some sort of art specialist.
>
> Nice hotel, right? I booked all the hotels myself. Enjoy, mate.
>
> W.

Liddell smiled. "Yes, Will, this is indeed funny," he said out loud. "Neither of the two people who were meant to make this trip are here. I bet you told Brenda that I was 'some sort of art specialist,' too." He laughed wholeheartedly.

⊨⊣ ⊦⊨

Connie hung up the phone and frowned in confusion. Her cell phone rang. It was Brenda on the caller ID.

"Hello, Brenda."

"Hi, Connie. How was your journey to Rome?"

"It was fine, until now. It looks like Mr. Bale is not in this hotel. I'm confused, and I was going to call you."

"Yeah, that's why I'm calling you. Mr. Bale had a family emergency on Sunday night involving his daughter; he called me a few minutes ago. He thought I was on a plane, which is why he waited until now. He sent one of his best travel and art consultants, a man called Liddell Lockheed. According to Bale, Lockheed is very experienced, and a great photographer also. Ask the front desk for his name instead."

"Can you repeat his name, please?"

"Liddell Lockheed. I just e-mailed you his contact information as well."

*What an odd name.* "Okay, Brenda, I'll call him and head out to the museum. Thank you!"

"Bye." Brenda hung up.

The phone on her nightstand rang.

"Hello, this is Connie."

It was the dry and somewhat unappealing voice, with a strange accent, of the man who'd answered her call earlier. "Hello. Mrs. Stewart, this is Liddell Lockheed. I'm sorry for the confusion. I came in place of Mr. Bale."

"Yes, hello, Mr. Lockheed. No problem, I just talked to Brenda. We're all on the same page now. By the way, we're supposed to leave for the Borghese Gallery soon, right? It's twelve thirty now."

"Yes, indeed. See you in the lobby in, say, ten minutes?"

"Sure." *Boy, he gets right down to business.*

Connie quickly dressed and glanced at the full-length mirror before leaving her room. She was wearing blue linen trousers, a dark-green blouse, and a pair of silver earrings that matched her barrette and the two bracelets on her right wrist. Her wedding ring was on her right hand and her small silver watch on the left. She wore just a dab of makeup, enough to disguise the night spent on the plane.

She went down to the lobby, a little nervous about meeting this man who might easily discover that she wasn't really up to speed with the art scene. Her thoughts quickly wandered as she explored the luxurious room, while the tapping of her heels on the marble floor reverberated in the high-ceilinged space.

But being immersed in such an elegant atmosphere soon calmed her down. Her mind spontaneously opened up to a subtle state of perception; she noticed the details in the carved-wood panels on the walls and over the doors, the patterns of the marble floor, and the natural veins on the marble columns. It felt somewhat strange being alone after so many years of constant companionship. She was now in a state of silence within herself. She felt as if she had time, in the most profound sense: time to be quiet, time to be without thoughts, time to be one with the beauty that surrounded her at that very moment. No hopes for future delights, no thoughts about past experiences; she realized that she was savoring that very moment with a new brand of intensity.

"Mrs. Stewart," she heard the dry-toned voice speak behind her. It wasn't unappealing anymore, but just formal.

She turned and saw Liddell Lockheed standing four feet away, his hand extended toward her, offering an introductory handshake. He was wearing a light-blue tailored shirt tucked into black jeans. His brown suede boots looked new and elegant.

"Hello, Mr. Lockheed." Connie shook his hand and smiled warmly at him. Liddell's green eyes met hers with no apparent emotion.

"I am sorry for the confusion, Mr. Lockheed. I guess our bosses had some delay in their communication."

"It looks like it. Please call me Liddell. May I call you Connie?"

"Sure, sure, of course," she said, rushing the words.

They went out to the curbside; the sun was shining brightly, though it wasn't hot. It had been a humid summer in Rome. The trees were a lush green, and the shrubs were laden with heavy masses of thick leaves, making a sharp contrast with the dominant pastel, beige, and cream tones of the stone buildings.

"How was your journey from America?"

"Long! I'm really feeling the jet lag now, but I am happy to be here. What about you? Are you based in London?"

"No, no. I live in a small town near Stockholm."

"Stockholm? Interesting." *Well, that explains the accent.*

They got in a taxi that was parked right outside of the hotel. After telling the driver they were going to the Galleria Borghese, Liddell pressed his lips together. "I'd rather confess now, before I get embarrassed, that I'm not very knowledgeable about art. The only reason I'm here is because Will couldn't make it. That being said, my opinion will be that of an amateur. But as a photography aficionado for many years, I can take good pictures of the art for the article."

Connie raised her eyebrows. "Then I guess I will also admit now that, although I have a degree in art history, I didn't have much time to prepare for this trip. But I filled up my iPad with information about the pieces we'll be visiting. I read most of it on the plane; you can borrow it if you want to." She shrugged and chuckled at the odd situation. "You know what we should do, Liddell?"

"No, I don't," he said, smiling for the first time.

"We should both look at all these works by ourselves and then exchange our impressions. Whatever either of us finds interesting,

I'll write down as a single review that we can submit to Brenda with your photos. What do you think?"

"It makes the most sense to me."

The taxi stopped. "Galleria Borghese," the driver announced.

The Galleria Borghese museum was one of the many residences of the immensely wealthy and influential Borghese family. Arguably one of the most spectacular private properties in Rome, the building and gardens were designed and built in the early seventeenth century by its first owner, Cardinal Scipione Borghese. The collection of ancient and renaissance art, famous from the start, was begun and led by the passionate cardinal himself—an insatiable art collector and nephew of Pope Paul V, Camillo Borghese—and had been continued, expanded, sold, and repurchased by subsequent generations of the Borghese family until 1902, when the whole villa and its art was purchased by the Italian government and turned into a public museum.

Connie and Liddell headed to the ticket-pickup queue, where there was a group of about fifty people ahead of them. Retirees, they looked German, or maybe Austrian.

Once they gained entry to the museum, they walked through the entrance hall straight into the Room of the Emperors. The place immediately impressed them with its luxurious grandeur. So much marble, gold leaf, and artwork—it was like being in a different world, completely removed from this one.

Connie looked around her. *This is the most beautiful room that I've ever been in…How is this even possible?* Oblivious to the other people swarming the room, Connie felt her eyes brim with emotion as she gazed at the sculpture, standing proud at the center of the space. She got closer to Bernini's *Rape of Proserpina*, stared at it, and then slid out her iPad. She wanted to reread the story of the myth that the statue represented before diving into its charms.

Liddell stood next to Connie, looking at her iPad. "Mind if I take a peek?"

"Please do. I'll read it out loud," she said.

Pluto, the solitary king of the underworld, was hit by one of Cupid's arrows and fell in love with Proserpina, who was the daughter of Ceres, queen of the harvests, and Jupiter, king of all the gods. One day, while Proserpina was playing in the forest, Pluto came out of the Etna volcano and abducted her. She resisted, but her struggles were in vain. The monstrous Pluto took her into the underworld with him, his intention to marry her and never let her return to the earth's surface again. With the queen of the harvests devastated by the loss of her daughter, all the crops failed, and the lands turned to desert. This caught the attention of Jupiter who, being the most powerful of all the gods, knew that his brother Pluto had Proserpina captive.

"Did she get free?" Liddell whispered.

"Yes, she does. Let me see." Her slender index finger gently touched the screen and moved up a few times. "Here it is," she said and read quietly.

Jupiter ordered Pluto to free his daughter, and the king of the dead obeyed, but before leaving the underworld, Proserpina ate three pomegranate seeds. Because pomegranate was believed to be the fruit of the dead, she would never be able to leave the underworld completely—she would have to return to it every year for three months at a time, one month for each one of the seeds she ate. So the myth goes to explain the four seasons: the three months that Proserpina spends in the underworld with Pluto became the winter; the spring comes when Proserpina returns to the earth and Ceres welcomes her with the blossom of all the flowers; summer is when both mother and daughter are happily together, and in autumn, Ceres turns all the greens into brown, orange, and yellow in a way to say farewell to her beloved daughter until the next spring.

"Fascinating story," Liddell said, and he walked around the sculpture.

Connie put away her iPad and raised her eyes to the magnificent marble. *The veins, muscles, and sinews all look so real. How could a human being have done this, so perfect, so true to life? And poor Proserpina, she is crying. Those tears are incredible; they are marble tears! She is being taken to a horrible place where she doesn't belong; and Cerberus, that three-headed dog, looks so terrifying.*

She walked around the sculpture, to catch a different angle. *Pluto is in love with her, but he doesn't care for her feelings. He is just taking what he wants, as if she were a trophy, a mere object. What a wrong way to understand love.*

She stared at the sculpture for a few minutes, marveling at the detail and wondering how Bernini had managed to have his models pose for him. There was so much movement, like a single moment in time, a split second of life that had been captured forever in marble.

She pulled a small black notebook and a blue ballpoint pen from her purse and started writing, "Physical aspect: pure white marble, larger than life. Three elements: Pluto, Proserpina, and Cerberus. Psychological aspect: Proserpina looks soft, malleable, vulnerable. Pluto is powerful, muscular, unstoppable. Cerberus seems like a mass of pure anger. Her useless efforts to escape are represented by her left hand pushing Pluto's head, and her disgust is shown by her head looking away from him. She is in complete shock, tears roll down her soft, childish cheeks, and even her toes seem to be tense. Pluto is impassible, as if he were grabbing a prey animal; there is no love depicted at all, but instead, brute force, struggle, desperation, and anger. A most devastating experience for a woman: to be taken by someone who doesn't know how to love her."

Connie closed her notebook and slid it in her purse. Then, raising her eyes, she observed how quietly Liddell stood in front of the sculpture, looking at it from the left side. His eyes were fixed on Pluto's muscular abdomen; he didn't seem to be looking at the details. Instead, he appeared to be carried away by the marble and its unspoken tidal force.

The room wasn't quiet. A group of young American students was talking about the different details and nuances of the sculpture. Some of them boasted about their knowledge of the sculpting techniques and tools that were in use back then, saying loudly that they were still in use by current figurative sculptors.

Liddell ignored the racket; he was in a bubble. His face didn't show any sign of emotion, and his green eyes slowly moved up and down the piece without stopping at any particular point. He didn't take any notes; he didn't even have a notebook. With his hands in his pockets, he walked around the sculpture at a very slow pace. Then he stopped to look at Pluto's face, and after a brief moment, he pulled out his camera from its case and started taking pictures.

Connie glanced at her watch; they had spent thirty minutes looking at the sculpture. She strolled through the rest of the rooms, stopping at every work in awe. Bernini's *Apollo and Daphne* seemed to be dancing to a light and eternal tune, while Caravaggio's *Boy with a Basket of Fruit* projected a deep weariness and disdain for life that made her quiver. The contrast with the harmonious Titian's *Sacred and Profane Love* and the eternal Canova's *Paolina* could not have been greater.

From the corner of her eye she noticed that Liddell was walking behind her, but he didn't show much interest in viewing each and every work, as she did. Only a handful of pieces seemed to kindle a spark in him: Bernini's *David*, Correggio's *Danaë*, and Barocci's *Madonna and Child with Saint Simon and Saint Jude*.

She stopped her stroll and waited until he got close to her. "Would you like to sit at a café to exchange notes?" Connie asked.

"As you may have noticed, I didn't take any notes. A few minutes at a coffee shop should be enough for our exchange. Are you ready to go now?" Liddell said without much interest.

"Oh, I see." Connie's enthusiasm plummeted. "Yes, I'm ready."

They walked two blocks down the Via Pinciana to a small coffee shop that had a few tiny tables arranged on the sidewalk. They sat at the one farthest from the shop entrance to avoid any people traffic. A young waitress approached them within seconds; Connie ordered a panino and an Americano, and Liddell asked for a double macchiato and a vegetarian wrap.

She read her notes out loud, and as she did so, she felt somewhat exposed. She realized that she hadn't spoken about art in many years. And speaking was different from thinking—the sound of her own voice describing the feelings aroused in her by the statue felt like a brand-new experience. *Speaking is disclosure. It is a conscious decision to engage with another person. How invigorating this feels. I wonder if he will feel the same way that I do.*

There was a stretch of silence after she finished.

Liddell stared at Connie's lively blue eyes. As she recited her notes, he was trying to read her. *What is it about her? What does she have that I wasn't expecting? This odd sense of bliss, or childish joy, so uncommon in people of our age. She takes this little job much more seriously than I do. How interesting.*

"Now it's your turn, Liddell," she said, pen in hand, ready to take notes.

The waitress came back. She set a small silver tray with their food on the side of the table, and with a shy smile, she placed the white Illy porcelain cups with their coffees before each one of them. Then she nodded and left.

The afternoon sun came out from behind a group of fluffy clouds; its warm yellow light shone on Connie's right profile and projected a golden glow over her face.

Liddell slowly sipped his coffee; he wanted to take a few more seconds to admire the scene before he started to speak.

"I wasn't so much taken by the myth that inspired the marble, although it represents the story quite well—don't get me wrong. But instead, I was taken by the thought of Gian Lorenzo, the sculptor, chipping the lifeless piece of rock, sweating, swearing, second-guessing himself about this or that detail, getting chips of marble in his eyes and blood on his hands after missed blows of his mallet. Blisters on his rough hands and white marble powder all over his hair, on his eyebrows, and inside his lungs as he frenetically polished it. I imagine Gian Lorenzo working endless hours, with the indomitable passion of a twenty-three-year-old young man who knows that he's incredibly talented. I imagined his rage when things didn't go his way, but also his attention to detail while dealing with the people involved: stonecutters, middlemen, and cart drivers who delivered the block of stone. I saw his well-known passion for women: his restless body working so hard during the day and making love during the night. I imagined his fingers, just like Pluto's pressing Proserpina's waist and thigh, pressing his own mistresses' bodies. I guess I was taken by the physicality of the sculpture more than what it actually represents."

He looked down to his coffee and picked it up for another sip. As he did so, he felt Connie's intent gaze on him; she seemed surprised to find in him a passion that she had probably not imagined he would possess. Neither did he, but after a rather long silence, he continued. "How much drive and energy does it take to singlehand-edly achieve such a monumental work as that? How much imagination does it take to even dream about it? How much passion does it take to go through the difficulties of the practical and mundane tasks that go with it? What is the measure of all this passion? When I was looking at the sculpture, I almost heard Bernini yelling at me: Look how much you can achieve with the right amount of passion! Look how much else there is besides and beyond that dull life of yours, mere observer—" Liddell abruptly bit back his words; his eyes grew wet, and he blushed. "I'm sorry, Connie, I went a bit too far. I apologize," he said, lowering his tone to an almost humble whisper. "Anyway, this was what I had to say."

Connie had not written anything down; she had stared at him the whole time as he spoke. There was an element of surprise in her look, as if she had discovered something in him or experienced a new emotion for the very first time. *There is so much tenderness in her gaze. I feel like she is looking deep inside of me, trying to understand me.*

"Well, that was pretty deep coming from someone who doesn't know anything about art," she said, softly. "Can we say that, for you, the central idea of the sculpture is passion?"

"I guess we can say that. My take on the *Rape of Proserpina* is that it took a burst of passion for Pluto to go and take Proserpina as a prisoner or a forced wife, but it also took Bernini a tremendous amount of passion to produce the statue and to transmit both Pluto's and his own passions to the viewer. Certainly, for me, the whole piece is about different expressions of passion."

After writing down his comments, Connie closed her notebook and put it in her purse. Then silence fell down upon them like a heavy cloth.

Connie looked at her watch. Two thirty. "I—I think I'll head back to the hotel for a couple of hours," she said to fill in the awkward moment, "I'm exhausted. We're supposed to go to Saint Peter's Basilica at five. Should we leave the hotel at four thirty?"

"Oh...yes, please go. You had a very tough night with all that flying. Four thirty sounds perfect to me. I'll arrange the taxi with the concierge." His voice recovered the formal tone it had before.

"Thank you," Connie said, standing up. She pulled a ten-euro bill from her wallet, but Liddell waved his hand in dismissal.

"I got this," he said, standing up. "It was a pleasure to meet you and to share this first visit with you. I'm looking forward to the rest of them." He was trying to sound as formal as he could. Such an unexpected—and unnecessary—display of emotion on his part had left him feeling uneasy.

"Sure, I enjoyed it too. Thanks for lunch. The next one will be on me. See you in a bit." She slowly draped her purse strap over her right shoulder and left.

He watched her walking away. Her body moved with a gentle, natural swing as she headed to a taxi that had just stopped a few yards from the café. When the taxi drove past him, their eyes briefly met.

⋈ ⋈

Liddell went to a small bar filled with locals. He hated touristy spots. The bar was small and almost empty. He sat at a table tucked in a corner and asked, in Italian, for the wine list. He ordered a bottle of Valpolicella—the people's wine—along with a plate of prosciutto and melon.

He engaged in a mental dialogue. *Where did that show of emotion come from? I hope she doesn't think you are some sort of eccentric. Why did you have to speak like that? Damn! Once I started talking about the sculpture, I got wrapped up in my own feelings. I don't understand why.* He drank a full glass of wine in one go. *But it doesn't matter. I'm not going to see her ever again after this trip. I wonder if this display was a good thing or not. Anyway, it's good to be back in Rome.*

He poured more wine and drank generously from his short glass, in an attempt to soften his memories of the day.

＝⊹ ⊹＝

Back in her room, Connie rushed to her computer. She didn't want to think about what had just happened. *I have to call the family. I want to tell Nick how great this is.*

She logged in on Skype and dialed her home number. It was 3:00 p.m. in Rome, meaning that it was 8:00 a.m. in Minneapolis. She hung up. Nobody was at home on Monday morning. She tried Nick's cell phone. He picked it up right away.

"Hello, this is Nick."

"Hello, honey!" Connie was pleased to hear Nick's voice, even though they really hadn't cleared the air after their argument.

"Oh, honey! How is it going? How is Europe treating you?"

She noticed that he said that just a bit too effusively. *Maybe he's around other people. Or maybe he decided to move on and be nice to me. Why not?*

"It is so nice to hear your voice, Nick. All is good here—a bit different, but good. Do you have a minute to talk?" *I want to end this stupid grudge.*

"Hey, John," she heard him say. "I gotta take this call; it'll be quick."

"Nick?"

"Yeah, sorry, Connie, but I'm really busy today. What's up?"

Now it was Nick's typical tone.

"Nothing. I mean, I just wanted to talk to you for a few minutes."

"Well, this isn't the right time. I'm busy. Your talk will have to wait."

She looked down, and her voice lost all emotion. "We'll talk tomorrow."

"Yeah, that sounds good. Have fun."

She hung up. The kids were at school, and Deb was at a day spa. There was no use calling anybody else.

As she closed her laptop, a deep and unexpected sense of loneliness crept up on her and unveiled a feeling that had surged while she listened to Liddell speak about the sculpture—a feeling of inadequacy as a wife, and as a woman. If there existed a man capable of exploring the subtleties of art and willing to reflect upon the human emotions, if somewhere on earth there existed a man who could not feel ashamed of feeling vulnerable, and was capable of opening up to her in just the way that Liddell had done during their brief encounter, then why had she chosen Nick to be her partner in life? Why did she choose the unapologetic Nick—who was never ashamed of anything, who was always right in his manly reasons for being right, to whom life had nothing else to offer but what could be seen, touched, or possessed?

*Nonsense. I need a drink; that's what it is.*

A minute later she was in the elevator on her way down to the lobby bar.

Two couples and a businessman were sitting at the coffee tables, but the bar was empty. Connie sat on a stool as the bartender placed a thick menu in front of her.

"The wine list," he said.

She flipped the pages as she barely read the multitude of unfamiliar names. The selection of Chiantis was impressive. She pointed to one of the names; the bartender gave her a look of approval and told her that it was the best one they had by the glass. It was also the most expensive.

She thought of Robert, her father. *How would Dad have reacted to the sculpture? There is something about Liddell that reminds me of him. That muted passion, ready to spring up when the right moment comes. His eyes lit up with tears when he talked about the Bernini. And I thought I was opening myself up. But he made a good point: What is the measure of passion? How much of it does it take to feel really alive? I wish Nick made me feel at least warm.*

She swirled, smelled, and tasted her wine; it had just the right balance of fruit and tannins. The earthy flavors washed and then cleansed her mouth after each sip. The combination was irresistible: ripe prunes and violets, with an aftertaste of sweet tobacco that lingered on her palate. She closed her eyes and had the last sip, emptying the glass.

The feeling of inadequacy—now morphed with a sense of missed opportunity—not only did not wane but grew stronger, monopolizing all her thoughts.

*I'll call Dad.* She opened her eyes and placed the empty glass on the bar. She put a twenty-euro bill next to it and went up to her room.

*He's probably standing by the dining-room window with a cup of coffee in his hand, looking at the front garden.*

"Hello, Connie!" Her father's voice surged from her laptop's speakers.

"How did you know it was me? I'm calling from Skype, not my cell." She laughed.

"Ha. I impressed you. It was a calculated risk."

"What?"

"The chances that it was you who was calling were high. It's almost four o'clock in Rome, and besides, nobody ever calls me. According to the itinerary you sent me, you're probably getting ready to see the *Pietà*."

"Well done, Dad."

"By the way, how's the trip going?"

"It only started, but it's been intense. This man that I'm with, his name is Liddell, is very pleasant company. I know this is weird, because I just met him, but in a way he reminds me of you."

"Really? Why?"

"I'm not sure, but he got excited about the Bernini sculpture in the same way that I think you would have." She paused. "Dad, have you ever felt that you've missed out?" Connie listened as the words spilled out of her mouth.

"Missed out on what?"

*Okay. I'll let it all out.*

"On life. That you rushed into it, and you didn't pay enough attention to the things around you. Then one day you realize that the choices you've made didn't take you where you wished yourself to be. You realize that you spent a lot of time—"

"Barking up the wrong tree?" her father finished for her. "And by the time you figured it out, it seems too late to change?"

"Yes." Connie's voice turned into a whisper.

Robert remained quiet while Connie continued. "I'm…I'm having second thoughts about the way I've lived my life up until now. I know it sounds stupid, Dad, but I'm a bit confused."

"Did you know that your mother wrote?"

"No—but what does it have to do with what I just told you?"

Her father exhaled. "I've been confused, too." His voice suddenly turned dark.

"Dad, you're worrying me. What is it?" Connie knew by bitter experience that when her dad's voice lost its forced vim, it meant that a drastic change in his mood had taken place, and it could last for days. She regretted having told him how she felt. If he had a nervous breakdown, she wouldn't be able to help.

"After your mother's funeral, when I got back at home, I felt terribly alone. I was alone—only me in the house. I walked through every room slowly, very slowly. I looked at the things that had been there for years. It was like seeing a ghost. I could see her hands on the dishes we used every day. The mirror in our room showed me an image of her smoothing down her dress before going out to the grocery store. Our bed was just waiting for her to lie down with a book.

"One of her wineglasses was still on the countertop, and I could have sworn that Amy was just about to show up in the corridor, back from her cellar, bottle in hand, and gently pour some wine in it."

Connie had a flashback of her mother. She saw her sitting on a stool by the countertop, as she used to do every day, glass of wine in hand, her brown eyes staring out the kitchen window.

Robert continued. "As the days passed by, the portraits on the dining-room shelves looked like images of someone else's life. The smiles in the pictures, the souvenirs from our trips, the couch we used to sit on...it all seemed to belong to a different life altogether. Everything had lost its meaning to me. If Amy wasn't there, what did it all matter?

"I went through her wardrobe. It was full of all the things that belonged to her family, all the French stuff she'd inherited from her parents. I had decided to give it all away to Goodwill, when I found this box, a pretty big box. Gosh, it's not even that I found it...I mean, I'd always seen it. It had been *there* all the time, tucked in the corner of her closet. I'd just never paid any attention to it before. So I opened it, expecting to find more shawls and scarves and gloves...but instead, I found hundreds of letters. Her letters." He sighed loudly and continued.

"I didn't know if I wanted to read them. I didn't know what to expect. Why would she write so many letters and not send them to anyone? Up to that day I'd thought we knew pretty much everything about each other. I closed the box and took some time to think about it. What if I found out that she had a lover? I didn't want to risk ruining my memories of her. After all, she was dead and gone, with no chance to defend herself. And more important, had she wanted me to read them, she would've said something.

"Those letters haunted me for a few days until I made up my mind. I was going to read them without judging her. So I did." Her father paused. "Are you still there?"

"Yes, Dad."

"They were all handwritten in her mother tongue, so I had to send them to a French translator. It took this girl almost two months to translate them and type them in English. Anyway, I got this thick folder, with all her writings arranged by date, as your mother had kept them.

"There were all sorts of things: poems, journals, letters. One odd thing is that although they were all addressed to 'My Dearest,' there were no replies and no other person's writing. I think they were addressed to herself at different periods of her life, like to when she was a child, or to when she'd gotten old; but she also wrote down ideas, advice about situations and people, things that she'd done during the day, and whatnot.

"Connie, she was a much more sensitive woman than she appeared to be. She could write about an event, say, a Thanksgiving dinner, for pages! Writing exactly how she felt that day and even the conversations that caught her attention. For instance, I discovered that she didn't like going to your in-laws' house. She found Pam and Joe superficial and silly."

"She always looked so happy when we went to Pam and Joe's," Connie said.

"Exactly! She kept it all to herself. She wrote poems too, beautiful poems...I mean...who am I to tell? But I think they're pretty good. Some of them are so sad, you wouldn't believe it was your mother who wrote them...she, of all people, who was always so happy, or now should I say, seemed to be so happy."

"You think she wasn't?"

"I think she was happy about some things, but she was obviously extremely unhappy or dissatisfied with others. She missed her life back in France; there's no doubt about it. I'll e-mail you her first poem. I guess she had a boyfriend whom she left behind when they all moved to America. It's a farewell to this boy—maybe a summer love. Who knows? She never told me anything about it."

He continued, "Although I remembered every gesture that she made when she spoke, and every nuance of her gestures, I realized how little I really knew her. And there was nothing I could do about it—she was gone, and I would never see her again. But I figured that I could redeem myself for being so blind by breaking away from all the nonsense around me and trying to connect with my private self, as she did by writing those letters—" His voice quivered, and he stopped. A long, trembling sigh followed as he tried to contain his emotions. "I felt completely lost. I was a stranger in my own skin." Robert's voice finally broke up. "Sometimes I wonder if she loved me. If she loved me as much as I loved her."

"Maybe she put herself second simply because she loved you and she loved us so much," Connie said encouragingly.

"Maybe you're right…but we'll never know." Emotion still choked his voice. "I'm not crazy, as some people like to think. I'm just making up for lost time. You never realized it because you weren't paying attention. Now you are."

"Mom's letters made you change, not the fact that she passed away."

"Yes. And they helped me to get here."

"Where?" Connie was baffled.

Robert slowly recovered his composure. "To a state of mind where I reflect upon what I wish I'd done differently, but instead of feeling regret, I feel *pietà*."

"*Pietà*, like in the artwork?"

"Exactly." Her father explained, "The word doesn't quite translate to the English 'piety.' In the Romance languages, it refers to a feeling of veneration and love *for the sacred*. In art, they use the word *pietà* to name any piece showing the Virgin Mary holding her son's dead body. And there you have it; what's done is done. There's nothing else she could have felt but *pietà*. She lost what she loved the most, but her reaction to it was acceptance and veneration of what was sacred to her: Jesus.

"I guess, going back to your question, the answer is yes, I too now feel that I've been living a different life than the one I should have lived. I was immersed in my own world, embarrassingly oblivious to the true feelings of the only woman I ever loved. And maybe your mother had that feeling too, of being torn between two worlds—the one she left behind in France and the one in which she actually lived, here in America, with you and me. It's funny how it is. I wish I'd known her better, but maybe she wished she had stayed in France and never knew about me." He made a loud sob, and a cry welled up. "We'll have to talk later, Connie. I'm sorry."

"It's okay, Dad. I love you."

"Me too, dear...I love you too."

Silence pervaded the room once again, but this time it felt deep and somber. Connie lay down on the king-size bed and dug deep into her past, trying to find any cracks in her mom's daily, happy-looking mask. Among the whirlwind of memories, something came right up to the forefront—the way in which Amy used to stare out the kitchen window.

Her mother loved cooking, and as a typical Frenchwoman, she always had a glass of wine at hand. Oftentimes, when the meal was in the oven and the sauce was simmering on the stove, she would lean on the countertop and look out the window. During those moments, while she slowly sipped from her glass, her cloudy gaze seemed to turn inward. As the years went by, those moments of mental absence became longer and more frequent, and not only during cooking time, but at any time of day. Connie never gave it too much thought; as far as she was concerned, her mom was taking a break. It never occurred to her to wonder what her mom was thinking about.

Connie's computer chimed with a new e-mail. She dragged herself back to the desk and looked at the screen. Robert had just sent her an e-mail, the subject: "Amy's first poem." She immediately read it, whispering every word.

Farewell
Keep on kissing me, My Darling Love,
for our time is now and ours to live.
Tomorrow's been laid out for us,
apart and far, two specks in the sea of life.
Let's stretch this moment, thin as thin air,
for times like these are scarce and few.
Rush, rush! And melt in my arms, so we will become
a single and bright reflection of light.
I will keep you in my heart, forever alive,
the perfume of roses, a breeze in the fall.
The heat of our passion, the tears of our love,
captured in an instant, in a whiff, in a thought.

She read it a few more times while she imagined a younger Amy, back in sunny Provence, writing those lines before leaving the house that she grew up in, never to return again. *I wonder whom she wrote it to.*

Her room phone rang. Connie instinctively looked at her watch. It was 4:35.

"Do you need more time?" Liddell asked before she could say anything.

"No, I'll be down in a minute."

Saint Peter's Square expanded widely in all directions. An enormous chunk of open blue sky hovered over its gray cobbled courtyard, while Bernini's colonnade enclosed its human occupants with mighty stone. As they walked, Connie looked up at the almost two hundred statues that watched over them from the cathedral frontispiece and from above the columns surrounding the square. She felt the cold gaze of that stone assemblage rest on her, as if

Saint Peter's Square weren't really a square, but a stage—the stage of the theater of life.

They strode up to the obelisk. The four-thousand-year-old monument had pierced the Roman air ever since Emperor Caligula ordered its transfer from Egypt, almost two millennia ago.

They zigzagged through the crowd of tourists, photographers, clerics, and passersby. Liddell walked with the confidence of familiarity, and every so often he looked back to make sure Connie was still following him. Connie watched the different groups of tourists. To her left, a contingent of what she thought were Eastern Europeans listened attentively to a tall, slim, gorgeous woman with blond hair and a prominent nose, who spoke through a small speaker. Next to them she recognized a group from Japan by a small flag printed on their white bracelets. A second later she looked to Saint Peter's main entrance, and saw a sea of people flowing out of the church. Her eyes were drawn to a group of six African nuns neatly dressed in their habits. Their faces were lit up with what Connie thought was a heavenly peace.

As they got closer to the cathedral doors, the space seemed to shrink, and the crowd closed in. She heard Italian, German, Spanish, and Russian mixed with Asian and American voices, creating a uniform, unintelligible, and overwhelming clamor.

Inside the vast basilica, a new sense of dimension struck her with more intensity than she'd expected. Connie never imagined that so much space, height, and solemnity could ever be real. Liddell turned around once again to check if she was still with him, and after looking at Connie's face, he smiled.

She looked at Liddell while his eyes went to the distant *Baldacchino*, Bernini's massive bronze structure that hovered over the main altar. Connie moved closer to him. An unknown feeling of possession crept up inside her, a desire to be left alone with him.

"Would you like to walk around first?" Liddell suggested.

"Yes. Leave the *Pietà* for last," Connie replied.

They made their way across the nave toward the left aisle, strolling close to each other in silence. The mass of tourists that packed the basilica rumbled in a dissonant mix of camera flashes, sighs of appreciation, and the scripted explanations of the tour guides.

Connie pointed at the floor stonework. "Have you looked at this?" she asked. "Bernini was involved in its design."

"Bernini is all over the place," Liddell replied.

She explored the side altars, and was drawn to the grandiose sculptures just as much as she was to the minutiae of their settings: the frames surrounding the frescos and sculptures, with their multiple moldings and beaded woodwork; the columns and their elaborate capitals and complex profiles; the small steps near the altars, worn down by hundreds of years of use; and the rounded, shiny edges of the marble pieces, softened by the touch of infinite pilgrims over the passing ages. The perfectly shaped vaults, spotless gilded plaster, and countless additional details made the surroundings of the main works masterpieces in their own right.

But the towering *Baldacchino* wasn't like anything she had ever seen before. A huge, overwhelming canopy raised on four twisted brass columns; it was the most unique blend of architecture, art, and engineering she'd ever seen. Her eyes got lost in the intricacies of the work: its endless twists, turns, arabesques, images, lines, and textures. She scanned the monumental structure from top to bottom, and then her eyes, as if attracted by an irresistible magnetic force, rested on Liddell's, who stood not far from her.

Liddell couldn't help watching her and feeling at ease, even now that she was staring back at him. His muscles relaxed, and his heart's slow beating turned imperceptible. It took him one calm blink to focus his entire attention on the depths of Connie's still and contemplative eyes. Even three feet away from her and surrounded by people, he felt a complete, solitary union with Connie, an indescribable state of grace that somehow could only exist inside such a monumental building.

"Let's see her now," she whispered.

They walked around the *Baldacchino* and headed toward the entrance, where the *Pietà* chapel was located. Moving at an even slower pace, Liddell looked at the altars along the right aisle, which seemed never-ending.

Being a civil engineer himself, he thought about the immense effort it must have taken to erect the church, the masonry, and the statues—for it all to be there, ready to be seen by people like him. He saw the work of thousands of men and women over hundreds of years, carving, painting, polishing, framing, cooking, laughing, getting frustrated, yelling, praying, getting sick, cursing, mopping, dreaming, and dying. New workers coming in—using the same worn-out tools from the ones who'd left—to undertake endless hours of cleaning and rubbing, restoring and changing. Those forgotten faces presented themselves in surreal succession, among the details and the grandiosity of the cathedral. The fruit of entire lives of effort—devotion and labor, inspiration and hard work, great visions from a few and slim wages to many, genius and misery—humankind represented in its whole.

They finally arrived at the *Pietà* chapel. Liddell's eyes opened wide when he saw the polished marble masterpiece at the back of the altar. Next to him, Connie sighed.

They walked out of Saint Peter's Basilica and headed toward the left colonnade. The still air imprinted a solemn atmosphere on the piazza.

"Where do you want to go?" Liddell asked.

"I need a quiet place, really quiet…and some wine." Connie felt her voice softening, winding down to a whisper.

"Let's go back to the hotel. They have a nice private patio."

The small terrace outside the hotel's top floor offered a monumental panoramic view of the city, its ages-old buildings mingled with a two-millennium span of architectural masterpieces. The sun had just disappeared from the sky and was setting behind the horizon; this short-lived clarity announced the end of the day, as dense and dark shadows were cast over the gabled roofs, the innumerable cupolas, and the solid stonewalls.

A waiter approached their table; he was a middle-aged man, almost bald, with black, lively eyes and dexterous movements. He placed a menu in front of each of them, and in less than a minute he came back with a candle, which he set in the center of the table and lit up.

"Do you drink wine?" Liddell asked.

"Very much so. It runs in my family. And you?"

"Occasionally, but I don't know much about it. Would you like to order it?"

Connie smiled and opened the leather-bound menu.

The waiter came back. "*Signora. Signore,*" he said, nodding at Connie first.

"We'll have the 1997 Barolo, please," Connie said to the waiter, pointing at a line on the well-populated menu.

The waiter brought a large crystal decanter, which he placed on the round table. Then he presented the bottle to Connie and pronounced the full name and vintage of the wine as if reciting a line from a poem. He carefully took off the capsule, and after a gentle pop, he slowly poured the wine into the decanter and placed the bottle next to it with such choreographed moves and utter delicacy that it seemed as if he were handling a masterpiece that belonged in a museum.

"What would you like to accompany this exceptional wine?" he asked in English.

"Charcuterie with your vintage cheese selection, please," Connie said.

"Excellent choice, signora." Then he turned around and walked away.

Liddell winked and poured a small amount of wine into Connie's glass.

Connie picked up the glass by the stem, studied its garnet color, and swirled it a few times. She dipped her nose inside the glass and inhaled, and then she swirled it some more before smelling it for a second time. She looked at Liddell and nodded. She closed her eyes and sipped the Barolo, holding it in her mouth for a few seconds before swallowing. She opened her eyes. Immobile, Liddell's expectant gaze was completely focused on her. She kept her eyes on his and immersed herself in a brief, intense moment of connection.

"Forest, dark fruits," she whispered. "Sublime."

Liddell's hint of a smile turned into a full grin, crinkling the sides of his eyes and giving them a lively light.

The waiter returned, this time pushing a trolley, and placed two water glasses, a bottle of sparkling water, and a large platter of cheese, meats, and breads on the table. He looked at the already used wineglass and gave them an amused glance.

"My fault. I couldn't wait," Liddell said, grinning back at him.

The waiter nodded in understanding and poured more wine into their glasses. "*Buon appetito*," he said and left.

Liddell lifted his glass. "A toast. To life."

"Cheers," Connie said. "To life. And its surprises."

Liddell sipped and put his glass back on the table. "Have you been to Europe before?" he asked while grabbing a piece of bread.

"Yes, in my gap year. I went to France with Deb, who's still my best friend. We spent a few days in Paris, wandered a bit around the country, and ended up at my mom's hometown."

"So you are half-French? But your mother lives in America?"

"She passed away nine years ago, but yes, she lived most of her adult life in the States. My grandfather was a wine merchant in Bandol, in Southern France, and got offered a job at a big wine importer in Minnesota."

"And they moved from Southern France to Minnesota. I can only imagine how that must have felt."

"Different, for sure. But they never looked back. Mom was in her late teens or maybe early twenties."

"Is your father French, too?"

"No. Dad is fifth-generation American. He's an accountant, now retired, and was one of my grandfather's coworkers. He met my mom at a company Christmas party."

"Wine does run in your blood." Liddell sipped more Barolo.

"It does. I've been drinking wine since I was—gosh—thirteen? It was illegal, but my mom and my grandparents didn't care, and being wine lovers, they taught me everything they knew about it. My grandfather drank it all day long, even at work, but he rarely got drunk. I think they let it pass because he was French. He used to say that wine was the 'natural beverage' for him. Anyway, Mom inherited the love for wine from him and the passion for cooking from my grandmother, but I only got the love for wine."

Liddell was taken over by curiosity and attraction for Connie. Her confidence while ordering the wine and then tasting it, the unusual way in which she held the wineglass—by the base—and the idea that she had a family history related to the world of wine, with roots all the way back to France, added up to a sophistication in her that he surely didn't foresee. But there was something else in her that made her so special in his eyes: while with her, he had finally been able to feel, after such a long period of emotional numbness.

"Let's talk about the *Pietà*. What do you think about it?" Connie asked in what he thought was the most soothing voice he had ever heard, comparable only to the memory of Sigrid's.

Liddell gently leaned back in the chair. Then, settling his left arm on the armrest, he said in a low voice, "It's the most sublime and revealing piece of art that I've ever seen. It captures the most painful experience of humankind: a mother holding the lifeless body of her son—who hasn't just died, or even been killed. He's been crucified." He paused and looked at the distant ruins for a few seconds, searching for the right words. "She is outstandingly beautiful, serene, almost stern. There is no anger or pain in her face. How would you describe it? Acceptance? Resignation?"

"Love," Connie said. "I imagine that the only feeling that's left in a mother's heart at a moment like that is love. And it's of the deepest kind, which is the love between a mother and her son. She's not looking at his face. To me it's as if she's remembering him as a boy, growing up, becoming a teenager, brief moments of their life together...remembering better days, while at the same time she is confronted with the reality that her child, now a grown man, is dead, lying in her own arms."

"I agree. The sculpture seems to be about her, and Jesus is a secondary figure. It shows a kind of love so strong that even when all went wrong and the mother had to bury her own son, part of her is still at peace. Part of her knows love goes beyond distance, time, and death. She loves her son, and that love will stay within her, undisturbed by the external circumstances, be they departure, separation, or death."

"What other feelings do you see in her?" Connie asked.

"Loneliness, sadness, acceptance, and detachment."

"Detachment?"

"Her right hand is holding Jesus's body, keeping it from sliding off to the ground. To me it represents that she is holding on to the physical aspect of her son. A part of her wants to have him back and alive, of course. But if you look at her left hand, it's not touching him. Instead it is open and pointing out, as if she is saying, 'We all have to let go; life is just a journey, and we must go on.' I feel that Michelangelo wanted to show that there is also something to say about letting things go. Am I too far off on this one? What do you think?" he asked as he leaned forward and took up his glass of wine.

"It's a difficult concept, to me at least. I'm not good at letting things go. But I had this weird thought while we were at Saint Peter's. I decided I'd try to imagine myself as Mary, and that I was holding my son's, Bryan's, dead body. It was strange…I never had such a thought before. But I realized that after crying and weeping and asking why a thing like that could have happened, I would have also had to let it go. It was as if a universal truth struck me, right there…saying…we will all pass…It's just the way things are, and you have to let him go. It's interesting that we both arrived at the same thought, but through different channels."

"She is so beautiful, so young," he said.

"Do you want to know why Michelangelo made her so young when realistically she would have been in her fifties?" Connie asked with a smile.

"Pray, tell me."

"In Dante's *Divine Comedy* there is a verse that says something like 'Virgin mother, daughter of your son,' and it's the beginning of a prayer by Saint Bernard. Michelangelo revered Dante, and he figured that if Mary was, spiritually speaking, the daughter of Jesus, then she must have looked younger than him. There's another theory that says that because Mary was a virgin, she didn't show the signs of aging. And yet another story says that Michelangelo used the memory of his own mother as a model, who died very young, when he was a kid."

"I like the third one better. Michelangelo as a boy captured the essence of his mother in a memory, encapsulated her beauty, and then carried it within him for the rest of his life." He sipped more wine while images of his own mother flashed in his mind. "Tell me more about the statue."

"It was commissioned by the French ambassador to the Vatican, who was a cardinal. The pope had granted him a spot for his tomb inside Saint Peter's, so the cardinal ambassador thought that he ought to have the most beautiful statue for his tomb, because it would also represent France."

"So he hired Michelangelo."

"At that time Michelangelo was very young and not widely known; he'd only carved the *Bacchus*. An art dealer, I can't remember his name now, spoke to the ambassador about Michelangelo. When the ambassador saw the *Bacchus*, he was immediately convinced of Michelangelo's talent."

Liddell was entirely focused on Connie: her soft voice with American accent; the way her hair trembled slightly at times when she spoke; and the joyous light that seemed to come from inside her eyes—as if illuminated by a blue backlight—and made her look so alive. It seemed to him that Connie projected a singular type of energy, a unique radiation that wrapped all around him and enchanted him with its warm power.

She continued, "In the contract, the ambassador stipulated that Michelangelo should make the most beautiful statue ever seen in Rome. Isn't that naïve? Imagine putting something like that in a contract today," she said with a shake of her head. "The funny part is that he actually did make the most beautiful statue ever seen, but not only in Rome—arguably in the whole world."

"You make the story so exciting to hear."

"I'm glad, because I heard it from my dad like a hundred times. He's a Michelangelo geek."

"Please go on. I love listening to you."

"What else...Oh, the way the drapery folds. Some experts say that it shows the influence of Verrocchio, who was another Florentine sculptor." She looked up, as if trying to remember more facts that she had heard from her father. "Michelangelo was twenty-three years old when he carved it, and as in everything else, he was very precocious for his age. It's said that when the French ambassador visited his studio to see how the *Pietà* was going, he was impressed not only by the sculpture itself but by how much Michelangelo knew about theology."

"Was Michelangelo really religious?" Liddell asked. "I know that most of the Renaissance artists were religious on the outside because they had to be, otherwise they wouldn't get any commissions from the Church, but they were really more classically oriented, in a humanistic way."

"Apparently Michelangelo was a truly religious man. Some say that's why he not only impressed people with his craftsmanship, but he also moved their souls, because his faith was so profound that it permeated his work." She paused. "I gather you're not religious, but something tells me that you once were. Is that right?"

"It is exactly right. And I wonder how you guessed it."

"I don't know. Maybe we see in other people what we would like to see in them."

"I was raised Catholic, but my father's influence was stronger. He was a classicist. When I was twelve, he introduced me to Cicero, whom I still deeply love, but when I turned thirteen, he gave me Lucretius's *De Rerum Natura*. And that was the beginning of the end of religion for me."

"What's that?" Connie asked.

"*De Rerum Natura*? It's a poem, a long one. It means 'On the Nature of Things,' and it was written by a Roman philosopher called Lucretius, who was in turn a follower of Epicurus, a Greek philosopher. The book is really about Epicurus's thoughts, even though he had been dead for almost three hundred years by the time Lucretius wrote the poem."

"And what is it about?"

"It's about the universe and how it works according to very strict logic. But it also touches on other things: like how bad religion can be when taken too seriously; the idea that God as a Father does not exist, so he cannot answer any prayers; and the surprisingly advanced idea—that no one believed in when Lucretius wrote it—that everything is made out of atoms. Lucretius planted in me the idea that there is nothing after death, and it is on us to figure out a way to live a happy and virtuous life. It's very interesting, and convincing as well. For me it was like having my father tell me to my face that Santa Claus isn't real. It sparked in me a lot of questions that religion just couldn't answer." Liddell smiled, visited by old memories. "I remember my mother was very upset with my father, and for a very long time. She said that he was guilty of one of the gravest sins: shattering an innocent child's faith."

"Very dramatic words! So she was the religious one in your family."

"Very much so. She went to mass every Sunday and observed every festival on the Catholic calendar. I used to go to church with her until I read Lucretius."

"Maybe she really blamed your father for taking those moments with you away from her, and not so much for religious matters."

"I never thought about it in that way, but it's very possible. Mother and I used to walk to church every Sunday morning; we would leave the house at eight and stop at a small café to have breakfast. A frugal one: a croissant and a cup of coffee, with milk for me, while we read the Bible in silence. At exactly eight forty-five we would leave for the church and sit at the same places in the same pew, Sunday after Sunday, year after year."

"Until you read Lucretius!" Connie joked.

"Exactly!" Liddell said with a smile, as he forked up a piece of Reggiano cheese.

"What about your father? Did he ever go to church with you?" Connie asked.

"Not even once. He used to say that religion, like art and philosophy, is only for those who need it, and that he was fine with just art and philosophy."

"So what happened after you stopped going to church? Did you turn to art and philosophy, like him?"

"No. I thought I didn't need any of them. I just wanted to travel and see the world on my own terms. How bold, right? Later on I realized that I needed art, in my case through photography, and after all we've talked about on this trip, I probably need some philosophy too."

Connie poured more wine into their empty glasses. "You said you thought there's acceptance in the *Pietà* too. What do you mean by that?"

"Acceptance that she had to endure something painful for the sake of a greater good, in this case the redemption of humankind. If Jesus wasn't crucified, he never could've saved the world. Acceptance of the good and the bad." Liddell sipped his wine. "Maybe I'm theorizing too much."

Connie followed Liddell's hands as he slowly moved them forward. A firm delicacy showed in their every move. He held the glass by the stem with one hand while the other rested on the table. She was surprised to find an evidently masculine man—he was well built and lean—with such delicate gestures and controlled movements. It was a departure from Nick's wrongly understood and exaggerated manliness.

She looked him in the eye. "It reminds me of something that my father just told me a couple of hours ago: to accept the cards we've been dealt, to accept what we are, but also what we will never be. Now you gave it a twist: to accept because there may be a greater good to be achieved."

"But I admit that I've never endured anything painful for a greater good," he whispered. "Instead, I've always pursued what was within reason, never taking big risks, never feeling much joy, never feeling much pain. Besides my grandmother when I was a child, I never lost a loved one. I never had to make any sacrifices or even move out of my comfort zone. My life is not precisely full of passion or strong feelings." He looked down at his glass and swirled the wine around.

"By the way you reacted to the art, I would have thought it was the opposite."

"Connie, this trip is proving to be very revealing to me, in more than one way. I enjoy your company very much, and in some strange way, unknown to me, your presence lets me express feelings I never knew I had."

Connie felt the warmth of shared emotions—the subtle and quiet peace of two people feeling the same way. "It's like that for me too, Liddell."

The waiter came back to the table and asked if they wanted anything else. They both shook their heads and remained quiet until the waiter returned with the check.

⇒⊱ ⊰⇐

"What time should we leave tomorrow?" she asked, entering the elevator.

"Our flight is at nine; let's leave at seven. We'll skip all the lines since we have premium access."

"Perfect. Good night, Liddell," she said, as the doors opened at his floor.

"Sleep well." Liddell reached out to her.

Connie stood still, immobile, as he kissed her on one cheek and then moved to kiss the other. His scent surrounded her like a halo, wrapping her whole self with his unexpected closeness. She closed her eyes and felt her heart speeding up its rhythm. She tried to kiss him back, or to make some reaction, any reaction, to this European custom that she had completely forgotten about. But she just could not move. After what could have been one second or one whole day, she opened her eyes and watched him pull away and step out of the elevator.

Once in her room, Connie dropped her purse on the chest and kicked her shoes off. It had been quite a day, but still she wanted to call home. She lay down on the soft mattress—the white sheets were impeccable and felt fresh—put a few pillows behind her back, and rested her open laptop on her thighs.

The Skype symbol bounced a few times, she clicked on her home phone number, and after a long procession of rings, Amanda's voice finally came out of the laptop's speakers.

"Hello."

"Hello, sweetie. How are you?"

"Hi, Mom." Amanda's voice was dull.

"What's going on?"

"Not much. Bored to tears."

"Oh dear, cheer up!"

"Sorry, Mom. But I don't feel like talking right now."

"Oh...Is Dad around?" Connie's voice lowered, pierced by Amanda's words.

"Yep. I'm walking over to him as we speak."

Nick picked up the phone. "Hi there."

"Hi, honey. How are you?"

"Same old…How's it going over there? Bored of visiting museums yet?"

"Actually, not at all. This is great! I wish you were here. There are so many beautiful places to visit." *Why am I saying this? I don't wish he were here.*

"Yeah, I bet it's great. Anyhow…what time do you land on Saturday? There's a get-together at Eric's man cave. Vikings play the Packers."

"Let me see." She pulled up her flight information, and while her eyes scanned the computer screen, her desire to talk to Nick evaporated.

"I land in Minneapolis at six thirty in the evening. I say be at the airport at seven. But I can take a cab if you're busy."

"Whoa…no, no. I'll pick you up. That will work out. I'll drop you off at home and go back to Eric's house."

Connie remained silent.

"So…what else? Is the food too terrible over there? I heard the portions are really small."

"The food is delicious. And the portions are fine." Connie compressed her lips, containing a groan of frustration.

"Cool…"

"I'm sorry, Nick, I'm really tired. I've been walking all day. Let's talk tomorrow, okay?"

"Sure. Have a good one."

She closed the computer's top and set it on the nightstand. Then she rapidly undressed, turned the lights off, and got in the bed.

Connie closed her eyes, and wished things were different: that Nick had just one more ounce of sensibility and that Liddell attracted her less, but she shook her head with frustration, waving away the thought as ridiculous. Diverting her mind, she remembered the sense of peace and timeless silence she felt that morning at the hotel lobby, the astonishment as she walked the Borghese Gallery, and the awe and complex harmony of architecture and art she experienced at the Vatican. Her lips slowly curved up, and the frustration she felt after talking to Nick slowly subsided. Then, she fell asleep.

# CHAPTER 4

# LONDON. TUESDAY.

Liddell watched Connie as she headed slowly down the corridor from the elevators, pulling her roller bag. By the looks of her slightly puffy eyes and swollen lips, Liddell assumed that she hadn't slept well.

"Morning," he said. "May I take your bag? The taxi is outside."

"Good morning. Sure, thanks."

He had already checked out, and his bag was in the trunk. He put Connie's bag beside it and opened the taxi door for her as she came out of the hotel—she had put her sunglasses on.

The ride to the airport was longer than he had expected, but once they arrived at the check-in counter, they dropped their bags and walked to the security checkpoint. The line was long and moved slowly. *I wonder why she's so quiet today.* He tried to push his thoughts aside. *It's none of my business.*

They cleared security, and Liddell looked at his watch—they still had thirty minutes before boarding.

"Coffee?" He tried to sound upbeat.

"I would love some."

"Latte, as usual?"

"No, I'll have a macchiato, please."

"Nice change."

She took off her sunglasses, opened her purse, and delicately put them back in their case. She tucked a lock of her hair behind her ear and zipped the purse shut. Her movements had a rare but assured serenity that made Liddell think that something was going on. Like a change in the tide: slow, gentle, but irrevocable.

Liddell ordered a double espresso. They sat down by the gate and sipped their coffees.

"Are you all right, Connie?"

"Yeah...I'm okay. I'm fine. Thanks for asking."

"It's just that I noticed—" He stopped short. "It doesn't matter." He turned his head away from her in an attempt to erase what he had just said.

"What did you notice?"

"Nothing. It doesn't matter."

"I would like to know, please. What did you notice?" she asked again, gently but firmly.

"You seem to be a bit pensive today. Maybe it's just me, but something has changed in the way you look."

Connie stared at him. The muscles in her face seemed relaxed, but her eyes looked tired. "You're probably right."

The boarding announcement came through the PA system; they strolled toward the gate in silence.

⇒⊹ ⊹⇐

It was a small plane, and Connie's seat was next to Liddell's. The flight attendant closed the door and made the usual safety announcements. A few minutes later, they were in the air, headed to London.

Connie closed her eyes, trying to get a little rest, but the effort was fruitless. Instead, she found herself caught up in thoughts about her mother.

*Why did you never say anything? I would've understood if you'd told us you wanted a different life. We could've worked it out. Why keep it to yourself like that?*

*I've always thought that our daily life as a family was enough for you, as it was for me. But I get it now. The daily routine is just not enough. Maybe you did the right thing. Could we have understood you back then? I know I understand you now, a bit too late. I just got here to the point where you were for who knows how long. How I wish you were alive, Mom. I wish I could tell you that I understand.*

The flight attendant asked her if she wanted anything to drink. She muttered a no for an answer and pulled her sunglasses out of her purse.

*We were we all too worried about our own lives, but you were always ready to help. Pam always needed something from you: help with the cooking, help choosing the wine for their guests, help with the gardening. You were always busy doing things that you thought meant something to someone. Did they mean anything to you?*

*I remember how excited you were when I got back from France. You wanted to know everything about your friend, Monsieur Gagolin. I remember the dreamy look in your eyes when I described his old farmhouse, the vineyards, the people working with ancient tools, the food he cooked for us, the ingredients he used. Your face brightened immediately when I put the letter into your hands, like a little girl who'd been given a present, though you were about my age now.*

*I didn't think much of it back then, but that letter was the only link to your past, the last vestige of your beloved Bandol. Why did none of us ever ask you about your life before moving to the United States? Nobody really cared.*

*Oh, Mom, I feel there's so much I don't know about you. Why did I waste our time together thinking only about me, assuming that you were there only to help us? Now it's too late. You're gone.*

As the plane started its descent, she pulled a tissue from her pocket and dried the tears that leaked under her sunglasses.

⇌ ⇌

They landed at Heathrow at ten and walked together through immigration and security.

"Have you done any research on Rodin's *The Kiss*, our next piece?" Liddell asked on their way to baggage claim.

"I studied it in art school, of course, and I also refreshed myself on the facts while I was on the plane to Rome. What about you?"

"I did some research, too. I went through the works we'll be visiting and read as much as I could about them. I wanted to have a better understanding of the context in which they were produced."

"I thought you were called at the last minute, just like I was," she said, raising her eyebrows.

"Okay. I've said too much. To be precise, I was not called at last minute. I'll explain it later if you don't mind. It's complicated."

"Oh, never mind, it's none of my business," she said, turning her head away from him. *I'm getting used to being turned down.*

"Can I be honest with you, Connie?" Liddell asked.

She looked at him, and noticing a hint of guilt in his eyes, she smiled. "Of course."

"I knew about this trip for months in advance. I had plenty of time to prepare myself and to study the works of art. I shouldn't be telling you this, but I trust you will not repeat it. Will and I are very good friends. We have an agreement: I travel and take photos, and he writes. We both enjoy it, and it has been working fine so far. We've been doing it for the last six years."

"As far as I'm concerned, you are the art consultant whom Will sent in his place. The rest, as I said, is none of my business." *Our little secret.*

"Well, hold on a minute," she added with affected surprise. "That means that you are not the amateur you said you were. You're probably better prepared than I am."

"I'm still an amateur, regardless of the few things I've read about art. I can guarantee my amateurism!" he said, laughing.

Outside the terminal, they took a taxi to the Langham Hotel. At rush hour, it took them more than an hour to get into the city.

The Langham's entrance was on a small roundabout right across from the BBC Radio building and the circular All Souls Church. A few yards down, after a bend on Regent Street, the quiet road turned into a busy thoroughfare, with heavy traffic and packed with shops.

"Good. No confusion with the reservations today." Connie looked at the number on her room card while they walked across the lobby.

"Would you like to go for lunch before we go to the Tate?" Liddell asked once they were in the elevator.

"Sure. Lobby at one?"

"Perfect. See you downstairs at one."

Connie stepped out the elevator and headed for her room. She had almost two hours for herself.

Liddell put on his running clothes, splashed his face with cold water, and hurried out the door into the hall. He purposely left his iPod at the hotel—he wanted to think about Sigrid without any distractions.

Regent's Park was sparsely populated with pedestrians and other joggers. A light but cold drizzle came down from the thick sky and made the traffic seem to move slower. Liddell jogged at a fast pace, oblivious of the coat-clad people opening their umbrellas. His gaze was lost in the space ahead of him, and his thoughts were lost in the time behind.

His mind went back to that summer trip to the Philippines, where he and Sigrid had first met ten years earlier. They had left the shabby hostel where they had both spent the night and headed to the beach, backpacks on, when Sigrid teased him. "What can be worse than those bad beds? Let's spend the night right here." *The sound of her laughter had something so pure about it.* He agreed to her suggestion. It was a random decision, as random as any other that they made on that trip. After a full day of walking on the beach and swimming, they lay down on the sand and had an improvised dinner of some canned edibles and a couple of bananas. They talked about the places they had been to and the places that they would like to visit. They talked about writers and books, movies and music. *The sun falling on the ocean was a blurry orange ember.* They stared at the empty beach in front of them. The warm darkness of the summer night got closer... *like a welcomed guest who just joined us, I said, feeling poetic.* He moved closer to Sigrid, and their bodies brushed. She looked at him for brief moment. *There was no doubt in her eyes.* Liddell leaned forward and kissed her. She embraced him and pushed him back onto the sand, easing herself on top of him. *We kissed for a long time, in silence.* Sigrid took off her sarong, Liddell discarded his shorts and summer shirt, and they'd made love. It had been magical. *Where did all that go?*

He realized that he was running faster than usual—he felt the stress on his legs and on his knees, but he carried on. He wanted to catch the certainty of the love he had felt that night in the Philippines, a certainty that was so evasive now that it seemed to be running away from him.

The drizzle turned into heavier drops and fell relentlessly over the city. Liddell stopped at a store entrance to catch his breath, and then he turned around and headed back.

Back in his room, he shut the shades on the windows, undressed, turned all the lights off, and walked into the shower. He stood still under the hot stream of water for a few minutes. He couldn't help crying. He cried profusely as the water pelted down on his head and washed his tears away. *I'm empty. And it feels permanent.*

⇌ ⇋

Connie borrowed an umbrella from the front desk and went out for a walk. She visited shops, had a proper English breakfast that came with a humble sparkling wine, and bought some souvenirs to take home. She stopped at a few newsstands, hoping to purchase a few issues of the British edition of *Life with Style,* but she couldn't find any.

She thought about Liddell as she strolled around Covent Garden Market. The contrast was evident—Liddell's understated passion and Nick's absolute lack of it. And Liddell noticing a change in her that morning—and taking the trouble to bring it up—only exacerbated his differences from Nick. Liddell had made the effort to really look at her, and he noticed the change in her mood.

*Maybe when we stop being noticed—and stop noticing—it's the indication that something has faded, that love has lost its potency. But then… what? Start it all over with someone else, just to watch it fade again? What is the point in doing that? Why go through the pain of a separation, the longing for love while in solitude, and finally the childlike hope of finding true love, when one knows that it's futile? Is this thought right, or am I just making up excuses for not doing what I know I should do?*

She looked at her watch—twelve thirty—time to head back to the hotel.

⇌ ⇋

They found a small café on the busy part of Regent Street that looked promising. They ordered some salads and sat outside. The rain had stopped, and the sky was spotted with gray, moving clouds, and a timid sun struggled to shine above the crowded street.

"How did you meet Will?"

"We were roommates, here in London, around twenty years ago. We had a friend in common who put us in touch. Will was having some trouble with his finances, and I needed a cheap place to stay, so I paid him some money, and he let me sleep on his couch. I lived with him and his parents for almost two years. He still lives in the same flat, but his parents passed. I eventually moved out, but we've stayed very good friends. We're like cousins." He smiled. "What about you? How did you get involved in art writing?"

"As I told you, I studied art history in college. I didn't want to be an artist myself, but I liked the idea of being around artists. Maybe all I really wanted was a degree just like everybody else around me. Right after I graduated, I worked at a couple of local magazines, helping them out with the editing, getting advertisements, and whatnot. That was when I realized that I enjoyed writing."

"Writing is an art—"

"Yes, but what I wrote for those magazines was very basic. At one of them I put together a sort of local indie art schedule for the Minneapolis area, mostly facts. Then I worked at another one writing about pets; then I was at one writing about wedding planning, kind of all over the map, and I never really pursued…" She paused and, looking down, contemplated her plate for a few seconds. Her eyes went back to Liddell's. "Then I got married and had kids right away. Nick and I decided I should stop working until they were older."

"But you didn't stop writing, did you?"

She shook her head slowly. "I didn't write a single word for years."

"Your kids are old enough by now?"

"Sort of. I needed motivation. I took this part-time job at a teen magazine last year." She grinned shyly. "I just write what I think will make the girls read my short pieces on what is *cool*. I don't know if I would do it full time, but it's what I have now. And thanks to that work, Brenda got me involved in this trip, which turned out to be so important for me."

"May I ask why?"

"I hadn't been to Europe since I was nineteen. I always wanted to come back, but it just never happened. Now I realize how much I needed this." She gestured, waving her open palms. "The emotion, the art, and a bit of time for myself too." Then she slowly clasped her hands together and set them on the table. "I've been talking too much. I'm sorry. What about you? Do you find this art trip interesting?"

"I do. Although what I really enjoy is traveling, and taking photos. I like the feeling of going somewhere different from my house or my job, which for me are in the same place. I like being with people I don't know, who speak languages I don't understand. The whole culture change, I guess. I also like the feeling of returning. I've found that traveling is one of those very few things in life as sweet when they begin as when they end. I'm happy to leave for a new trip, and I'm happy to go back home."

"You go back to your happy life and wife."

"How do you know I'm married?"

"You wear a ring."

"Oh, yes." He rubbed his wedding ring with his thumb. "Well, I can't say that she is very pleased about me being gone. Unfortunately, she is very busy at work, and besides, she's not interested in traveling that much anymore. For her, being away from work is a waste of her time, so I go solo. I still enjoy getting away every now and then." He smiled and forked up the last of his salad.

They finished lunch and took a taxi to the Tate Modern. On their way, Connie gazed out the window—she liked the diversity of people in London: a white-collared man opened his way through a group of Asian tourists, and a few steps behind a young woman strode confidently, shopping bags in both hands. Across the street, an older man with a stern gaze looked as if he'd been walking those streets forever and the whole city belonged to him. Then suddenly, coming out of nowhere, two heavily tattooed teenagers wearing tank tops and huge, shiny headphones, zipped right next to the old man on their skateboards. The contrast of the scene appealed to Connie.

The taxi dropped them off at the museum's entrance on Holland Street. They entered and strolled across the atrium, heading to the Rodin sculpture in the gallery without stopping at any other work.

"Here it is," Liddell said. "Rodin's *The Kiss*."

The wide gallery with its amber bare-stone walls and minimalistic decor stretched in all directions, letting *The Kiss* be the centerpiece of the section. Flooded by overhead light fixtures, the people paraded around the sculpture in a silent, endless procession.

Connie was immediately absorbed by the marble's sensual energy. The piece wasn't as smoothly finished as Bernini's *Rape*, but she thought that only increased its effect.

Although the gallery was crowded, she felt alone with the marble. *This conveys raw emotion, but at the same time it has such a delicacy of movement. She is pulling him down, to make him lie on her. He looks so solid.*

Connie felt her heart beating faster as she got closer to the marble and farther away from reality. *They are close, so close; they are becoming one. Why have I never felt that way when I make love with Nick? What is it that we don't seem to have but that this sculpture is all about? The sense of closeness of the two lovers is overwhelming. How old are they? They don't seem to be that young. Could I ever feel like her? I don't think so. Nick and I live in different worlds; he'd never be interested in any of this. I wonder if he's ever imagined feeling what I'm feeling now. But how could he? He's not that kind of guy.*

She closed her eyes tight, pushing the tears back. *What am I thinking? This is wrong. Wrong and unfair. Nick is a good man; he is just not interested in this sort of stuff. He is not into art or into talking about his feelings, or mine, or sharing them. I wish he were, though. This feeling of missing out is haunting me again.*

She opened her eyes and tried to focus on the sculpture. *Is it tenderness? Is it closeness? Or is it the purest love between two people that this work is representing? The same purest love that I don't feel. The same purest love that Nick doesn't even know exists.*

Liddell approached the sculpture in the same way as he had the Bernini: he stared at the marble for a few seconds, walked around it, and stopped a few times to pay more attention to the details. He looked for the book that the man was supposed to be holding with his left hand. *There it is, barely noticeable.*

His eyes then rested on Connie, who stood on the opposite side of the sculpture. She was staring at the female element of the composition. *She is not taking any notes today.* Her hands were locked together in front of her, holding her small purse with her long fingers tightly wrapped around the handle. *She's completely still.* He couldn't stop looking at her. The sculpture suddenly lost all importance. *She's got such a sad look in her eyes. I wonder what she's thinking about.* He briefly thought of Sigrid. He'd never seen his wife in such a deep state of concentration.

He ambled around the statue, still looking at Connie. *There's a timeless beauty in Connie now, so lost in introversion, above the material world, beyond the frenzies of life, a still beauty.* He tried to focus on the sculpture, but as he walked past her, a gentle whiff of Connie's jasmine perfume caught his attention. He closed his eyes. *I can't think about the marble.* He wanted to ask Connie what was on her mind, what she was feeling, but he dismissed the idea; he didn't want to rouse her from her state of deep reflection.

Liddell forced himself to look at the statue. Minutes felt like hours, until finally Connie turned around and looked at him.

"Intense, isn't it?" she said in the lowest whisper.

"Indeed." Liddell nodded.

Connie exhaled. "I think I'm ready to go. I've got a pretty good idea of what the work represents."

They ambled the museum's surroundings, looking for a coffee shop—the evening felt lazy, and the breeze, pleasant. The colorful leaves, still on the trees, swung with a down-tempo cadence, projecting a quiet autumn pensiveness. After passing several busy coffee shops, they stopped at a small café, staffed solely by the owner.

"Inside?" Liddell asked, pointing at a small table by the window.

"I was going to suggest the same table," Connie said.

Liddell ordered an Americano, Connie, a café latte.

"Do you know the story behind *The Kiss*?" Connie asked. "Because I don't think I remember it that well."

"Actually, I do. The two lovers are taken from Dante's *Inferno*. Their names are Francesca and Paolo. Paolo was the younger brother of Francesca's husband. The statue shows them after they read the romance of Guinevere and Lancelot, which as you may know, is the story of the forbidden love between Arthur's wife, Queen Guinevere, and Sir Lancelot, the best and most trusted of all of Arthur's knights. Apparently, Francesca and Paolo discovered that their love was in fact possible, however much against all conventions, after they read the book, which is still in Paolo's hand."

"So the man is holding a book! I wondered what it was."

"Unfortunately for them, Giovanni, the mean and unpleasant husband, discovered them in the act of kissing when he entered Francesca's room."

"Oh, no."

"Yes. And in a bout of fury, he killed them both. Oh, I forgot to mention—Paolo was married as well."

"That's terrible! A double adultery story." She paused, but her eyes quickly recovered the soft look that they had momentarily lost. "But the sculpture is so beautiful, so pure."

Liddell chuckled. "Let's pretend we haven't heard anything about the adultery business. What are your thoughts about the piece?"

"Let's pretend. I know this will sound pretty obvious, but I think the piece is about love. Now, let me be more specific: it's about that uncontrollable physical force that is unleashed when two people really love each other."

"Ah!" Liddell nodded.

"In its purest form, love bonds people, unites, mixes up, melds them together. Just like in the marble, they become one. And I think that to show this, Rodin made them out of the same block of stone, so one lover is part of the identity of the other. The significance of one depends on the other. To me, loving and being loved is the ultimate form of communicating: through each and every part of our being. Does it make any sense?" Connie's eyes shone with a bright blue hue.

"I think it does." Liddell remained still. "Now let's stop pretending," he said, moving his chair a few inches closer to the table. "Is *that* love pure even if it's the result of not a single, but a double adultery? I too find the sculpture quite powerful and convincing; however, the fact that both of them are being untruthful to their respective partners baffles me. What's your take on that?"

"I don't know. I wish they weren't cheaters. I just see the immensity of love melting them together as one, in the most perfect communion imaginable. I don't know what to think about the moral issue."

"If I may, there's an anecdote about that." Liddell took a sip of his black Americano.

"Please go ahead." Connie looked surprised and smiled in her usual shy way.

"I'll take a small detour first. I agree that love has the power to unify, or as you've very nicely put it, 'meld' the lovers together. But I'm also a bit of a pragmatic, in the sense that I believe love is quite unpredictable. Just look around: people getting together and breaking up all the time. None of them got married thinking they would eventually stop loving the person they were marrying. I relate this to the myth of Cupid, this little winged, blindfolded boy whose arrows hurt the victims by inflicting them with uncontrollable desire and love. Therefore, according to the myth, love can change. It's capricious and often irrational, not unlike the whims of the little lad, Cupid."

"Is this your way to justify adultery?"

"Hold that thought for a minute, and let's go back to Rodin. He took that particular story from Dante's *Inferno* for a commission he'd gotten to decorate a pair of huge bronze doors known as the 'gates of hell,' which would represent, quite obviously, the entrance to hell and the stories of the sinners that went through them."

"I think I remember something about those doors, but it's a bit blurry in my mind," Connie said. "But go on, I shouldn't have interrupted."

"The doors were commissioned for a new art museum in Paris—which was never built—and Rodin had the liberty to pick the theme. And what's more universally sinful and despised, however common, than adultery? And not just adultery, but also treachery, because Paolo and Giovanni were brothers. What's interesting is that because the image of these two lovers was so pure, Rodin ended up removing the original bronze figures from the door and making the larger, marble piece that we just saw, this time away from the gates of hell. All this goes to say that, adulterous or not, this sculpture wasn't perceived as conveying any sin at all. However, I'm afraid that the two lovers did go to hell, at least according to Dante."

"So you don't think the main theme of the sculpture is love, but sin?"

"Hmm." Liddell pressed his lips together and looked up.

"I think it's both," he said, looking back at Connie. "I think the idea is that love, even real love, can be sinful as well, given the circumstances—and if you believe in sin, of course."

"Well," Connie said, "a sin is still a sin."

"But how deep and intense love can be regardless. What's open to debate is the moral issue, and I have no idea what Rodin really thought about it, but it's known that he had many affairs throughout his life, even when he was already involved with the woman who was to become his wife. But you know, there's a difference between what is presented to the public at large and what one truly believes in." He took a breath. "Would you blame the lovers?"

"I think I would." Connie looked perplexed. "Yes, I would blame them, because they shouldn't have done it while they were still married to other people. It's not fair to their partners."

"In this particular case, I think that finishing their relationships with their partners and making their love public was not an option. Paolo and Francesca lived back in the eleventh century."

"You're not religious, and that's why you don't see a problem in what they did."

"I'm not sure if that's the reason why. But nobody is religious anymore in this day and age."

Their eyes locked. "I am. I am religious." She slowly pronounced the words, as if she were reminding herself of her own beliefs. "I think we have enough to write about."

*Liddell, you spoke too much, again.* "Indeed." He nodded once.

When the waiter brought the check to the table, Connie was swift to pick it up. "My turn."

Liddell watched her as she pulled her wallet from her purse and her long, manicured fingers carefully searched for a twenty-euro bill, which she gently placed on the center of table. He recalled how sad she looked at the Tate while she gazed at the sculpture.

*She is so different from Sigrid. She tried to hide her tears. Cry in front of a marble? There's got to be more to it. She seems so tender and delicate, so vulnerable at times. I wish I could help her. Help her with what? I don't know. I'm just feeling the need to truly appreciate her.*

"Connie, I know that we've just met. I've no idea of who you are and vice versa, but at the Tate, you seemed to be having a difficult time. And it's none of my business, I know, but I just see it fit to offer you my help, if there is anything in my power to do."

Connie looked down at her empty cup, and then back at him. "Thank you. I appreciate it, but I'm fine. I just got distracted by other thoughts, personal stuff that has nothing to do with what we're here for."

*There you have it, Liddell. Two in a row. Mind your own business.*

They took a taxi back to the hotel. London at this hour was bustling with people going places. Liddell saw small groups waiting at the bus stops, others going for a drink, and others walking by shops on their way home. *Just another day.*

His mind wandered. *Tides of people going in different directions, all living in their own separate worlds, carrying their own all-too-well-known set of emotions: hope, love, guilt, greed, beliefs. The constant state of change of such an immense mass of an unchanging element: humanity.*

Connie rushed into her room, fighting off an uneasy feeling in the pit of her stomach. She opened her computer and clicked on the Skype icon. *Why is it taking so long? Come on!* She looked at her watch. It was six o'clock in London, and noon in Minneapolis.

"Hi, honey, what's up?" Nick asked.

"I just wanted to hear your voice and to tell you that I love you."

*I do love you.*

There was a long silence on the line.

"Uh, okay. I love you too, honey. What is it?"

"Well, *that's* it. I wanted to tell you that I love you."

"Well, now I'm kind of worried, with you calling me just to say that. Are you sure you're fine?"

"Yes, I'm fine. I just got back from the Tate. We were looking at Rodin's *The Kiss*."

"Are you with Brenda?"

"No, she couldn't make it. They sent this guy instead."

"I knew this trip was wrong, right off the bat. It's about this guy that's traveling with you. Do you feel safe out there?"

"It has nothing to do with him. Why is it strange that I'm calling to say I love you?"

"Well...a) you've never done it before, b) you sound kind of strange, c) you just left everything behind for that stupid trip, d) who knows who that guy out there with you is. You want me to keep going?"

"Oh, no. You're right. I've never called just for that. Maybe it's the distance, you know. I'm a bit homesick."

*You don't get it, do you?*

"Of course I'm right, but you'll be back here in two days, so try not to worry about it too much. Everything will be just fine, like it's always been. Okay?"

"All right," she whispered.

"Do you want to come back home now?" Nick's voice grew in intensity, as it always did when he wanted to solve a problem in his own definitive way. "Just go buy a damn ticket and get on a plane tonight. Forget about Brenda. You don't need that stupid job." He sounded almost angry.

*What?* "No, no, I said I'm fine. I'm fine, Nick. One hundred percent fine."

"Okay." Nick gave a loud sigh. "Just wanted to help you out there, but you just wouldn't let me, would you?" he grumbled. "Do what you wanna do, I gotta get going. I have a few meetings ahead, and stuff keeps piling up on my desk. Can we talk later?"

"Sure. Bye, Nick."

Back in his room, Liddell sat on the chair beside the desk. After spending a few minutes on his computer, he picked up his cell phone and called Sigrid. She didn't pick up. He tried again, with the same luck. *I'll call the house.*

"Hello?" Elga's voice had a timeless calm that Liddell attributed to her strict religious beliefs and stern upbringing. It somehow soothed him.

"Hello, Elga! How are you?"

"Mr. Liddell! I am very well, thank you. How are you, sir?"

"I'm fine, thank you. I guess if you are there it means that Sigrid is not at home."

"Yes, sir. Mrs. Sigrid had a meeting tonight. I'm with the boys, and they are quite fine, sir."

"Did she say what kind of meeting?"

"I believe it's about a certain website, sir. She was talking about it on the phone right before she left."

*Of course.* "How are the boys doing?"

"Very well, sir. I made sure they did their homework before they had their shower. Rutger's handwriting has improved a lot lately, sir—one can actually read what he writes now, instead of guessing it. A lovely young man he's turned into, little Rutger; and Klas, oh, Klas was awarded a prize. He was the best in his class at mathematics during the last month. He is quite happy about it, sir."

"That's good news, Elga."

"Indeed. I'm so proud of both of them, sir. When I think about how quickly time has passed, how fast they grew up. I can't believe it."

"Yes, they grow up fast." He sighed. "All right then, please tell Sigrid that I called. I will call tomorrow."

"I will do that, sir. Have a good night."

"Thank you, Elga. You too."

He placed his cell phone back on the desk and picked up the room's phone.

"Hello?" Connie's voice sounded dark.

"Hello, this is Liddell."

"Oh, hello," she said, sounding surprised. "What can I do for you?"

"Well, I'm going to have a glass of wine at the hotel's bar, and I wondered if you wanted to join me."

"Thank you, you are so thoughtful. But I'll have an early night tonight. I'm still tired."

"Oh, sure, I understand. Then have a good night, and I will see you tomorrow."

"Yes, thanks. See you tomorrow."

Liddell left his room and went to the elevator. Shortly after, a soft bell chimed, the elevator doors opened and Liddell stepped inside. As the doors closed, he patted the breast pocket of his jacket and realized he had left his money clip in the room. *What was I thinking?* He quickly pushed the door-open button and dashed back to his room.

Connie's hair was damp: she had just come out of the shower. After the unexpected call from Liddell inviting her for a drink, she'd hung up the phone and sat down on the bed. *What am I going to do*

*in here?* She picked up her watch from the nightstand. *It's only six thirty. There's nothing wrong with a drink.*

She picked up the phone and dialed Liddell's room number. It rang one, two, three, four times. Connie shrugged and was putting the handset down when she heard Liddell's voice.

"Yes?"

"Liddell!" she said, hastening the handset back to her ear.

"Oh, hello."

"I was wondering if you're still going for a drink. I changed my mind."

"Absolutely. See you downstairs."

Connie hurriedly brushed her hair, put on her earrings, and rushed out of the room.

She left the elevator and went past a group of men in tuxedos and elegantly dressed women. She immediately felt underdressed. Once in the lobby, she saw a lot more people ambling to and from the main entrance, filling up the bar, talking and greeting one another in a relaxed manner.

She stood by the bar, looking at the tables, and tried to spot Liddell, with no luck. Then she heard a familiar voice from behind her. "I'm glad you decided to come along."

She turned around. "Well, there's not a whole lot to do in the room."

"It's so crowded in here," Liddell said. "What about going for a drink elsewhere?"

"Sure, why not?"

A line of chauffeured cars was picking up people at the hotel entrance. Once they walked past them, they hopped into a taxi that had just dropped off a passenger.

Liddell gave an address to the driver and turned to Connie. "We'll go to a quiet bar around Soho. It's quite close. It used to be one of my favorites, back when I lived here."

Connie nodded.

The taxi stopped at the entrance to a small bar on a narrow side street. As Connie got out of the taxi and waited for Liddell to pay, a young couple stepped out through the thick wooden door, holding hands.

Inside, the atmosphere was casual, but the sleek modern furniture added some sophistication to the place. There were about a dozen tables, only half of them occupied, and a large, wide, marble-topped bar with small white candles artfully placed along it.

"Let's go to the bar," Connie said. *It's more appropriate.*

They sat on the red-velvet-covered stools. The bartender swiftly placed the menus and wine lists in front of them.

"I don't need this one," Liddell said and returned his wine list to the waiter. "She'll pick the wine."

Connie flipped the pages and stopped at the new-world reds section. "This Malbec from Mendoza is really good, and they have it by the glass," she said, pointing to a name on the list.

"If we are both having the same wine, why not order a bottle? It would be more practical."

"Practical? Sure, let's be practical." Her lips slowly curved. "And I'm hungry too!"

They ordered food, and then Connie showed the name of the wine to the bartender. Soon afterward, the young man poured a small amount of the deep-ruby wine into her glass. Connie swirled it and smelled it. She swirled it again, and closing her eyes for a moment, she tasted it. She nodded at the bartender, who filled both glasses and left the bottle in front of them.

Liddell hadn't turned his eyes away from her. "You look so naturally sophisticated when you do that with the glass of wine."

There was a large mirror on the opposite side of the bar, with a variety of liquors and spirits lined up against it. Connie glanced at her reflection. Her damp hair was dry by then. She gently tucked a lock behind her ear as the soft candlelight flickered on her earrings and in her eyes. There was a rosy glow on her cheeks. She smiled, relaxed.

"Thank you. Now, Liddell, would you mind if I asked you something about the Rodin? I'm trying to wrap up our thoughts before we move on to the next work."

"Go ahead."

"Do you really think it's about love *and* sin? I find the sculpture so pure, so full of love, that I can't get my head around the fact that there is any sin in it. I just don't see it in the marble."

"Well, now that you mention it, I brought up the subject of sin only because it's in the story behind the sculpture. For me, the idea of sin gets somewhat diluted in the whole interpretation."

"But do you believe in God?" *This feels weird. I don't remember ever asking this question of anybody.*

"First I'd like to apologize for my comment on religious people. I didn't mean to offend you, and I shouldn't have spoken like that."

"Apology accepted."

"Thank you. Regarding god, I have a rational approach to things, both material and moral. I don't believe in an active god, in heaven and hell, or for that matter, in sin. I believe in human law and in the rational pursuit of the good life. And last but not least, I believe in my own thoughts and emotions, which sometimes I understand, but at other times I don't." He looked straight ahead and sipped some wine.

Connie examined his face. She thought she could see a trace of regret in his green, and now softened, eyes.

He turned to her and continued, "Now, going back to the sculpture, if we ignore the tale and everything that is said *about* the sculpture, then no. I don't see anything wrong in it. Just two people deeply in love with each other."

Connie clasped her hands together and leaned forward. "I discovered a way to feel that was unknown to me. *The Kiss* is like a force of nature. It is raw energy, surging inevitably, ever present and all-embracing, but so delicate and gentle at the same time. When I looked at it, I saw two people, but one single being." She took a small sip; the wine barely touched her lips. "I didn't have much time to read about it, and I didn't know their names, or their stories, but does it really matter? It triggered such a beautiful set of feelings inside me that I just can't accept that there can be any wrong in it. I see love between two individuals in perfect communion, like we said before, love in its purest form."

They looked at each other, and the background music stopped. Connie felt awkward. She turned to the mirror, picked up her glass, and drank some wine.

"I imagine that in order to recognize that kind of love, one must have felt it," Liddell said.

"Well, I haven't," Connie automatically answered. *Did I just say that?* "But I want to believe that it's possible." *Oh, God.* She finished her glass.

Liddell bent his head over his empty glass. He seemed to be thinking about something or someone. Then he picked up the bottle and filled both glasses. "I haven't felt that kind of love either, but I imagine that it would be a hard one to find. Besides, how many people even know that that kind of love is possible?"

*I don't think Nick ever cared to think about love, much less about the intensity of love. But who does?* "Who does?" she said. "I mean, who thinks about love in those terms? It may not be the smartest thing to do to dream about something that you are most likely never going to get."

"Are you backtracking?" Curiosity sparked in Liddell's eyes.

"I'm just realizing that to imagine a love like that would only expose the defects of our current partner, and it would make us feel miserable, or sorry, or both. It's a risky business. We'd be setting ourselves up to fail."

"It takes a wake-up call to think about our lives, and real love as well."

"What do you mean?"

"We usually don't think about the way we live our lives. We just do it. And this is a crass generalization, I know, but I think that most of us get so used to the way of life that, for whatever reason, we have chosen or ended up with, that we become blind to it, and we get stuck in a self-made rut, unable to break free from the beliefs that we've developed over time."

"Including love."

"Yes, but it gets worse. As time goes by—especially if we have a certain feeling of success in life—a reason to think about change gets harder and harder to come across until we become unaware of the possibility of change; we end up accepting and justifying the way we are, what we do, how we feel, and how we relate to others. We use the same tricks to get what we want in life, over and over; we expose the same part of ourselves to the world, and ultimately, we get stuck in the smallness of our own made-up world."

"And the wake-up call is..."

"It can be anything. The death of a loved one, a car accident, maybe even admiring art, for that matter. Any intense moment that shakes us hard enough to make us consider change a possible, or even a desirable option. I relate my little theory to what you just said about dreaming of a perfect love. Maybe a thought like that could be powerful enough to make us opt for change, to think about what's important in our lives." He slowly shook his head. "But honestly, I don't think that a lot of people will be willing to shake things up, just because."

"Unless they have no other choice."

"Correct."

"Have you ever had a wake-up call?" She had that same feeling of asking too much again, but this time it felt good.

"When I was younger, I thought that if I traveled enough, I wouldn't get stuck in any of those *mental habits,* as I like to call them, because life would surprise me time after time. Every trip was a novelty, and I could reinvent myself as I discovered new people and new places." His face lit up with joy. "If that proved to be true, then I wouldn't need a wake-up call at all. I would stay always fresh and free, forever young!" He paused and looked perplexed. "But when I think about it…it didn't work out like that. I just got used to traveling. And here I am, stuck with my own small self, too, just like everybody else." He chuckled. "So finally, my answer to your question is no. I have not had a wake-up call…yet."

"What an interesting thought," she said.

She drank more wine and closed her eyes. She imagined having that same conversation with Nick. *We are both too stuck in our own ways. Was it time that imposed on us the same empty words, expressions, and feelings, forcing us to repeat them over and over again, day after day? Or is it the lack of love that made them all too evident?*

She remained silent until they finished the bottle. Liddell didn't speak either; he seemed absorbed in his own thoughts.

"Are you ready to go back to the hotel?" she softly asked, disguising her emotions behind a calm smile.

Liddell nodded and raised his hand to the bartender. "Have you ever been to the opera?"

"What? No. Why?"

"There's *Madama Butterfly* at Covent Garden tonight, starts in an hour. Would you like to come with me?" Liddell pulled a few bills from his money clip and stood up, signaling toward the bar door. "We better get going if we want to make it in time."

"But—how?"

"I bought two tickets online when I got to my room. I imagined you would be interested."

Connie took her purse and followed him. "I need to change clothes," she finally managed to say.

⊯ ⊱

Connie spotted Liddell immediately. He was standing beside a red upholstered bergère across the lobby, with his left elbow on the backrest. His eyes were on the piano next to the bar, where a young man played a jazz standard. There was something that made Liddell stand out from the people around him. A certain aura, an indefinable light, made him appear unique in Connie's eyes.

As if he had sensed her entering the lobby, Liddell turned to Connie, and then he slowly straightened and watched her approach. His eyes looked alert, engaged with her.

Connie felt at ease in her long navy-blue dress. *Not a bad purchase after all.* Topped with a silvery-gray silk shawl around her shoulders, her gown emphasized the better features of her body.

"Connie," Liddell said without hiding his surprise, "you look fantastic. I'll be the envy of all the gentlemen at the opera house."

"Thank you, Liddell. You look very smart too." She reached out to Liddell's gray tie and slightly centered it.

The taxi was waiting outside.

"I can't believe I'm going to the opera." Connie said, entering the cab. "But you've been before."

"Covent Garden, please," Liddell said to the driver, and as the car took speed, he turned to Connie. "Yes, I've gone many times. I love opera. Not all of it, though...I enjoy Italian opera in particular."

"How did you get to like it?"

"My father loves opera. Growing up, I listened to it almost every evening, from vinyl records to shortwave radio. Father was always trying to find something new: a new singer, a different production, a different orchestra."

"Is he a musician?"

"No. Barrister. He likes facts. He used to read everything and anything about opera...and I was always around. We used to play chess, his other passion, while we listened to classical music."

"When was your first time at the opera?"

"Let me see. Father took me to the opera for the first time when I was fifteen years old. Mother was ill that day and couldn't come, so it was just the two of us. And it was actually this same one, *Madama Butterfly.*"

"Does your father live in Sweden too?"

"No. He and Mother still live in Cape Town."

"So that's where you're from."

"Yes."

"Then I guess you don't see them that often."

"True, they don't like traveling, and Mother's health is very fragile; even if Father wanted to come visit, he wouldn't leave her alone. The last time I saw them was three years ago." He frowned, as if remembering an unpleasant moment. "I went by myself. Sigrid didn't want to come."

"Sigrid...your wife?"

"Yes. She stayed with the boys."

Connie's heart beat harder. She felt the urge to know everything about Liddell: about his sons, his wife, and his parents. About his thoughts, his feelings, his memories. But she couldn't utter a word; instead, she looked into his eyes. Her whole self was drawn into his deep-green eyes—eyes with the obstinate zeal of keeping his private world locked up behind them.

"Covent Garden," the driver announced.

Liddell paid, and they rushed into the theater. As soon as they entered the foyer, a bell sound played over the speakers, signaling that the patrons should go to their seats.

"Right on time!" he said.

Connie followed Liddell into the opera hall. Their seats were at the orchestra level, near the center.

According to the program, this was the second to last of the eleven performances the Royal Opera had staged of Puccini's *Madama Butterfly* during that season. Connie read the enthusiastic reviews in the program pages; evidently, the expectations were high. The soprano playing Butterfly's role was a Russian star. Connie looked at her picture: a middle-aged, well-built woman with an apparently very powerful voice and great experience in drama. Pinkerton was played by a world-famous Italian tenor, known for his "bright vocal power and the perfect diction of his singing." Connie closed the program and tucked it on the side of her seat.

Around her were people from all walks of life. A few rows down, a man in a tuxedo stood up, looking toward the balcony. To her right, a tourist couple, dressed in khaki pants and light-beige shirts were taking pictures with their phones. Up in the balcony, on the sides, Connie thought she could see the habitués who came to the opera after work. She wondered how many happy couples there might be in the hall, at that very moment, enjoying each other's company on a special night out.

"I like the multicultural feeling to this audience," she said after listening to the different languages being spoken around her.

Liddell nodded. "Opera houses are a haven for the stranger in a strange land."

The musicians slowly took their seats. A few scattered notes from the brass section, a cello melody, and the reeds playing a scale up and down warmed up the theater's atmosphere.

The oboist played a long, elastic A note. The whole string section played along, the brass joined in, and then the rest of the instruments followed. Then they all stopped at the same time. Connie felt the tension in the air growing. The lights went out, and a reverential silence took its place.

A spotlight followed the conductor as he made his way to the podium through the music stands. People applauded. He bowed to the public, and once the clapping faded, he turned toward the orchestra. His baton slashed the air three times, and the overture started.

The sound of the violins seemed to come in waves, from everywhere. The stage lights came on, washing over two singers as they entered the stage. Connie could hear the restrained sighs of the audience, already in rapture.

The opera was set in Japan, during the late nineteenth century. The actors sang in Italian, but Connie quickly read the English subtitles on a small screen placed at the back of the seat in front of her. Her eyes went back and forth from the stage to the little screen. The music wasn't loud, just the natural sound that came out of the instruments and the power of the singers' own voices.

During the first act, Pinkerton, a US Navy lieutenant, buys and marries a young girl, a singer called Cio-Cio-San, Japanese for butterfly.

Butterfly has an irresistible air of innocence that Pinkerton wants to possess, even knowing that he will soon leave her and go back to America to "marry a real, American bride," as he put it. Sharpless, the US consul, warns Pinkerton that by doing so, he will break Butterfly's heart. Connie felt a gust of foreboding fear when she saw the young, fragile, and oblivious Butterfly, surrounded by her joyful girlfriends, walking up the steep hill leading to Pinkerton's house.

**Butterfly**
I am the happiest maiden,
the happiest in Japan,
in all the world!

**Girl Friends**
Best of fortune attend on you,
gentle maiden, but here
you cross over the threshold.
Pause and look behind you,
and admire the things you hold the dearest!

Pinkerton disregards Sharpless's advice and marries Butterfly anyway. Minutes after the marriage, during the party, Butterfly is harshly attacked by her own family with questions. They've found out that she has abandoned their traditional religion to become a Christian, thus totally surrendering to Pinkerton. When Butterfly admits to her conversion, her family renounces her. She bursts into tears as Pinkerton expels her family from his house. Then he consoles her.

### Butterfly
I used to think: if anyone should want me,
then perhaps for a time I might have married...
...now I am happy.
Yes, I am happy...

### Pinkerton
Give me your darling hands that I may kiss them.
My Butterfly! Aptly your name was chosen,
Gossamer creation.

The dialogue between them continues. Connie sadly watched Butterfly fall deeper and deeper into Pinkerton's deception. The newlywed couple finally retires to the nuptial chamber, and Pinkerton closes the sliding door behind them.

The curtain fell. The first act finished with a heavy round of applause, and shortly after, the lights came back on.

Some people stood up and left the concert hall during the intermission. Connie and Liddell stayed in their seats.

"What do you think?" Liddell asked.

"I've always thought that the opera was dull, old-fashioned entertainment for snobby people. I was so wrong!"

"Glad to hear that."

"I noticed that you barely read the subtitles. Do you understand Italian?" she asked.

"I've seen this opera so many times. I know some bits of the recitatives and most of the arias by heart. I still listen to them now, twenty-seven years after that first time with my father."

"What's your favorite memory of that performance?"

"Let me see…it was the first time I ever saw my father cry. Actually, it was the only time," he added in a casual tone.

Connie wasn't expecting that kind of self-disclosing answer. "Hold on…Are you forty-two?" she asked, changing the subject.

"Good math. Yes, I am forty-two. Surprised?" He grinned.

"I thought you were older than me. I'm forty-seven. I mean, you look so formal."

Liddell pulled his vibrating cell phone out of his pocket. Connie thought she could read "Sigrid" on the screen.

"Thank you. I appreciate maturity," he replied and looked at the phone screen. "I need to take this call. Sorry," he added. He stood up and walked to the corridor.

Connie tried to imagine Sigrid. *What would she be like? She's Swedish, so she's probably a tall, sophisticated, and gorgeous woman. I wonder if she's still infatuated by Liddell's charm, after the decade that they've been together. Does she know him as well as I want to know him? Does she still crave his presence when he is not around, as I do? Do they still make love and mean love? Making love with Nick, back when it used to happen, was just the satisfaction of his own needs—never saying that he loves me, never asking, either. I can't imagine Liddell's marriage being as forsaken as mine. No. He looks like an active man, ready and willing to fulfill his wife's deepest needs—of love, of companionship, of communication. They think about each other, she calls him, he picks up the phone, and they talk. He makes Nick look like a real brute, which is what Nick probably turned into, but I just never realized it, until now.*

Liddell returned to his seat right before the lights went out.

In the second act, Butterfly and her maid, Suzuki, are alone in the house that Pinkerton bought for them and then abandoned. The two women are in financial ruin. Three years have passed since Pinkerton left for America. Against all evidence, she has been waiting for his return, and she scolds Suzuki when she shows doubts about Pinkerton's return. Then, full of faith and smiling, Butterfly says,

> Weeping? And why? And why?
> Ah, it's faith you are lacking!
> Hear me.

Connie's skin tingled. The opera house became deathly silent, as if something major was about to happen. She held her breath, and completely immobile, she fixed her eyes on the stage, without even blinking.

The soprano quietly begins singing a humble melody. The soft, plush sound of her voice caressed Connie's ears, as the orchestra entered in crescendo. The notes grew louder and more dramatic with every word, playing along with the sad melody.

> One fine day we'll notice
> a thread of smoke arising on the sea, in the far horizon.
> And then the ship appearing;
> then the trim white vessel
> glides into the harbor, thunders forth her cannon.
> You see? Now he is coming!

Butterfly's sadness mingles with hope—hope for a happy life with Pinkerton. Connie's skin hardened with chills, and her hands felt cold. *This is divine. Magic.*

Five minutes passed in a heartbeat, and the aria finished. Connie felt light, ethereal. In awe.

Before the end of the second act, Butterfly calls Sharpless and lovingly shows him the son whom she gave birth to a few months after Pinkerton had left. She named him Dolore—Sorrow. Sharpless looks at the blond-haired three-year-old boy and understands how deep, but also how doomed, Butterfly's love for Pinkerton is.

In the next act, Sharpless and the newly arrived Pinkerton, with his American wife, Kate, go to Butterfly's house early in the morning. Pinkerton has returned to Japan for a brief time, and when they learn of the existence of Sorrow, they decide that the best course of action is to take the child back to America with them, where the boy will be loved as their own son and will receive a proper education. The party quietly arrives at Butterfly's house, and only the maid is there to receive them. Pinkerton sees how nicely decorated the house is to celebrate his return and realizes how much Butterfly still loves him. Filled with guilt, he is ashamed for what he has done to her and cries bitterly. Overwhelmed by remorse, he flees the house without seeing Butterfly.

Butterfly wakes and learns that Pinkerton will soon leave for America again, this time probably never to return. Butterfly sees Sharpless and Kate standing in the distance and realizes who she is. After a brief but painful conversation, Butterfly agrees to give her child away to Kate. Butterfly's only condition is that Pinkerton himself should come pick up the boy.

After Kate and Sharpless leave, Butterfly dismisses Suzuki and goes to her room. She returns with a dagger, as she says:

> Death with honor is
> better than life with dishonor.

Unexpectedly, the boy comes into her presence. Butterfly hastily hides the dagger, kisses him dearly, and sits him on a mat as she lulls him,

My son, sent to me from heaven,
take one last and careful look
at your poor mother's face!
That its memory may linger,
one last look!
Farewell, beloved! Farewell, my dearest heart!
Go, play, play.

Oblivious of what's about to happen, the small boy picks up an American flag that Butterfly gave him to play with as she gently blindfolds his eyes.

Out of her son's view, she thrusts the dagger deep into her abdomen and slashes it open.

Right before her last breath, she hears Pinkerton's voice calling her name as he hurries into the house to see her for the last time. Butterfly weakly points at the small boy, and then she collapses and dies.

The heavy velvet curtain came down one more time. The house shook with roars of applause and bravos from the audience, now on its feet. People were in tears—handkerchiefs in hand, they clapped, cried, and clapped again.

Connie got carried away by the moment. With tear-brimmed eyes, she clasped her hands and whispered bravos.

The curtain went back up, and the performers, coming back onstage one by one, bowed to the cheering public and the ovation. The crowd members didn't want to leave the hall, reviving their applause each time the singers bowed or waved.

"They all want a little bit more of this feeling that you only get at the opera house," Liddell said, raising his voice over the clapping and cheering.

Connie nodded.

As the clapping faded out, Liddell looked at his watch. "Ready for coffee?"

"Coffee? It is eleven o'clock! How am I supposed to sleep after that?"

"Come on! Let's stay up a little longer! Our flight is not until eleven in the morning!"

Connie felt relieved, and against her better judgment, she decided to go for coffee with Liddell, even at eleven at night. "Let's go."

"The Delaunay is still open," he said.

⇥ ⇤

"Double macchiato," Liddell ordered.

"Same, please," Connie said.

The waiter nodded and rapidly zigzagged through the busy tables, heading back to the bar.

Liddell felt a subtle joy mixed with a different kind of feeling that he tried to pinpoint. *I want to get closer to her—in every sense.*

Connie showed the glow of a woman who had just experienced something transcendent; her eyes were filled with light and emotion.

*She looks exultant and unaffected. She looks true.*

Connie's lips parted, and after a moment searching for the right words, she began talking. "This was just marvelous. The whole experience: being dressed up like this, the music, the singing, and even the people around us. So beautiful! How did I miss out on this for all these years?"

"Well, this is a good start," Liddell said.

Her smile was wide, intense. *The lines on the sides of her mouth, her smooth lips, and white teeth—they remind me of young, fresh hopes.*

"Okay. Let's treat this as the art we've been looking at. Who speaks first?" she asked, clasping her hands.

"You first, please," he said.

"I think this work of art is about the tragic ending of unbalanced relationships. The typical case when someone is deeply in love but the other is not, or at least not anymore. Such imbalance also affects the way people in a relationship understand their love: what commitments they are willing to accept; what things they give up…I was moved that Butterfly gave up so much; she even rejected her religion because of love."

She paused as the waiter placed their cups in front of them.

"You're right. Pinkerton never moved a jot for her," he added.

Connie picked up the small silver spoon and swirled her coffee. "That imbalance was everywhere: cultural, financial, religious… It was as if such love was destined to fail…They didn't have anything in common." She paused and turned her head sideways, as if catching a thought, and went on. "But it could've worked, if only Pinkerton had loved her a little bit."

Liddell nodded. "Pinkerton was always aware of that. But why didn't Butterfly notice it until the very end? She was told multiple times—by her maid, the matchmaker, the consul; in fact, everybody seemed to know it, except for her. Her conviction, which eventually turned into stubbornness, made her blind to the truth that she wasn't loved."

Connie puckered her lips. "I think that once you've given up that much of yourself because of someone else, then you believe that all you have is the other person. You'd think that if that person stopped loving you, then you would be left with nothing. Her love for Pinkerton isolated her; and once she realized that she wasn't loved by the one for whom she had given up everything, she felt completely worthless, so devastated that she decided to kill herself." She paused, looking for the right words. "Coming from such different worlds, their concept of what love really is, of how deep it can go, was completely different. Pinkerton assumed that Butterfly would understand that he didn't love her and move on, but he was wrong."

Liddell remained quiet. He looked down at his cup.

"Now it's your turn, Liddell. You're the opera specialist here."

"I agree with your interpretation. There are plenty of imbalances in their relationship. They couldn't have been more different, as you say, in all regards. But to me there is another element just as important, and that element is the power of the decisions that they made.

"When you think about it," he continued, "nothing in the story happened by chance. No accidents, no murders, not even a disease or some natural disaster. Everything that happened in the story was the result of the characters' own decisions: Pinkerton decided to marry Butterfly for his sole pleasure, and Butterfly decided to accept. She decided to reject her religion—Pinkerton never asked her to do that. Pinkerton decided to leave her and get married in the US—he wasn't forced to go off to war or something of the sort. Butterfly decided to wait for him, even when all the facts were against her hopes. He never even wrote to her; she found out about him through a letter he sent to Sharpless, three years after his departure. And when he eventually returned, he didn't have the courage to see her."

"Pinkerton was a scoundrel," Connie pronounced, shaking her head.

"An absolute scoundrel. And poor Butterfly...after agreeing to give up her son to Pinkerton, because the boy is intentionally delivered to him and his wife, she finds herself without a husband and without a son. Left with nothing, she makes her final decision and commits seppuku. Decisions have consequences—we make our own beds. My father used to say that this opera is more about decisions than it is about love."

"How did he come about that conclusion?"

"It's a bit personal. I don't know if you—"

"I'd love to hear it," she interrupted.

"This is odd. I've never talked about this with anybody, not even with Sigrid."

Connie leaned forward.

Liddell closed his eyes and saw himself with his father, Sean, at the opera, twenty-seven years earlier. The memories of that night had stayed with him as clearly as Puccini's arias.

He opened his eyes and stared into Connie's receptive gaze. "As I told you, my father took me to the opera for the first time when I was fifteen. *Madama Butterfly.* Everything was new to me—from the opera house at night, to the people so dressed up, to the loud chatter in the foyer. I remember Father had a glass of Champagne at the small bar before we got inside the hall; he always did that. Then we took our seats, the lights went down, and the opera started.

"I thought the performance was good. But what did I know? It was my first time. Anyway, it all went fine until 'Un bel di vedremo,' Butterfly's aria at the top of second act. Do you remember that one?"

"Of course."

"I turned to him to see his reaction and to share my excitement with him, but to my surprise, he was crying. And quite profusely. His eyes seemed lost; he was looking at the stage, but I knew he was looking beyond the stage. His mind was somewhere else, far away. His face didn't move; tears came rolling down his cheeks, and he did nothing to stop them. I was shocked because he's such a rational and harsh man."

"What did you do?"

"Nothing. I slowly turned my face back to the stage and didn't look at him again until the lights came back on. Once they did, he looked absolutely normal, as if nothing ever happened. He even smiled. On our drive back home, we had a little chat about my first time at the opera, my impressions about it, and such."

"Did you mention it to him?"

"No, but he noticed I was acting strange. It was around midnight by the time we got home. He stopped the car in the garage and looked at me with his inquisitive lawyer's gaze. He read me right through. "We will talk," he said. So we went inside the house and sat in the drawing room. Mother was asleep. He picked up a bottle of scotch and brought two glasses. He poured a good measure into both, picked one up, and pointed at the other one with his open palm."

"He offered scotch to a fifteen-year-old?"

"He's unorthodox. Always been. I picked it up, and we made a toast. 'You're not a child anymore,' he said."

Liddell felt transported back to that night. He saw his younger self, sitting on one of the plush Bordeaux-red armchairs. His father sat on the one beside him. He recognized the small, long-legged square table with the amber bottle of scotch sitting between them. He was witnessing, once again, the dialogue that had burdened him so heavily ever since. He had paraphrased that conversation to himself hundreds of times before, but this time he did it out loud, with all detail, and shared it with this woman who had captivated him so intensely.

Sean, his father, gulped some scotch and started the conversation. "I assume you saw me crying at the opera, and you were surprised to see me in such a state. I also assume that you remember it was during 'Un bel di' that this happened. You were slightly embarrassed, but you tried to act normally. Now you wonder why I was crying. You know it takes more than a melody to make me cry. Am I right?"

"Yes, Father," an insecure teenager answered.

"Your mother is seriously ill."

"Mother? What is it?"

"Depression. She has lived with it for the last nine years. But as it turns out, after suffering so intensely from it for so long, depression has prevailed over her mind, keeping her now in a constant state of melancholy and with a certain unawareness of reality. I am sure you have noticed her slow decay in the last couple of years."

"I've noticed she's been a little slower than she used to be—"

"She is now just the shadow of the woman I once loved."

"But didn't you say it was her hormones that weren't right? That the medication she is taking will solve it? Why...why is she depressed?"

"The pills do what they can, which is not much." Sean swallowed another generous mouthful of scotch. "I'm not a good husband. I've got flaws, like everyone else. I must admit that sometimes I lose my temper, and I'm not the kindest of men. But you already know that, right?"

Liddell was immobile. Sean hesitated, shook his head in self-reproach, and continued. "I've done a great deal of harm to your mother. I'm just as guilty as Pinkerton. I enjoy women too much. I've always done." He swallowed the remaining scotch in his glass and poured more into it. "I've always had a woman on the side, even when you were born and in the months that followed. Women are too busy to care for their husbands' needs during that time. That's just the way it is. She knew about my affairs, and she tolerated my tantrums for a number of years, without a word of complaint." He drank more. "She kept it all inside for far too long. By the time you were a small boy, she began to get moody, more and more often. I paid no attention to those signs; I took it for granted that they were transitory—just the way women are sometimes. I was wrong. She never got better. Do you remember the week I sent you to your grandmother's house for a few days?"

"Yes, I remember. Grandma Johanne was finishing a painting of mother and me."

"I took your mother to the hospital. She was delirious. They had to sedate her just to stop her from hurting herself. I stayed by her bed during those four dreadful days. I thought she was going to die. During the night she would talk in her dreams; those drugs they gave her were so strong...One night she said such horrible things about me. I found out that she despised me, but somehow it didn't surprise me." He finished the second glass of scotch and poured more.

Liddell wrinkled his nose in disgust and put his untouched glass back on the small table.

Sean continued. "Then she calmed down. Her face relaxed, and a shy smile appeared on her lips. The muscles of her arms lost all tension, she put her hands together, and with the sweetest voice, full of tenderness, she said that she loved me. That alone," he emphasized with a raised pointer finger, "that alone, made me think that it wasn't too late to mend my ways. If she still loved me, there was a chance that I could have her back."

"So she will get better soon?" young Liddell had asked, wishing that all that his father had told him was a thing of the past and that his mother was now on the path of recovery.

"Un bel di vedremo, son," Sean said. "Like in the opera, my decisions can have dire consequences. I just hope that one day she will come back from the darkness she's been in for all these years, she will forgive me, and we will love each other again." Sean finished his third glass of scotch, and with it, the conversation. He had said as much as he would ever say about it.

Connie remained immobile under Liddell's spell. "Did you ever talk to your mother about it?" she asked.

"No. She doesn't know that I know." Liddell sipped his now cold macchiato.

Connie watched Liddell as he slowly put the cup back on the saucer. She saw the opaque light of regret blurring his eyes. She recognized that feeling. If some things had just been different. If one could steer those moments away from one's past, or at least from one's memory, that would be enough.

She looked at her watch. "It's almost one in the morning. Should we go back to the hotel?"

⊨ ⊨

Once in her room, Connie sat in front of her computer. It was 7:30 p.m. in Minnesota at that moment. She realized how silent her room was, and after the unexpected dose of caffeine, she didn't feel ready to go to bed. She opened the curtains and looked at the BBC building right across the street. Then she turned to look at All Saints Church—its small round shape and single spire caught her eye. *I feel out of place. Something is missing.* She felt the urge to hear a familiar voice, to talk to somebody about her day, about her feelings.

Connie launched Skype and called Deb's cell phone number. At the third ring, Deb's energetic voice came out of the computer speakers, her voice loud and clear.

"Hello, this is Deb."

"It's me, Connie!"

"Why did I see all zeros on my phone instead of your name?"

"Because I'm calling you from my computer."

"Oh, I see. How's the European excursion going so far?"

"It's going great. We're having these wonderful conversations—"

"Who else is out there with you?"

"I'm with this man called Liddell, who is filling in for the UK editor who couldn't make it either. Isn't it strange?"

"Hmm."

"We went to see Bernini's *Rape of Proserpina*, Michelangelo's *Pietà*, Rodin's *The Kiss*, and now we just came back from the opera, *Madama Butterfly*. It was amazing, Deb."

"What does he say about it?"

"Well, he's into opera, and he has seen *Butterfly* many times before. After the show he told me this really sad story about his parents. We've been talking a lot." Connie paused. A shy smile had appeared on her lips. "He's a very interesting guy—handsome too."

"I meant what Nick says. How does he feel about you hanging out with another man?"

Connie's smile disappeared. "I don't think he'd be happy if he knew how *I* feel about it." She paused. "I guess that's why I called you. I've been thinking about things I've never thought about before."

"What kind of things?"

"For instance...love. I discovered feelings that I'm sure Nick would never understand, feelings that are so foreign to him. When I was looking at Rodin's *The Kiss,* I felt the need to be loved just like that: I felt that anything less than *that* kind of love, tenderness, connection, passion..." She hesitated. "Anything less...is not really love. Love should feel like that. Not the way I..." She stopped to think about what she was about to say. *The writing is on the wall.* "But at the same time, before seeing the statue and opening myself up to those feelings, I never thought that love could be so passionate and deep. Does it make any sense? I'm so confused. I never thought I'd feel so vulnerable—not at this age."

"Go on..." Deb's voice was soft and soothing.

"At the opera, I felt like I was on cloud nine. Beauty surrounded me, the music was pure, the singers like angels. And then after the show, when we were discussing our impressions, I felt connected to Liddell in such a deep way, a way unknown to me. He told me about his life, and I told him some things about mine. Nothing special, but we shared time, we looked at each other, we actually listened to each other...and I realized that I've never had any deep and open conversations with Nick. I mean, ever! I'm embarrassed, Deb. Here I am, with this man I met two days ago, talking about things that I've never talked about with my own husband. Don't you think this is wrong?"

"Why should it be? You're just talking." Deb sounded assertive, as usual.

"But I feel I'm not being honest with Nick. He's the one I should be having these chats with, but I don't know where to start...I don't know if he'll get it, or if he'll even care..."

Connie knew that Deb never liked Nick. When she first met him, Deb had said that he was a simpleminded man, below what Connie deserved; but she never said a word again after Connie and Nick got married.

"You can't transfer your experience, Connie. There's no way Nick will be on the same page that you are on now. Why blame yourself for your feelings? You should live the moments that are only yours to live."

Connie took a deep breath and exhaled slowly; she could feel the tension inside her subside. "I don't know me anymore, Deb. I opened a Pandora's box...and it feels like I've been oblivious, distracted for all these years, and suddenly my mind and my heart are upside down."

"I don't know what to say to that, Connie." Deb sighed. "But it may be a good idea to think twice before you do something drastic."

The chime of the incoming mail caught her attention. She instinctively brought the mail program to the forefront of the screen, and to her surprise, she saw Liddell's name at the top of her in-box.

"Oh—" Connie covered her mouth with her hand. "I—I'll call you later, Deb. Something came up."

"Okay...bye, I guess?" Deb sounded surprised.

Her eyes remained on his name for a moment. *Liddell Lockheed.* She forced herself to wait a few seconds before opening it. She wanted to savor that unexpected rush a little bit longer. Her heart pounded in her chest. She took a deep breath and clicked it open.

Hello Connie,

Thanks for coming to opera with me tonight, I know how tired you must be.

It was truly lovely to share time and thoughts together.

Liddell

She whispered the words "truly lovely" and "together."

*I haven't had a lovely moment in a long time. Tonight was lovely, absolutely lovely.*

She quickly wrote him back.

Liddell,

Thank you for your kind words. I enjoyed the opera very much...and your company too. Also, thank you for buying the tickets and thinking of me!

Have a good night of sleep and see you in the morning. Paris awaits us!

xx—Connie

She closed her computer, set the alarm for 6:00 a.m., and then quickly undressed and got under the covers.

# CHAPTER 5

# PARIS. WEDNESDAY.

Connie stepped outside the hotel and gazed up at the pale English sky. *Wednesday morning. Last day of the trip.* A stream of puffy white clouds slowly floated across the brisk September-morning air. She took in a deep breath. *I'll remember London like this.* She then turned to Liddell, who was standing next to the taxi, and nodded.

He slid into the car after her. "Heathrow, please."

The driver pulled away into the moving traffic.

Forty-five minutes later, the taxi dropped them off at the airport. It was a busy morning—people filled almost every space of the check-in area. They went to the less-crowded first-class counter and checked their bags, and then zipped through security's priority lane.

"It'll be hard to fly coach ever again. I feel spoiled!"

"Will is not cheap when it comes to spending the magazine's money," Liddell said and chuckled.

"I just wish this trip were a little longer."

"Me too."

As they arrived to the gate, a British Airways employee announced the boarding of their flight to Paris. "First-class passengers are welcome to board now," she said over the PA in heavily accented British English. They slowly headed for the open gate.

⇥ ⇤

It was a bumpy flight. They flew through a few stormy pockets until they reached cruising altitude. The captain asked the passengers to keep their seat belts on and announced that the beverage service would be delayed due to more turbulence ahead. Liddell ignored the plane's rough movements—he'd flown enough times to feel unperturbed.

His mind went to Sigrid. The night before, she had called him just to let him know that Sean wanted to talk to him, but Sean wouldn't call Liddell's cell phone. She had complained that his father didn't want to tell her the motive of his call and had been rude and dismissive with her; she was very upset and said that Sean was a misogynist bully.

Liddell wondered if she still cared to think about him as her husband. *We don't have much of a present together, but we have a fairly well-populated past: the trips, the nights of conversation and drinks, the laughter, the kids. I wonder if she ever stops to remember any of that, if she has any love left for me after all these years. I should call her today. I should tell her that I miss her and ask her to give us another chance. This isn't lost after all; we have the boys, and we have history. It should work out.*

They left the windy skies behind. The flight attendants finally pushed their carts through the aisles, and handing out napkins, they asked the usual questions.

"Would you like something to drink, sir?"

"No, thank you," he said and closed his eyes.

He remembered when Sigrid was pregnant with Rutger. *She looked gorgeous. Such a warm glow in her face, so much life in her eyes.* During the last weeks of pregnancy, Sigrid had always been smiling and touching her belly, as if she were including baby Rutger in all her

124

conversations and thoughts. She worked until the last minute. On her due date, she had called him from her office to let him know that she would be at the hospital delivering Rutger. *Sigrid, you've always been such a brave, fearless woman. I've always admired your resolution, your will to get things done, your hunger to succeed. Am I a burden on your life now? Are you done with me? I feel so excluded, it's as if I'm just another chore to check off on your mental list. I'll understand if you've changed your mind and now want to go on alone. I know people change. I know it all too well.*

His thoughts went back to one particular moment from his childhood. It had been a sunny spring morning in Cape Town, but more so, it had been a Saturday, the most awaited day of the week, when he had enough time to wander around before tennis practice at eleven o'clock with Felix, his best friend.

He left his bicycle outside his house, leaning against the three-foot-high wall that separated the main door from the garage. It seemed much higher back then. Later on, he realized how big things look through a child's eyes.

The front door was wide open, and a smooth melody issued from inside the house. The air felt light; it was a splendid morning. The smell emerging from the kitchen announced that his mother was cooking his favorite meal for lunch—oven-roasted chicken with potatoes. *She made it every Saturday.*

He went through the front door, across the small hall into the corridor, toward the kitchen, which was at the back of the two-bedroom house. Now he could hear his mother humming the song that was playing on the turntable in the drawing room: "Va Pensiero," sung by the inimitable Nana Mouskouri.

He entered the kitchen without knowing that the image he was about to see would stay with him for years to come: his mother was smiling, singing small bits of the song, and moving around the kitchen. She was wearing a ruffled white blouse, an ankle-length brown skirt, and a white apron with a floral motif that she had made herself. And she hadn't noticed his presence.

Liddell stood by the door. A peaceful, warm, yellow light entered from the window above the sink and washed over the whole room; it was a light that, later in his life, he would often dream of. Both casements were open, and the bigger window on the adjacent wall, facing the back garden, was open too. The white cotton curtains moved to the rhythm of the breeze, as if trying to dance along with the content woman who was immersed in her intimate, daily world. A small world indeed, a tessellate of indefinable yet significant details: the apron she had sewn herself; the exact place where she kept her favorite pan; the same short Italian glass she used for drinking water, always on the countertop; her brown leather notepad—where she used to write short sentences, recipes, and bits of thoughts—tucked away beside the spice jars.

She turned around and faced Liddell's innocent smile and wide-open green eyes. "Liddell," she said with her soothing low voice, smiling back at him. She rapidly swept across the kitchen and kissed him on the cheek. Then, with her soft, warm hands, she caressed his face. Their deep-green eyes, identical in hue, met each other. A second later, she went back to her chores.

Even after the many recurring bouts of depression that his mother had suffered over the years, Liddell had always managed to pull up that single memory, that dynamic picture in his mind, which contained what he believed was the real essence of his mother. No matter how far away in space and time it now was from him, he always felt as if it had just happened.

"This is the captain speaking. Please fasten your seat belts. We are starting our descent into Paris, the city of light."

The plane stopped near the runway for a few minutes, waiting for a gate to be assigned. The captain welcomed them to Paris, mentioned the local time, thanked them for flying with British Airways, and said he was sorry for this delay. He said it should only take a few more minutes and told them to have a great day. As soon as his spiel was over, the flight attendant picked up the microphone and repeated the captain's speech in several languages. Liddell kept his eyes closed. Airline talk invariably annoyed him.

They walked to the baggage claim in silence. A calm, French, female voice sounded through the PA speakers; Connie mentioned that she had not heard anybody speaking French since her mother passed.

Once outside the terminal, they looked around for a taxi stop. Connie spotted it almost immediately, as if she'd been at that airport many times. When they pulled their bags toward the line of people getting in the cars, a warm breeze blew through her hair—he looked at her as she smiled.

"I can't believe I'm in Paris," Connie said, clicking the seat belt on. "There is so much I want to visit, but I'll only be here for less that twenty-four hours."

"Next time," Liddell said.

"I don't know if there'll be a next time."

"Just believe there will. Always think you will return to the places you like. It makes leaving them less painful, and besides, you actually don't know what the future will bring."

"A nice thought, Liddell, but I'm pretty sure this trip is a one-off for me."

"Don't you think you might come back with your family on vacation?"

"Not really. I want my girls to visit Europe, but Nick is not even into traveling in Minnesota, much less outside the United States."

Liddell noticed a change in Connie's voice. It was somehow devoid of hope, slightly somber. *Maybe the fact that the trip is coming to an end makes her think about her life back at home, about her husband. Fair enough. It made me think about my wife. But she seems restrained, less ambitious. Her dream is coming to an end. Tomorrow she'll head back home, to the real world as she knows it. She's getting ready for it. She's protecting herself from her own hopes. Liddell, you're making things up again.*

⫸ ⫷

Connie observed the passing landscape out the taxi window. She daydreamed of a conversation with Nick about going back to Europe, this time with the whole family. She pictured him getting excited about the trip, the kids packing their bags, and the entire family talking about it. Then she imagined the five of them walking around museums, little cobbled streets, having a coffee here and there, and even at a picnic in a park. *It's never going to happen.* She shook off those thoughts and stared at the never-ending postcard-style landscape that scrolled through the window.

The taxi took them to the Millennium Opera Hotel, a forty-minute ride from Charles de Gaulle airport. It was a fresh morning in Paris. The city was in full motion: busy people going to work, nannies pushing strollers, couples chatting at cafés, and students carrying their backpacks. Life flooded the streets.

They arrived at the hotel on Boulevard Haussmann at eleven. The lobby had a manicured art-deco atmosphere with delicate geometric patterns on the doors and wooden furniture, pale stucco walls and ocher marble columns, and a black-and-white-checkered marble floor—she felt immediately relaxed.

"*Bonjour*, welcome to the Millennium Hotel," the woman at the front desk said.

"Hello, we have a reservation," Liddell said, pulling his slim money clip from the breast pocket of his blue jacket. Connie stood next to him, fiddling with her purse, looking for her passport.

"You have a reservation for two rooms. Is the other couple coming later?" the receptionist asked.

"No. We are taking the two rooms. One for me and one for the lady."

The hotel employee nodded earnestly. "Oh, of course." She typed a few words on her computer and handed them the key cards. "My colleague will show you the way to the elevator. Enjoy your stay."

They followed a slim, blond-haired young porter across the lobby.

The elevator moved at an incredibly slow speed. "I'll call you in a minute. What's your room number?" Liddell asked.

"302."

"Good. Mine is 202," he said, stepping out of the elevator.

Connie sighed in awe when she entered her room. It was thoughtfully decorated, with lush ornamented brocade curtains on the windows, damask blankets with intricate motifs, and a white veil canopy around the four-poster Renaissance-style bed, which created a soft contrast with the wood-paneled walls. The bed was flanked by two gilded rococo nightstands, and the parquet floor around it was covered with a plush beige rug, woven with crimson arabesques.

She took a shower, changed clothes, and lay down on the bed for a few minutes. She gave a quick look at her watch and counted the hours back to Central Time: almost seven in the morning in Minneapolis. Surely Nick was awake, already checking e-mails. Amanda should be up by now too.

Lately, Amanda liked to go to the basement bathroom and spend time working on her hair. Connie didn't let her use any makeup to go to school, but Amanda still put just a little bit on, enough to make her feel that she got away with it. Connie let that slide.

Connie looked up Nick's number on Skype, but just before clicking on it, she held her finger up. She didn't want to hear his voice.

Her room phone rang. Connie rushed to the nightstand and picked it up after the first ring.

"Ready to go to Musée de l'Orangerie?" Liddell's voice was expectant, excited.

"Yes. Give me just one minute, please."

Connie washed her face with cold water and dabbed some concealer on the dark circles under her eyes. Turning the lights off, she went to the door. But then she stopped short, spun around, and went back to the bathroom. She flicked the light back on and searched in her toiletry bag. She put on a hint of light-red lipstick and changed her earrings; then she brushed her hair and tucked in a small violet barrette above her right temple. She grabbed her purse, and without smiling, she left the room and headed to the lobby.

Liddell was sitting on a couch, flipping the pages of *Le Figaro* with indifference. As soon as he saw her approaching, he quickly put the paper down and stood up.

⚔

They walked down the Boulevard des Italiens toward the Opera Garnier, where they briefly stopped to take pictures of its monumental facade. They headed down the Rue de la Paix, across the Place Vendôme, and turned right at the Rue de Rivoli. The quiet stroll with Liddell and the view of the Tuileries Garden gave her a comforting sense of peace. *There's nothing wrong with feeling at ease when I'm alone with him. We could become friends.*

Liddell suggested stopping for lunch at L'Impérial. The bistro was full with office workers and tourists and had no tables left, but just when they were about to leave, a young couple got up from one of the small tables outside. They immediately took their places.

Connie held the menu with both hands, but her eyes went to Liddell; he was reading his out loud, trying to pronounce the words in ridiculously broken French.

"Our last lunch together deserves a celebration, French style. Would you order the wine, please?" Liddell said.

"*Oh là là!* Of course!" The sense of peace turned into exhilaration, but the word "last" stung her with a bittersweet note. She ordered two glasses of Beaujolais, a word she pronounced in perfect French to the waiter.

"Beaujolais? May I ask why?" Liddell asked once the waiter left.

130

"For me, Beaujolais means a fresh start: lighthearted and wonderful conversation, perfect weather, nice company, light, seasonal food. Midday glory!"

"That's a lot of meaning packed in a glass of wine! Who would've thought?"

The waiter came back and placed the glasses in front of them. Connie nodded, and looking at Liddell, picked up her glass. "Wine is all about meaning."

"To all of the above," Liddell said, raising his glass too. "*Santé!*"

They each ordered a salad and another glass of Beaujolais. The waiter also brought them a square basket of bread and a one-liter bottle of water.

"Here we are in France, your motherland. Do you still have family in Bandol?"

"Not anymore. There used to be a couple of my grandfather's cousins, but we lost contact many years ago. When Deb and I went there, we visited one of Mom's friends, a winemaker, Monsieur Gagolin. He may still be alive. He was such a warm, lovely man... he left a great impression on me."

"In what way?"

The clear, transparent light of the midday sun shone on Liddell, making his eyes look greener than usual. Connie found an odd familiarity in his countenance, as if they had spent not just three days together, but a timeless, indefinable period.

"Monsieur Gagolin..." Connie whispered. Her time in Bandol came flooding back, when she was nineteen years old and her whole life lay ahead. She narrated her time there with every detail she could recollect.

⥱ ⥰

It had been a hot summer in Bandol. Connie and Deb spent a few days at her mother's village and stayed at the small bed-and-breakfast of Monsieur Gagolin. It was a small centuries-old manor house, not precisely up-to-date, located in the midst of his vineyards, very close to the house where her mother was born and had grown up—according to what Monsieur Gagolin told them.

Monsieur Gagolin took the bread out of the oven. It was an extremely old oven, but solidly built. Its squeaky door was worn-out, and the two racks inside were black, slightly bent, and contained a few gaps after decades of use. He placed the fresh-baked loaf on a white rectangular dish and slowly brought it to the table where the girls were waiting for breakfast.

"Why do you think he keeps that oven?" Connie whispered into Deb's ear.

"I don't know, but he doesn't care much about things." Deb pointed at the ceiling with her eyes. "Look at this place; it's falling apart. I bet he doesn't make a lot of money with the vineyard and this small B and B."

Monsieur Gagolin put the plate on the table without saying a word. A minute later, he was back with two cups of coffee on saucers, which he placed in front of each of his guests. He glanced at Connie, turned around, and left for the vineyard.

The table was simply but perfectly set. Two small plates—one with a block of yellow butter and the other with a dollop of grape jam—were at the center of the round oak table. An old-looking, white porcelain sugar pot and a creamer with milk were on one side. Opposite to them was a short, pale-pink vase with two fresh cream-colored roses. The silverware was probably as old as the oven, very much like the rest of the place; but it all had a strange harmony that only resonated when Monsieur Gagolin was around.

After breakfast, they went out for a walk. They stopped on the side of a hill, but still close to the house, from which they could see about a dozen workers, both men and women, walking the aisles between the vines. They were pruning, tying, moving the soil around the old vine trunks, and cutting leaves. Connie spotted Monsieur Gagolin working alongside the others.

"Look at this scene, Connie. Isn't it romantic? The green vine-yard, the workers, the simple life..." Deb said.

"Romantic? That's because you are not one of them. Can you imagine yourself working every day doing that?" Connie laughed at the thought of Deb doing any physical work at all.

"I would do it if I found the love of my life here," Deb said in a sigh. The light of possibility shone in her eyes.

That night, Monsieur Gagolin prepared a rabbit cassoulet. There were other people staying at the bed-and-breakfast: an American woman in her fifties who was traveling alone, and a sommelier student from Germany who was on a field trip to the Bandol wine appellation. That night, one of Monsieur Gagolin's friends joined them at the table, too. He was in his late forties, or maybe early fifties, who went by the name of Quiqui. A vigneron as well, his calloused hands were wide and generous, his gaze warm, and his clothes worn and tattered.

The cassoulet was excellent, and the wine sublime. At just nineteen, Connie was already a very experienced wine connoisseur.

The atmosphere at the table was relaxed. Connie translated bits and pieces of it into English so Deb could take part. Connie spoke very good French—her mother had made sure of that.

The German student asked a lot of technical questions, monopolizing the conversation. He seemed determined to learn every nuance of the winemaking process, and his attention was entirely focused on Monsieur Gagolin.

"That kid's kind of rude. He doesn't even look at us," Deb whispered.

"And Monsieur Gagolin's not teaching him that much, either," the American woman said under her breath, signaling to Monsieur Gagolin with her eyes. "His answers are really vague and very abstract."

Connie looked at Monsieur Gagolin and smiled with secret satisfaction.

After the meal, their host brought a plate with cheeses and another bottle of red wine. He sat down and gave Connie an intense, pensive look—what seemed to be a shadow of old things and times long gone by glowed from deep inside his eyes. Then, addressing the whole table, he said, in French, "Winemaking is a process. Some people call it science; others try to call it art. For me, it's something greater than both of those. It's an act of love.

"I was born here, and I've been doing this since I was a small child, helping my father, and his father as well. We were never great landlords, and we never used fancy terms to describe our farming; we just did what we've always done: loving and tending the vines.

"I love the workers who have been helping me for years and years, as their parents helped my parents; I love the crackling sound of the carts full of grapes, pulled by my old Percheron horses; I love the mornings when I walk up the steep hills to see my vines; I love the afternoons when I drink past vintages and remember times now gone." He briefly looked at Connie and continued.

"I love tasting my wines and seeing them develop as time goes by. They change, like real people do: rough, loud, and wild when young; quiet, complex, and expressive when mature." He paused again and grinned. His face wrinkled, and his brilliant eyes sank below his dense, white eyebrows. Then, puckering his lips, he went on.

"This young man here has been asking me a lot of questions about great wines and how to make them, and I hope he understands me when I say this. There's good wine, and there's bad wine—with all the degrees of quality in between—we all know that. Is there an ideal, perfect wine? To say yes to that would be as ridiculous as saying that one particular woman is the most beautiful in the world, so all the others are less beautiful compared to her. So the question then is: what makes a good wine exceptional?

The answer is that a great wine turns exceptional when you drink it with the people you love. And I daresay that it's only as good as the memories of the moments you made while drinking it. The moments when you *really* lived."

The German student shook his head. "But that is not objective! You have to admit that a great vintage and a great terroir will always produce a great wine, regardless of whom you drink it with. And even if you spat it out before swallowing, it would still be great. It's chemistry!"

Monsieur Gagolin looked at him with tender eyes. "You are only half-right. Let me explain. I like to compare winemaking to the work of a seamstress. A dress must be done following a plan, and with the right method—the analogy to a good year and honest winemaking techniques; we must also choose the appropriate fabric of the best possible make—this is terroir and grape quality; but in the end, the total beauty of this perfect dress will depend on the love that we feel for the woman who wears it. There is where the subjective and the objective mix together and become something different, more important: they become meaning. And if you don't understand this dimension in which wine operates within us when we drink it, then what you are talking about is just another beverage, burdened by affectation and senseless consumerism."

After his speech, Monsieur Gagolin lifted his glass and a toast to the memories of times past. Connie had always remembered the subject of the toast.

⊫ ⊨

"He was a romantic," Liddell said.

"Oh yes, but so authentic...so true. That was the way he really was; he never cared to impress anybody. It's all coming back to me, these memories...I'd forgotten I even had them."

They finished lunch, and they walked to the Musée de l'Orangerie—the sun's rays felt mild, and a fresh breeze stirred the air at the Tuileries Garden. A sense of calm pervaded their stroll.

The museum queue was long but moved at a steady pace. "We'll be inside in fifteen minutes at the most. What do you know about Monet?" Liddell asked.

"I studied him at college, but I don't remember much. This morning I downloaded an essay about this particular *Water Lilies* series." She pulled her iPad out of her purse and handed it to Liddell.

"I left my glasses at the hotel. Could you read it to me, please?"

*Read to him?* Connie cleared her throat. "Sure. I didn't know you wore glasses. Anyway, here it goes."

At the end of World War I, the French government wanted to exhibit some of Monet's work in order to venerate the fallen ones and to celebrate the victory of France, but also to create a place for contemplation and for reflection on the idea of peace.

Monet donated this collection of *Water Lilies* to the French government, although it was delivered after the artist's demise.

During the time when he painted these panels, Monet's existing cataracts had gotten worse. He couldn't tell the difference between tones of the same colors; however, he could still clearly discern between different degrees of shades.

While experimenting with new approaches to his art, he realized that if he looked at the canvases from a farther distance, he could actually tell the differences in tone that he could not tell when looking at them up close.

Liddell sidled close to Connie in an attempt to look at her iPad. She felt Liddell's body getting closer to hers, gently brushing her arm. A whiff of his scent caught her attention. *Lemongrass. Passion.*

*Tender.* Her heart pounded, and a light hum began to reverberate inside her eardrums. She forced her body not to pull away and kept reading.

> He painted numerous canvases, but as a result of his frequent tantrums, he destroyed a great deal of them. His sense of sight went from bad to worse, until he became almost blind; then he agreed to have surgery. He had two operations in one eye, which gave him a short-lived relief. Soon thereafter he began to notice strange symptoms: all colors would suddenly turn to blue, then to yellow.
>
> This was a brutal period for him. Bursts of joy during the short moments of acceptable vision were followed by a great intensity at work. But with daunting moments of deep insecurity about his art and the whole *Lilies* project, yet more paintings were destroyed out of rage.

"You even have a few pictures," Liddell whispered while looking at the iPad. "Look at the size of those easels. May I take a closer look?"

Connie nodded. Words escaped her, and heat flushed her cheeks. Liddell swiped his finger over the iPad and pulled up a photograph that showed an immaculate studio with Monet's imposing figure smoking a cigarette. Connie's gaze rested on Liddell's wedding ring. She shut her eyes.

"Look at how shiny his shoes are," Liddell said, now looking at her. "Are you okay?"

Connie opened her eyes and nodded, blinking rapidly. She kept her eyes fixed on the iPad.

"Sorry I interrupted, please go on."

> The one eye that had had surgery slowly normalized, providing him with longer periods of relative calm, and

soon he was able to use a set of custom-made spectacles that improved his vision even more. With renewed energy, he focused on finishing the *Lilies* commission, but unfortunately, his mood remained extremely volatile for the rest of his life.

The goal of the *Lilies* project was to create a "decoration," as Monet called it, big and overwhelming enough to immerse the viewers into a continuum of water, water lilies, weeping willows, reflections of light, transparencies, movement, and change, all in one room, with no beginning and no end.

Connie read automatically, without listening to her own words. She tried to make sense of her babbling, but the closeness to Liddell's body wrapped her in a newfound state of confusion, preventing her from noticing anything else. She tried to recall the last time she had felt the closeness to a man with such intensity. Nick came to mind and then quickly went away. *This is primal. I can feel his warmth. The tension of his body transcends his clothes, and my clothes.* An imagined idea of plenitude grew inside of her, which then morphed into déjà vu of the fulfillment of an innate craving that she just realized she still had. Words kept pouring out of her mouth.

Monet envisioned a place where people could go to relax, contemplate, and think, and the paintings would help them do that.

When the paintings were close to being finished, the negotiations for where to physically place the huge canvases proved to be excruciating. The actual museum wasn't built yet, and the various authorities in charge of the project, representing many governmental factions—each with their own agenda—made very little progress.

By his final days, Monet was so emotionally unstable that they had to wait until he passed away to take the canvases out of his studio and to put them into this custom-made museum, built on what used to be the orange trees garden inside the Tuileries, hence its name: Musée de l'Orangerie.

Liddell nodded. "Very informative. Thank you," he said, pulling away from her.

The queue moved forward. Connie took a deep breath as a strong ache of longing swept over her. The sense of completeness disappeared, but the memory of its possibility remained.

They entered the first of two large oval rooms. A powerful but diffused light came through the roof and expanded downward, washing the immense canvases with an even and ethereal light. Monet's lily pond paintings stretched all around the room, fixed to the concave walls.

Connie and Liddell sat on the center bench, looking in opposite directions. Shortly after, Connie stood up and walked around the hall.

She got inches close to one of the paintings, fixed her eyes on a spot, and slowly walked away from it. *The colors, the strokes, and the shades blend with one another, and the meaning comes forward.*

She walked around the hall, her eyes lost on the slowly passing canvases. *The meaning comes forward. What is it? What did I just feel?* She stopped and looked at Liddell. He seemed absentminded, staring at a single spot on the painting right in front of him. *I wonder what he's thinking.* As if hearing her question, Liddell turned to her, and their eyes met. *Those eyes, they're yearning for something. Maybe the same thing that I'm yearning for?* She strolled to the second room. He stood up and followed her.

Liddell entered the second room; weeping willows, with their gloomy silhouettes, rose up from the sides of the pond. *The way she looked at me. Come on, Liddell. She's married. And you too. Does it mean I'm not supposed to examine my own feelings anymore? Not if you're attracted to her.*

He sat on the corner of a bench and intently gazed at the canvas on the end wall, opposite the entrance to the first room. Its lugubrious darkness captivated him like the memory of a familiar place. His eyes rested on the darker shades of the painting, and his thoughts looked for solace, digging out memories of happier times. He recalled that particular afternoon when, still oblivious of his mother's depression, he was sitting with his grandmother, Johanne, in the wide and luminous drawing room at her house, back in Cape Town. She was working on one of her canvases, entitled *Tender*. It was a painting of a full-leafed plane tree, with rolling hills in the background, scattered clouds in the orange, blue, and gray sky, and a golden sunset washing the whole scene from the right. Under the massive tree, which occupied most of the scene, Johanne had painted Liddell and his mother, merrily playing.

*Grandma Johanne.* He smiled at her memory. Johanne's unimposing way of looking, delicate way of talking, and peaceful way of staying silent were unique to her. He remembered her formal manners and Victorian demeanor. *Old school,* he chuckled. *Why do I remember her now? It's probably the paintings. Or Connie. There's something about her that's so…pure. It takes me back in time. A perfume of unspoiled virtue. Of possibility. Still.*

His mind switched to the phone conversation that he'd had with Sigrid the night before: facts about the kids and her job, and complaints about his father. Liddell wondered why his father had called. *Why didn't he call my cell? It was probably something irrelevant. He can wait. I'll call him when I get back home.* Uneased by the thought of his wife, he turned around to see where Connie was. She was standing a few yards behind him, in silence, looking at the same canvas he had been staring at. He stood up, pushed his hands into his pockets, and walked over to her.

They sat next to each other, in front of the weeping willows; the dark stillness of the painting pervaded Liddell's mind, and a few scattered notes of a half-remembered Vivaldi violin adagio danced inside of him. His muscles softened; his anxiety evaporated. As his eyes wandered over the canvas, those ethereal, almost unreal shades glowed over the water, back and forth, incessantly. The bucolic atmosphere inherent in the weeping willows and the shape of their languid branches gave the painting a certain flow, a liquid nature that seemed to move and tremble in an endless flutter.

He felt the urge to share this newfound state of mind with Connie. *She'll understand. She's probably feeling the same.* He almost said the first word when something shifted in him. Something broke loose—a violent rush. It was the same feeling he had had when he watched Connie in front of *The Kiss*, but this time with much more intensity: a thousand times more powerful. He felt it grow and stir his blood, heat up inside of him, and push outward: he realized he wanted to turn around and embrace her. He wanted to feel her body against his, to press her mouth with his lips, and to tell her, without using any words, what he was feeling. That he *was* feeling.

"If Claude wanted to make people contemplate life while in here, he succeeded, at least with me," Connie whispered.

Her voice reverberated inside him. *Her voice is like a siren's chant—the softest sound. It keeps taking me back. Back to my own unspoiled virtue.* Liddell inhaled deeply and slowly released the air. *What was that? Stay in control, Liddell. Stay in control.*

But he couldn't—his hand hovered over hers and slowly landed on top, his fingers feeling hers, his warmth sensing the same warmth in Connie's hand. She didn't look at him or move her hand away. Instead, she closed her eyes, and her flushed face showed her mixed emotions, her hesitancy about whether to hold his hand back or not.

Liddell waited for what seemed to be an eternity: a few seconds. He waited for her to decide if his whole life was going to change by a slight motion of approval on her side. In a split second he imagined a life with Connie: days of conversation and nights of love, moments of joy and shared thoughts, shared feelings—being relevant to someone.

Connie finally pulled her hand away, and her eyes opened back to the painting.

He stood up, pulled his camera, and started taking pictures. It was the perfect excuse to put some distance between them and give both the time to recover from his failed attempt.

"Ready for a walk?" he asked once he was done, trying to sound unaffected.

"Yes," she whispered without looking at him.

As they walked out of the museum, Liddell's legs felt light, a renewed energy surged inside him. Although it was fall, he thought the air smelled of green, new leaves.

The sun was setting over Paris, laying a chiaroscuro on the buildings and on the trees, washing the city with varied shades of light; Connie pointed out some of the glowing buildings as they crisscrossed the narrow and winding backstreets of Paris.

"We got a lot done on this trip, I think," Liddell ventured.

"It will be a really good article," Connie said with a nod.

"How long will it take you to put it together?"

"I have all of next week to do the text, and then an editor will take it from there. I still want to discuss the total length with Brenda. We could make it more in-depth, if she allows the space. There's a lot of material. And you took a lot of pictures too."

"I hope she gives you leeway to express yourself. I'll submit all the raw photos to Will and let them decide. They usually hire a professional to manipulate my shots. Look, there," Liddell said and pointed at a small statue of a winged angel that was hanging over a storefront.

Connie aimed her phone at it and snapped a photo.

"How old are your kids?" she asked while taking a picture of the quaint chocolate-shop storefront below the winged angel.

"Rutger is nine, and Klas, twelve."

"Two boys…nice. I have three kids, two girls and a boy."

"Ages?"

"Amanda is sixteen, Stacey, fourteen, and Bryan, twelve."

"Two girls! I've always wanted a girl."

"What about your wife? What does she do?" Connie put the phone in her purse, and they started walking.

"Marketing for a real state company. Hers are twelve-hour days. We also have our lifelong nanny, good old Elga. She's been with the family since Klas was born."

"She lives in your house?"

"Almost. She's with the kids most of the day. I work from home and try to help them with homework when I can, but lately I've been so busy that I barely leave my office."

"You never told me what you do."

"I'm a civil engineer; I design manufacturing plants. I also consult on upgrades and new technologies for those plants."

"How long have you been married?"

"Ten years. Sigrid got divorced when Klas was two. I met her a year later."

"Klas is your stepson."

"But we're so close that it's hard for me not to think of Klas as my son, just as much as Rutger is."

Connie turned toward him. "That's a lovely way to feel about it. And it speaks volumes about your heart, too." Her voice softened, and her eyes shone with a new, distinctive light.

*Her eyes. They couldn't be more expressive, pure, and open. Her eyes. They make time stand still, drawing me to her. I can't believe this is actually happening.* He fought his desire to wrap his arm around her waist, pull her body against his, and kiss her, right there, at that very moment. He was about to lose the battle and risk it all with a bold move, when he heard his own voice asking her, "How long have you been married?"

"Almost twenty years."

Liddell cocked his head forward. His self-control proved to work this time, but pity over the lost opportunity blurred his thoughts.

Connie continued, "Nick and I met in college, and we've been together ever since." She paused, as if weighing whether she wanted to keep talking about her personal life. Then she went on, "I just realized that neither Nick nor I had any prior experience when it came to partners. I had a couple of boyfriends in high school, and Nick had a girlfriend a few years before knowing me, but those were more summer romances. Neither of us had a serious relationship until we met. I guess that what I'm trying to say is that I never knew any other man, and Nick never knew any other woman, as far as I know."

"Do you think of it as a drawback?"

"Not necessarily. But sometimes I wish I had more experience with feelings like love, passion, loss, longing, change...I feel I'm very naïve, emotionally speaking. Nick and I always got along pretty well, never stayed away from each other, never really missed each other, but also never felt really passionate about each other. We ended up stuck in some ways, and it never changed."

"When did you realize that?"

"On this trip." She had a shy smile on her face. She briefly glanced at Liddell and then promptly looked straight ahead.

Liddell stopped walking and took her by the arm. "But then why..."

Connie looked at him intensely and held his hand. "Please, Liddell, don't ask. This isn't easy for me." She slowly pulled his hand off her arm and continued walking.

The sun had finally sunk in the horizon, and a cool breeze swept the streets. Liddell zipped up his jacket and suggested entering the next café.

La Mouette only had half a dozen tables, crammed into a space not much larger than a living room. Yellow light, coming from century-old lamps hanging from the walls, colored the oak tables and battered chairs with a warm sepia hue, and subtle music from vinyl records played in the background. Liddell immediately recognized the sound of the needle on the grooves, and the nostalgic voice of the French singer-songwriter icon from the sixties. *Barbara, Le Mal de Vivre. I like this place.*

They sat by the window. The three other couples in the café didn't seem to notice their arrival. Chatting in indistinguishable whispers, they looked like part of the decoration. An extremely thin young woman ambled around the tables and stood next to theirs, mumbling a few words in French. They both ordered a macchiato. The waitress nodded, walked behind the counter, and started making the coffees.

"Change," Connie said.

"Pardon me?"

"To me the *Water Lilies* are about change. The whole idea of a circular, continuous canvas with darkness and light in different scales, the trees and the water with different colors…I think Monet painted the seasons to represent change in our lives. But also, if you compare these last water lilies to the first ones he painted, in the early nineteen hundreds, they are quite different."

"Indeed. He painted the same garden over and over again. He had to make some changes, right?"

"He saw the garden in different ways as he grew older. You can argue that his sight got worse with age, that surgery affected him quite a bit too. And it's all true. But the most important factor was the passing of time. He changed his perception as he grew older, dismissing the superfluous and trying to capture the essence. The glows, the shades, the darkness, the movement…he departed from the material and explored the conceptual."

"We could link that idea to the classic concept that works of art remain the same, but we, the viewers, change and thus change the meaning we find in them," Liddell suggested.

"Yes. But it also resonates with what you said yesterday, after we saw the Rodin, that some of us try to hold on to the way we once thought things were. We try to have a routine, we fix our minds with concepts of right or wrong, and we hold strong opinions on things. But we tend to forget that time changes the world around us, and more important, time changes us." She clasped her hands. "That's my case anyway. I'm speaking for myself."

"The painter changed as he painted, the subject matter changed as it was being painted, and the viewer changed as he or she viewed it," Liddell said.

The waitress returned holding a round silver plate with two minuscule brown porcelain cups. She placed the coffees in front of them. "*Sucre?*"

Connie and Liddell shook their heads, and the young woman walked away.

"Change is all around us—either we like it or not. It is such a simple concept but one I never paid any attention to."

"Monet figured that one out," Liddell said.

Connie wrapped her long fingers around the cup with delicacy and slowly brought it to her lips. Her pale-blue eyes showed a hint of sadness. *Or is it regret? Unspoiled virtue. Is innocence a virtue? I'm making this up. I'm seeing who I'd like her to be, like Connie said. Not necessarily who she really is.* "I'm curious. How do you relate this idea to your own life?"

"Now that I look back, things were changing right in front of my eyes, and I seldom took notice: Mom and Dad, Nick and the kids…myself. But on the other hand, I did notice the last time

Amanda played with her favorite rag doll, and that was, in a sense, the end of a period in time for her."

"How did it happen?"

"Amanda was ten. Just another afternoon. She came home from school and was watching TV while she was holding the doll next to her. She always did that. I was going back and forth, doing random things, when I saw Amanda stand up and put the doll on one of the shelves next to the TV. Then she turned around and sat back on the couch. I had this strange feeling. For some reason I knew something was over for her. Something had changed. And I was right; she never touched that doll again."

"But that was the natural thing to happen. Kids grow up."

"Yes, I know, but sometimes when I think of Amanda, I still picture her playing with *that* doll, like she used to. At other times, I try to imagine how much else about her has changed, things that I will never know: thoughts, feelings, ideas, hopes. She turned into a different person...the same essence...but so different. And now I realize that the same happens to all of us."

Liddell nodded. "On the same note, when I remember things about my past, there are memories that seem to linger, to stick around. Moments that seem to have been there forever: scenes of my child-hood, a conversation with my father, the perfume my grandmother used to wear. Some days I imagine I smell fresh-baked bread coming from the bakery around the corner from my childhood home, or I hear the sounds of the beach in Cape Town. The tennis matches every Saturday morning with Félix, my best friend, when I was twelve. They are all somewhere in my mind, still and quiet. Sometimes I feel like those memories are about to become real again, just about... but then, like soap bubbles, they burst and disappear, and I remind myself that those worlds are gone forever, never to return."

Connie leaned forward, rested her forearms on the table, and clasped her hands together. "What do you think of the Monet? What does it trigger in you?"

"Self-reference," he said. "I think that we humans are self-referential creatures. We are always comparing the things around us to what we know from our past. Not from the historical, textbook type of past, but from *our* past: the very things that happened to us. Just look at us now! We live among memories from our childhood, from our youth, stories we heard from our parents, and snippets of the moments that meant something to us—and some of us even live among memories from our dreams. The pleasant memories soothe us, and we carry them fondly with us all throughout our lives; and the bad, or dark moments we lived, they come back again and again, haunting us. And while we live, we remember, we compare, we reference back...all the time. The continuity of the water lilies makes me think of the continuity of my own life, when the same feelings and thoughts reappear at different times, with slightly different shapes, changed by the shades of the seasons of life; but the essence remains the same."

"Don't we humans look for safety in our memories?" Connie asked.

"Yes. We search for familiarity, we want to feel secure, validated; our memories are that familiar place, where maybe we yearn to return, someday, sometime." He idly tapped his spoon against his saucer. "We know it's not possible. But still, there is this constant self-reference to our past as we move on to the future."

"I like that thought," Connie said. "It's reassuring to know that I'm not the only one who lives with memories." Her smile was relaxed and warm. She slowly closed her eyes and remained quiet.

Liddell looked intently at her face, scanning every detail. He observed the subtle wrinkles at the corners of her eyes and mouth. The skin on her cheeks that once must have been porcelain-smooth and spotless was now slightly burdened by the passing of time. The skin on her neck was not as firm as it must once have been. Her hands, now resting on the table side by side, showed hints of aging. But Liddell's only thoughts were how fascinating and profoundly beautiful Connie was at that particular moment. He didn't want to imagine what she once looked like. He delighted in admiring what she currently was: a perfect balance of beauty and wit, experience and sensibility. *Unspoiled virtue.*

Connie opened her eyes. "What?" she said, deadpan.

"What?"

"What's that look in your face?"

"Oh, nothing…I was just…looking at you," he said. He knew he was blushing, and he was surprised to find that he kept staring at Connie all the same.

Connie smiled. "Tell me more about your family. How do you get along with Sigrid?"

Sigrid's name was the last thing he expected to hear at that moment. He took a deep breath. "We are not the most in-tune couple, I'm afraid. For a number of reasons, we've been slowly growing apart through the years, and we are now caught up in this rut that seems so difficult to get out of. We've changed so much; we've gone in different directions, and something got lost along the way. I know, it doesn't sound like breaking news in the world of marriage, right?" He sighed and continued. "Sometimes I get this sense of lost opportunity. I remember when we met, how exciting it was: the plans we made, the moments we lived together, and the feeling that there was so much more ahead for us, that life was truly worth living, and that we were so lucky to be together. Then the routine started: work, chores, the kids, a kiss not really meant, thoughts not shared. We both took less care of ourselves as a couple…I think we got too used to each other."

"But you still love each other."

Liddell gave an uneasy smile. "Let's say we're working on it."

"Well, I would say that love, at our age, is more about companionship, about respect for the time and history together, about keeping a family, and maybe not about ourselves as individuals anymore."

"If we agree that love is *that*, then yes, I think Sigrid and I still love each other."

"But you are not so sure that love is *that*."

"I'm afraid not."

"I want to hear your definition of love, then." Connie pushed her empty cup to one side and cradled her cheeks between her hands.

He paused only a moment. "Love, to me, is the feeling of absolute fulfillment when you are with the person you love. Consequently, it is complemented with a feeling of deep solitude, or loss, when you are away from that person."

"Just that?"

"Basically, yes. I also think that even *at our age*, as you said, love has the same traits that it had when we were younger. As a matter of fact, I think that all the feelings that we have as adults have basically the same traits as when we first felt them. Some of them grow more intense, however, and others get tamed by the passing of time. But we still self-reference all of our feelings back to when we first had them when young, and they impressed us the most."

"And because we were so impressionable, those first feelings will always seem too strong when compared to what we feel now," Connie added.

"Exactly. For instance, take a man buying a brand-new car. Every time he buys a new car, which by the way is more powerful and better designed than its predecessor, maybe what he's really seeking is the same thrill he had when he bought his very first car. And I believe you could say the same for a gourmand who keeps trying different restaurants and foods—always comparing and self-referencing, maybe even back to the food her grandmother used to cook when she was a child. Does the food have less flavor because she has grown up? Does the new car create less excitement because he is older? Think about the passion of the artists we've been looking at. Did they lose any passion when they got older?

On the contrary, I think they were as passionate or even more passionate when old, *because* they grew older. When I think about love along those same lines, I gather that we can't tone down love just because we grow old; maybe it isn't that youthful extroverted energy anymore, but still…we either feel it, or we don't. And it should still feel like love."

Connie pressed her lips and took a few seconds before she started speaking. "It's an interesting point of view," she said, "but one that leaves me outside the definition of being in love."

"Go on."

"Well, I don't feel the same for Nick as I did when we were young. But even then, like I told you before, I was never really passionate about him, or he about me. We just were together, comfortable. Before we knew it, a few years had passed, and we got married. Why not? We liked each other, we knew each other, as did our families, and everything was so easy and predictable that we just did it. And I thought I was in love with him…at least, I thought *that* was love. When I listen to you talking about big love and great passion, it makes me think that maybe I never knew love in the way you knew it. Maybe what I've been feeling all these years is not love but companionship, or friendship, or something else. I don't know."

"I'm sorry. I shouldn't have exposed my thoughts so freely."

"Oh, it's okay…I'm just realizing that maybe I was never in love, or maybe I was never passionate about anything, and I never gave it too much thought. I was just never exposed to such levels of emotional intensity. Now, I feel that much of my life has passed by, and I've lost a lot of chances of feeling alive, really alive, as Monsieur Gagolin said. Maybe I never *got* what he was talking about. After looking at all these pieces of art and discussing them with you, I realize there's a deeper, more meaningful world—full of beautiful ideas, emotions, and passions—that's completely under the radar. I mean, for a woman like me, who has been living a practical, day-to-day life." She looked down. A strand of hair fell slightly over her face, covering her now brimming eyes. She pushed her hands together and stayed still, as if resisting an impulse to say or do something.

Liddell saw a tear running down her pale left cheek. *She is Venus. She is the most beautiful woman on earth.*

⊶ ⊷

A flurry of memories rushed through Connie's mind. Awash in a waterfall of images and sounds, she recalled endless moments of family chatter back when she was young: at her in-laws, Pam trying to impress Amy with her affected manners, Joe boasting about his investments and how much money he'd made in the stock market, Nick loudly talking nonsense about sports and cars.

Then she pictured her mother. She saw her alone in her kitchen, sitting on a stool, gaze on the window over the sink, with a glass of red wine in her slender hand, which looked just like Connie's looked now. Her angular, wrinkled face wore a hard expression, and her brown eyes seemed to wade through distant times and places. She was taking a break. Not from cooking, Connie now realized, but from a harder type of labor: from the task of keeping the surface of her life neat and tidy, merry and satisfied, to all appearances, with no stress or needs. She was taking a break from forcing a self-assured smile onto her face, and from pretending that life was a simple thing and that she, like everybody else around her, knew exactly what it was about.

Connie then recalled her father. Robert used to work at home over the weekends, carrying fat folders of papers around the house, rapidly pushing the square buttons on his large calculator, and repeatedly swapping out his two pairs of glasses—one for reading, one for distances.

Her thoughts went back to her mother. Maybe that was why she never said anything about her real feelings. Maybe that was why she kept doing what they all did. It would have been too hard to swim against the current. Her life was already set in stone: the husband, the kids, and the routine. Just like Connie's own life.

Connie raised her eyes to Liddell. "I would like to tell you a story about my grandfather," she said, wiping the tear and tucking her hair behind her ears. "It has to do with the idea of self-reference."

"I would love to hear it."

"His name was Pierre, and he was a small-time wine merchant in a tiny town near Bandol, in southern France. He used to buy bulk wine from small producers, and after blending and bottling it himself, he would sell it to the wine buyers who traveled from town to town, purchasing wines of the Bandol *appellation*, as they call it here in France. He got a reputation for selling really good wine, but always in small quantities. He was very picky about the wine he bought. My mother told me that he used to buy all of Gagolin's small output, and during the weekends, Pierre never failed to go to the vineyard to discuss wine concepts with Guy Gagolin, his best friend and the father of Gérard Gagolin, the man I told you about."

"Another Gagolin." Liddell sparked a half smile.

"Yeah…My mom used to go along with my grandfather, and while the men sat around a table, tasting wines and talking about them for hours, she would walk the vineyards with Gérard. She learned a lot from him, mostly about farming and the winemaking process.

One day Pierre was offered a job in America by a US importer who bought wine from him. The company had realized how much he knew about Bandol, but also about French wine in general, and wanted to have him at the company's headquarters in Minneapolis. It was a tough decision for the family—they loved Bandol."

"Was it a big family?"

"No, just my mother and her parents. Pierre was an ambitious and very determined man, and he knew that to make a leap forward in his career, he had to work for a big company."

"And they left town? Just like that?"

"The writing was on the wall. It was Pierre's once-in-a-lifetime opportunity. They sold everything, which wasn't much, and left France, never to return. My mom wanted to stay in Bandol, but my grandfather didn't let her."

"Why?"

The waitress came back to the table, and Liddell gestured that they were ready for the check.

"It wasn't an option. Mom told me that, back then, a young single woman had to obey her father."

"And you told me she was in her late teens. I guess it's understandable."

"So they left for Minneapolis. By the end of his career, Pierre had become a respected figure in the wine world, with thirty-something years of experience and having tasted the best wines from all over the world, year after year. But this is where I wanted to get to: a few months before he passed away, when he was in the hospital, my mom, trying to have an easy conversation with him, asked him which one was his favorite wine of all. 'Oh, that's easy,' Mom told me that he immediately said. He closed his eyes, as if remembering a taste, and said, 'Bandol Rouge. Domaine Gagolin, any one of the dry years, drinking it with Guy.' This little story makes more sense to me now than it ever did before."

"I love your story, and I like the love you projected as you told it," Liddell said.

Connie remained quiet. She had said all that she wanted to say.

The waitress returned with the check and left it on the table. Liddell took his money clip out of his breast pocket and gave her his credit card without looking at the piece of paper.

"I guess we can wrap up the Monet experience by saying that it kindles the ideas of change and self-reference." Liddell checked his watch. "And now, it's dinnertime, and I happen to know the perfect restaurant," he added with an open smile.

"Let's go." Connie grinned.

The taxi took them to 101 Rue de l'Ouest, a bistro Liddell said he visited every time he was in Paris. Connie scanned the place with curiosity as they walked inside. Slightly larger than a small American coffee shop, the restaurant was filled with local people, mostly middle-aged. The chatter was definitely louder than at the café they'd just come from, and the atmosphere felt lively and casual. Connie felt relaxed. *I'm starting to get why the French like small places. They feel more real.* A rectangular blackboard on the wall opposite the large-paned windows had the handwritten menu of the day on it. There were eight small square tables lined up along the windows, accommodating two comfortably, and a large table, which Connie figured must sit more than fourteen, extended along the blackboard wall. A long wooden bench was up against the wall, and seven or eight chairs were on the other side of the communal table, which was already nearly filled with diners.

"*Bonsoir.* Where would you like to sit?" the waitress asked as soon as they entered.

"At the big table," Liddell immediately said. "There's room right in the middle."

Connie gave him a look of surprise.

"It'll be fun," he said, deadpan. "Just look."

Connie covered her mouth, suppressing her laughter. "She's going to bother all those people because of us. Don't do it!" she said and pressed Liddell's arm with both hands.

She realized that she was sending him mixed messages. At l'Orangerie she had pulled her hand from his, even though she wanted so terribly to hold it and feel the reassurance of feeling noticed, heard, understood—loved. Then she had dismissed his questioning of why she wasn't consenting. *What am I doing?*

"Too late…" Liddell replied.

The waitress raised her arms, calling the attention of the people sitting at the table. "*Excusez-moi, s'il vous plaît. Faire de la place pour le beau couple*," she announced with a mischievous smile.

"She just called us a beautiful couple!" Connie said.

"The woman has good taste."

The guests on one side of the bench stood up without showing any sign of inconvenience and filed out into the aisle. The waitress signaled Connie to slide in.

After Connie took her place, the customers quickly slid back to their places, resuming their conversations.

"I like this place a lot already," she said, leaning across to Liddell as he took his own seat in the row of chairs.

The waitress brought two small cardboard menus featuring the same items that were written on the large blackboard.

"You've got to try the pig ears; it's one of their specialties," Liddell said, looking at the menu.

"Pig ears…? I know exactly the wine that will go with them. Let me see if they have it."

Connie zipped through the wine list, quickly turning the few pages. The waitress returned with a small notepad and looked at her, pencil in hand.

"*Voilà!* We will have a bottle of Bandol *rouge*, 2001, please." She grinned at Liddell.

They ordered different appetizers to share; the various orders came in small bowls, little plates, and cups. The pig ears were julienned and sautéed with local herbs, and came presented on a rectangular piece of wood. The table was a feast for the senses, and Connie realized that Liddell was in the same carefree mood as she was. A mood her mother would have described as *characteristic of great happiness.*

"*Santé!*" Connie lifted her glass.

Their eyes locked, and their glasses clinked.

"*Santé,*" Liddell said.

⇥⇤

They stepped out of the taxi and entered the hotel. It was 11:00 p.m., and it had been a long and intense day, in more than one way, but Connie didn't want it to finish just yet. After all, it was her last night in Europe—in Paris, of all places—and she wanted to savor it to its fullest. There would be time to sleep on the plane home the next day.

"One more drink to say good-bye?" Liddell suggested and pointed at the still-open lobby bar.

"Did you just read my mind?" Connie joked.

*Our last drink together, our last conversation, probably my last mean-ingful conversation with a man. Gosh...I'm playing with fire now.*

They sat at the bar, and Connie ordered a glass of brut nature Champagne, which is the driest version of all.

Liddell asked for one of the same. "As we entered the hotel, I wondered if we're ever going to meet again, or maybe just stay in touch."

"I thought about it too, and I don't think it is a good idea."

"Why not?"

"Why would we want to do it? With what purpose?" Connie's voice softened.

"I don't know, to check how the article is coming along, or how the other one is doing? This trip didn't promise much for me, and now I realized that I will..." Liddell hesitated.

The barman placed the glasses in front of each one of them. Connie felt that that simple task was taking much longer than necessary. She wanted to hear what Liddell would—miss.

When the young man behind the bar finally left, Liddell suggested a toast. Connie explained her choice. The Champagne she had chosen, which she knew very well, had the elegant yet masculine backbone of the Pinot Noir that had been used in its blend. *Stern, complex, ideal.*

"What were you saying, Liddell?" she asked nonchalantly and put her glass on the bar.

Liddell resumed. "I will miss—this."

"What is *this?*" Connie felt vulnerable, her mouth slightly open, her earnest expression beseeching Liddell.

"You," he murmured. He looked her square in the eyes.

The air eased out of her lungs in a long sigh. She wanted to clutch her glass of Champagne, but her trembling hands didn't feel safe anymore; instead, she slowly affixed her hair behind her ear, caressing her right cheek and the side of her chin. They felt hot. Her vision suddenly blurred; she had the feeling of being somewhere else she couldn't describe, and everything around her looked strange and distant. The only bright light she could see came from Liddell's eyes, which she couldn't stop staring into.

"I think I'm not feeling well," she whispered hoarsely, lowering her head to break that visual contact.

He remained immobile.

Connie stood up, clumsily pushing her stool back, and headed toward the hotel interior. But as she entered the lobby, her vision grew cloudy, and her hand grabbed the doorframe in an attempt to keep her balance. Her fingers clung to it with all their strength.

"Please let me take you to your room." Liddell's soothing voice came from behind as he firmly wrapped his arm around her waist. "I want to make sure you get there safely."

"I'm fine, I'm just…a little dizzy. I think I had too much wine." It was a lie. She was quite sober, but it was the only thing she could say without feeling embarrassed. The pressure of Liddell's hand on her hip only increased the awkwardness. Things around looked malleable, surreal. Liddell held her tight, and they moved together to the elevators. When they arrived, Liddell pulled his hand off her waist and pushed the button—as they waited in silence, the seconds seemed interminable.

Connie tried to put together an apology for such an odd, abrupt way of interrupting the conversation, but her mind was a whirlwind. *This is so embarrassing. I wonder what he's thinking now. Why should I care? I'm a mess, and I really care. His arm, his hands, his touch. So delicate, so warm, so strong. What am I feeling? Stop. Stop this now.*

The elevator chimed, and the door slowly opened. Connie stepped into the small car, and Liddell followed her. She pushed the number three on the panel, closed her eyes, and leaned against the elevator wall. Her mind started working again, and she gathered enough strength and composure for a reasonable apology.

She would say that she wasn't prepared for the amount of wine she'd just drunk, and that she hadn't had enough food. She would say that she felt really tired after walking all day, that the *Water Lilies* was the best visit of all, and that she had enjoyed the whole trip very much. She would then politely thank him for the time spent together, the good conversations, and the good wine. After that, she would extend her hand, shake his, and step out of the elevator. She would walk to her room as fast as she could; she would take a shower and go to bed. The next day she would fly back home to her family and her real life. She would never see or hear from Liddell again, and she would never feel this awkward again.

She opened her eyes, ready to recite her perfect prevarication. She looked at Liddell for an instant and leaned forward. Her right foot took a step, the left one followed, as if an outside force thrust her closer. She saw him clearly as her face got close to his. The warmth of his body and the scent of his cologne became closer too. She made one last step, and feeling as if she was jumping into a void, she leaned up and kissed Liddell's lips with an intensity and passion she had never felt before. Her hands ran through his hair, and her body pressed him against the elevator wall. His arms locked around her in return, and his hands ran up and down her spine. Their bodies thrust against each other, as if trying to become one.

Her sense of awkwardness disappeared, and instead, Connie felt a long-suppressed energy gushing out inside her. As she sighed, her innermost feelings came to the surface, and she imagined them perfectly matching Liddell's feelings. The elevator door slowly opened at the third floor, but neither of them could stop a deepening kiss that took so long to give and receive. They swung out of the elevator, still in an embrace, only an instant before the doors closed. Without saying a word, Liddell took Connie by the hips and kissed her again...her shaky hands searched her purse and pulled out her room key. They walked the short steps to her room; she opened the door and dragged Liddell inside. There was no space for words. They looked intently into each other's eyes, and she surrendered entirely to a passion she hadn't known she was capable of until the very moment when they became one.

She rose and sat on the bed. Pulling up the white sheet, she covered her naked hips. She looked around. It was dark, and the window was slightly open. The white drapes were lit from the outside and danced irreverently to the gentle breeze that blew in. She never left windows open in her room. After a second look around, she saw a small table near the canopied bed, a bottle of rosé Champagne inside an ice-filled chiller, two flute-shaped glasses, a white pillar candle, and a red rose, all gracefully arranged on the cast-iron, marble-topped table. Somebody had been inside her room before they came in and prepared the stage for their encounter. She turned to Liddell, who was lying on his side, watching her.

"Did you plan all this?" she asked.

"Just some of it," he said with a slow smile. "I wanted to give you a small present after dinner was over and we said good-bye, so I asked the concierge to put the Champagne in the chiller, light up the candle, place the rose next to it, and open the window slightly." He raised his torso from the bed, reached out to the bottle, and pointed at the open window. "My room is right below yours; they both face the west. It's a beautiful sight of Paris."

"And the two glasses?"

Liddell popped the bottle open and poured the rosé into the flutes. "I asked him to bring *a* glass, but I guess I did not make myself clear in my broken French." He handed Connie one of the glasses, and then his hand moved under the sheet and gently caressed her thigh. "I never dared to think that this would actually happen, believe me," he said in a whisper.

The glasses clinked, and they drank the crisp, delicate wine.

*Silk. Fresh Flowers. Release. Wonder.*

Connie took the glasses and placed them on the nightstand. She gently pushed Liddell back on the bed and slid on top of him, kissing his lips tenderly; the breeze was still blowing through the window.

"I never imagined this was even possible," she replied, her tear-filled eyes fixed on Liddell's.

He held her tightly against his body and kissed her passionately.

# CHAPTER 6
# LIDDELL

L iddell opened his eyes to the sound of chiming when the fasten-seatbelts light turned off. The passengers on the Scandinavian Airlines flight arriving from Paris began standing up and opening the overhead bins. From his seat he observed their calm faces and orderly procedure. *Back in Sweden, the land of order.* The front door opened, and the passengers filed out in relative silence. Liddell didn't stand up; instead, his eyes rested on the passing line of bodies next to him. Some passengers stopped before his seat, briefly waiting for him to stand up and then walking past him with a look of surprise. He waited until everyone left the plane, and then he slowly rose, pulled his carry-on bag from the bin, and walked out, nodding at the smiling flight attendant who stood by the plane door.

⚖

He paid the taxi fare and got out of the car. As he pulled his bag across the driveway, he looked at the house. Something felt different, as if he had been gone for a long time, and things had changed, but he couldn't come up with a logical explanation. He shook his head, turned the key, and walked inside.

The living room was lit by the waning evening sunlight coming through the windows. The silence was complete—there was no-body home. He thought that maybe he should have called Sigrid to tell her that he would arrive at five, but he didn't want to hear her voice. He left his roller bag in the living room and went to the boys' bedroom. The beds were made and the toys put away; the rooms looked in perfect order. Elga's simple and loving ways were palpable. He walked past his bedroom to his studio. Without turning the lights on, he sat in the roller armchair by his desk and gazed out the floor-to-ceiling window. The landscape had clearly changed—the leaves on the trees seemed scarcer, browner, and drier than when he left. He swung the chair around and looked at his office. The covers of the books on the shelves looked old, more worn-out than he remembered. Even his desk looked different; the pencil holder in front of him seemed out of place. He moved it to a corner.

He lifted a Post-it note from the middle of his writing area; he recognized Elga's writing. *What beautiful, thoughtful handwriting.*

Mr. Liddell, please call your father. He has called twice since you left. Blessings.

He picked up his office phone and pushed the memory button labeled "Father." Having no time difference between Stockholm and Cape Town had always made him feel closer to his parents. After all, they were just a phone call away.

"Go ahead." Sean's clipped voice and distinctive straightfor-wardness, so frequently misinterpreted as rudeness by the people who didn't know him well, sounded perfectly familiar to Liddell.

"Hello, Father."

There was a brief silence on the line. "Your mother passed away on Tuesday." Sean's tone was somber. Silence again, this time a longer one.

Memories rushed to Liddell as fast and copiously as the tears rolled down his cheeks. He closed his eyes and saw his mother again, dancing around the sunny kitchen in the small house in Cape Town, as Nana Mouskouri's singing came from the drawing room. The pots sat on the burner, and the pan was in the stove. The window to the backyard was open. A small boy looked at the joyous, beautiful woman whose long skirt waved as she turned around and sang. Her hair was loosely twisted in a knot at the crown of her head, and the bodice of the white apron with a floral motif that she had made covered her white blouse. Liddell watched her approach the little boy. Her warm hands caressed his rosy cheeks, and her deep-green eyes looked at the boy's identical eyes with the most pure, primal love. Her voice reverberated and withered in a dreamlike memory: "Liddell."

Tears kept spilling in an unstoppable stream.

Sean continued, "We went to bed on Monday night after tea, as usual; she went to her room, and I went to mine. On Tuesday morning, after noticing that she wasn't up by ten, I entered her room to wake her up...her body was already cold. No signs of pain. There was no funeral...she was cremated the following day, as she had expressed numerous times. There is no reason for you to come. Attend your businesses. I can take care of myself." Sean's voice was a monotone, like a judge giving a verdict.

"Was she sick?" Liddell asked through a muffed sob. The same set of feelings that he had when he was a teenager, and had asked the same question to his father after the opera overcame him: ignorance, unawareness—guilt.

"No...not at all. But I did notice a difference in her in the last few days."

"What difference?" Liddell regained his composure.

"She looked calm, very calm indeed. But she also looked... how shall I put it...not sad, no. Disappointed. That's it...she looked...disappointed." Sean sounded as if he was gathering scattered thoughts, and his voice now trembled. "I also found it peculiar that on Monday evening, before she went to bed for the last time, she slowly walked through the house and looked intently at almost every object, including the rather common ones, like the walls, the carpets, the furniture, even the ceiling. I meant to ask her what that was all about, but I hesitated. There was an element of solemnity to her whole person that I hadn't noticed in her in years—the way she walked, the distant look in her eyes. The tips of her fingers gently touched the things as she walked by them."

"As if she was saying farewell..." Liddell muttered. "Did she say anything?"

"No." Sean sighed heavily. "To be honest, Liddell, we barely spoke in the last few years. I guess life at old age tends to be quiet."

"Was she still on antidepressants?"

"Very much."

"Why didn't you call me on my cell?"

"You were out on a business trip, I was told. I didn't want to disturb you with news about something that you could do nothing about but grieve."

Liddell's guts twisted. "I'll visit you when I can."

"You know you don't need to."

"Good-bye," Liddell said and put down the phone.

By now the house was completely dark. Liddell went into the bathroom, the lights still off. He opened the shower door, turned on the tap, slowly undressed, and stepped under the hot, strong stream of water. He stayed there for a few minutes, immobile. His thoughts went back to his mother. *What would've happened if you'd left him? Would you have finished your life a little bit happier? Probably. I wish you'd had a sunnier end.*

Sigrid parked her car outside and jogged the short distance to the front door. She looked through the glass panes as she turned the key, and once inside, she flicked the lights on. Liddell's roller bag stood in the middle of living room. She shook her head. She walked across the entrance hall and threw the keys on the dining-room table, making a loud clank, and then headed to her bedroom at a steady pace. She stormed in, turned the lights on, and saw Liddell lying on the bed, with eyes closed, wearing only his underwear.

⇌ ⇌

"You could've called," she said. Her tone was assertive and void of affection. "What time did you get here?"

"A couple of hours ago," he said, with eyes still closed. "I told you I was coming back Thursday evening."

"Yes, but we haven't talked since Tuesday. Did you call your father?"

"Yes."

"What did he want?"

"Mother passed away on Tuesday." He opened his eyes, meeting Sigrid's.

"Oh, my God, Liddell, I'm so sorry—but why didn't he say anything? I talked to him, I told him you were on a business trip. He could've…What's wrong with your father? He doesn't trust me?"

"It doesn't matter. He's always been like that."

"It doesn't matter? I'm his daughter-in-law, the mother of his grandsons." She shook her head in disgust.

"Just stop, Sigrid. Stop. Leave Father alone." He tried to push his father's image out of his mind but couldn't do it as long as Sigrid kept bringing him back to the conversation.

"You support him. I should have known that you'd become a cold-hearted and distant man just like him—or maybe you always

167

were, but you managed to disguise it. You just don't care about anybody, do you?"

Liddell observed her intently. He tried to find the Sigrid whom he had met a decade before: the woman who had strolled with him at the beach in the Philippines; the one who liked to talk with him for hours on end, with a generous smile on her soft lips and a thirst for moments shared together. He tried to discover a glimpse, or even a hint of the woman with whom he had made love so many times, and whom he hoped he still loved. He wanted to see the woman he had dreamed of a life with—the mother of his sons.

But he couldn't find her. Instead, he saw his own reflection in her limpid blue eyes. And in that reflection he couldn't recognize the man with whom Sigrid had walked, talked, and fallen in love. In his own reflected image, he saw a different man altogether, a man he had not realized he'd become, until that moment. That vision scared him—if he was a different man, then Sigrid had no more reasons to love him, or him to love her.

Sigrid continued. "This time alone made me think about us, Liddell, and made me realize that we are both wasting our time."

"Why? Because I couldn't cancel this trip?"

"The trip was just the tip of the iceberg."

Liddell leaned forward from the headboard and looked at her. "What's this about?" His pupils lost focus of her. He felt everything sliding away.

"Come on, Liddell, you know better than this." Her mouth quivered, and she wrapped her arms around her waist.

Liddell knew her well, but he'd never seen her so determined or so vulnerable at the same time. "May I ask why you think we've come to this?"

"You tell me. You don't talk to me anymore. You don't communicate...I feel so neglected...I feel like someone you just need to deal with but whom you don't care about in the least. You're always locked up in your studio, as if you are avoiding me; you barely answer with monosyllables when I want to start a conversation—and it's been like this for years now, Liddell.

"You never say that you love me anymore. Do you remember the last time you did? Because I don't. Now you never even touch me—not a simple caress. When was the last time that you approached me to make love?" She sobbed. "I don't know what's wrong with you...or me...but the love we had has turned into that. Something we *had*. You're such a different, cold man now, and I just don't know who you really are anymore."

"Have you thought about the boys?" His tone was calm, controlled.

"This is so you, Liddell. What are you asking? The boys will adjust. I can't take your cynicism anymore. Do you think it's all about pros and cons? All your silly calculations in your head...but you can't fool me anymore. You feel no love for me, but you won't admit it. And I don't know why." She took two steps forward, drawing closer to the bed. "Tell me—do you love me or not?" she asked, sniffing back her tears.

"I wasn't aware that you had such a bad impression of me," he said with the same calm voice.

"Answer me!" she yelled at the top of her lungs. The echo in the room seemed to amplify her rage.

The way in which Sigrid had compared him to his father suddenly made perfect sense in his mind. She was right. Maybe he *was* just like Sean—he had stopped loving his wife, had hurt her with his indifference, and now had had an affair. For one second he imagined that Sigrid was his own mother, yelling at his cold-hearted father, in the way that Liddell had always wished she would.

"No. I don't feel love for you anymore," his tone was still controlled, but deeply sad—sad for having hurt the woman he once loved and sad for having become like the man he despised.

He felt a huge burden shifting off his shoulders, like a heavy load that had kept him severely hunched for so long. Now he could finally straighten up and look ahead. But all he saw was a barren landscape. He had no thoughts, no feelings, no emotions. His emptiness was too loud; blood rushed to his ears, his limbs felt fragile, and everything around him felt worthless and distant.

"Why didn't you say anything?" Sigrid broke down in tears, and her trembling voice became a ragged whisper. "Did you think we could go on like this forever?"

"I guess I thought we could," he said, wincing at the pain in her face, trying to find the words that had fled from his reach. "I realize I wasn't thinking about you or me..." His voice failed him, and he had to swallow before he could continue. "I've always thought about the boys...the gift of a family. What I felt or stopped feeling has been irrelevant to me...for many years now. How much good do you think we're doing them by ending our marriage?"

"I can't live with someone I don't love and who doesn't love me. I need real love, not formality and distance. I don't know when or how this happened, but I can't take it anymore." She waved her arms around. "This is all fake: our family, our chitchat...I don't even remember the last time I felt happy being next to you." Her eyes held a mixture of anger, pity, and sorrow.

"What about Harry?"

"Harry?"

"You've been seeing him. You think I couldn't tell?"

"God..." Sigrid exhaled. "Yes, I've been seeing him...to work on that damn website that's been sucking up my whole life."

"And am I supposed to believe that you two only worked together?" He realized that the conversation would take an inevitable turn, but if everything was crumbling down as it actually was, at least he wanted to know the truth about Harry.

"What?" Her jaw dropped, and she shook her head, with half-closed eyes. "Harry is gay. He lives with his male partner. Did you really think that I was...? Oh my God...get out of my life. We're done. Pack your things and leave. Now!"

Her hands trembled as she furiously swiped at her tears. "You can use the empty apartment in town. Elga will pack your things. Leave now…I don't want to see you ever again." She rushed into the bathroom, slamming the door behind her.

Liddell could hear her crying while he dressed. He walked to the bathroom door and spoke softly. "You are right about letting me go. You deserve better. I'm so sorry—so sorry."

He went to his studio, swept up a few folders and papers and was heading out when his eye caught sight of one of the paintings on the wall. He stopped and looked at it. A little boy played under a towering plane tree while a woman, seated in a chair, looked at him, gazing at him lovingly; the sun was setting behind the huge tree, bathing the scene with a warm, orange light.

"Who could have thought back then," he murmured, staring at the small child in the painting, "that life changes it all. It changes us all." He put the folders on the floor and gently took the painting off the wall.

⇒ ⇐

A whole week passed by, and Friday afternoon came around in the blink of an eye. Work had piled up while he was away on the trip, and the sheer amount of reports and phone calls he had to make, just to catch up, had been enough to keep him glued to his makeshift office.

The city apartment was spotless, but barely furnished: a table in the living room served both as an office workspace and dining table. Piles of papers, his laptop computer, and a coffee mug competed for the scarce space left on it. The small kitchenette, which he only used for making tea and coffee, had its narrow countertop scattered with supermarket plastic bags. A mattress on the floor of an otherwise empty bedroom was his bed. He had just bought a bunk bed for Klas and Rutger, which had been delivered during

171

the morning. The deliverymen put it together in the second bed-room, but the mattresses, pillows, and sheets were still in their plastic wraps, unpacked, sitting in a corner of the boys' room.

The doorbell rang. He opened the solid wooden door while still talking on his cell phone. He nodded at Elga, who stood behind Klas and Rutger. The kids kissed Elga good-bye and came inside the apartment with their duffel bags swung over their shoulders.

Elga timidly raised her hand, waved good-bye to the boys, and whispered, trying not to interrupt Liddell's phone conversation, "I'll pick them up on Sunday at five. Good-bye, Mr. Liddell." Her short, wrinkled fingers spread out, signaling a five.

Liddell nodded again, as his cheek pressed his cell phone against his shoulder. Elga turned around and walked away.

"Yes," he said, closing the door, "I'll have the report ready by Monday. You'll see that you are making the right decision. You'll have to buy the new machinery sooner rather than later." He paused, listening to his client's reaction. "Okay. Yes, I know, the board has to approve it." He looked at the boys. "Yes, Mr. Haabs. Have a nice weekend. Bye."

Klas and Rutger were sitting on the floor, looking up at him. He put his phone on the table and sat next to them.

"Done with work. Let's talk now. Rutger, how was your week?"

"Normal," the small boy said. "I miss doing my homework with you."

"Well, we can do some of it over the weekend and learn new things as well. And we'll go canoeing tomorrow morning. Would you like that?"

"I like being with you, Dad. Why did you leave?" Rutger asked. His voice didn't show grief, just curiosity.

"Because your mother and I decided that we would both feel better if we lived in two different places. You have two homes now."

"This is not my home, Dad. I don't have my bedroom or my toys in here." Rutger said.

"You are right, Rutger, this is not your home. Neither is it mine, to be honest. I may move. I don't know yet." Liddell's tone was flat.

"Are you going to South Africa with your parents?" Klas asked.

"They are your grandparents, Klas." He corrected him. He hadn't told the boys about his mother's death. The news about the separation was enough. "I'm not going anywhere."

<hr/>

He ordered pizza for dinner, and then they played Scrabble for about an hour. Before long, the night had closed in. Liddell made tea and asked the boys to prepare for bed. He felt exhausted, defeated. He pulled the plastic wraps off the mattresses and made the beds with the new white sheets. He tucked the boys in, kissed them goodnight, and turned the lights off. Then, lying down on his mattress, he clasped his hands over his chest and lay still. The memory of Connie was all too fresh. Her presence seemed to hover over everything he did or thought about.

*This is unbearable. What if I called her? I wouldn't say a word. I'd let her say hello a few times, until she hung up.* He groaned. *What are you thinking, Liddell? Don't be silly. What if I wrote? I'm supposed to know what happened with the article. You are so childish. Who cares about the article? Even so, it's her article, not yours. You didn't write a single word of it. You deserve no credit. But I gave her my opinions and took the photos. You gave her what? Stop it, please. She is gone. Get over it. She's as gone as Sigrid. As gone as Mother. They all left, one way or another.*

The mattress felt hot. He kicked the blanket away. He meant to force himself to sleep, but he couldn't control his feelings of guilt and longing. When he eventually fell asleep, he dreamed about Connie; the sound of her voice in his dreams soothed his rest.

<hr/>

He woke up to the echoing sounds of Klas and Rutger running around the empty apartment. It was nine thirty in the morning, and the light flooded his bedroom through the curtain-less windows. He grimaced at the bright light, rubbed his eyes, and turned away. The stomping of small feet came closer and closer to the door, until the boys finally stormed into his room and jumped on him, giving way to screaming and shouting. They had a brief wrestling session, after which they all lay down on the mattress. The sheets had been dispersed, and the pillows had flown to the corners of the room.

He looked at the faces of the two boys for a moment. Their rosy cheeks and easy smiles knew nothing about grief; their hands, eager to grab their toys and quick to reach out to him to play, were soft and pure. He couldn't help recalling when he was their age. *They have no past, and nothing to forget. Their time is ahead of them.*

He wondered what things life had in store for these two young boys. Would they fall prey to the same mistakes he had made? Was there a way for him to warn them? He knew the answer. He knew that life was going to teach them only as much as they were willing to learn. Not more, not less. And he made peace with that idea.

He poured Redbush tea into their cups while Rutger pulled two slices of bread out of the bag and placed them in the toaster. Klas, standing a few feet away, looked at them in silence, with his hands in his pockets.

"Come on, get the butter, Klas," Liddell said.

Klas dragged his feet to the fridge and took a stick of butter; he left it on the table and moved a few steps back with a sad expression in his eyes.

After their quiet and frugal breakfast, Rutger ran to his bedroom and came back with a pack of cards he had taken from his duffel bag. He poked Klas, asking him to play, but his brother wasn't in the mood. Rutger insisted until Klas agreed to play. Little Rutger sprinted to the empty living room, where he sat on the floor and dealt the cards. Klas followed him and sat next to his stepbrother in silence.

Liddell's cell phone rang; it was Will. Liddell realized he hadn't heard from him since the room confusion in Rome. *Maybe he has news from Connie.*

"Hi, Will. How are you?"

"Not too shabby, all things considered," Will sighed. His voice sounded tired.

"What's up?"

"I have a new boss. He thinks he knows it all and dares to tell me how to do my job, when it should be him who should listen to a few facts about what a manager ought to be."

"Is he giving you a hard time?" Liddell disguised a smile.

"This is bollocks, mate. He wants to trace all the expenses, one year back from now. He wants receipts from everything. Can you believe it?"

"Times are tough for everybody, Will. But I assume you have your finances in order."

"Of course not. You know me!"

"Funny that you called. I was going to call you to ask if you had news about the article or Connie. I never heard from her, I mean, not that I had to but...you know...I just wondered."

"Oh yeah, yeah. It all went fine, I suppose, but I don't know much. The American office was in charge of that one."

"I see..."

"This new guy has absolutely no clue. His name is Trevor High the Third, or something ridiculous like that—he's just one of those rich kids fresh out of school who thinks he can run companies because he attended some classes at university. You know what I mean? Fresh out of school. Unbelievable. Now, going back to business, they've opened a new little spa in Bath, and they've handsomely paid for a review in our world-famous magazine. Do you want to check it out? I could get you an extra pass for Sigrid. Just pay for her flight."

"Could you get me two passes? I'd like to take the boys instead. I don't think Sigrid will be interested."

"Why not? She'd love it…but as you wish. I'll schedule it for Friday and Saturday. I'll e-mail you the details."

"Do you want me to write a few comments?"

"About what? I already wrote the entire article, mate! I looked up the place online and came up with some gibberish. Just let me know about a couple of details that catch your attention—anything that I could mention, you know, to give the article some…legitimacy."

"For sure." Liddell smiled and shook his head.

"Cheers, mate."

He put the phone down and felt the desire to call Connie. *Just to hear her voice.* He thought he had her phone number, but he didn't; he would have to e-mail her or ask Will. *Damn.*

A casual e-mail would be much easier—just a few words, nothing compromising.

*You'd better leave her alone. She's got a life at home. Do you want to ruin her marriage, like you did yours? Besides, what's the point? You're too far apart. It'd never work.* Liddell tried to silence his inner voice, but again, his efforts were in vain. *You left Mother. She withered and died alone. You cheated on Sigrid. You couldn't love her, and you hurt her. Now the boys, you let them down by not being able to keep a marriage together. What do you want to talk to Connie for? You ruin everything you touch. Leave her alone. At least you won't be able to ruin a memory.*

Regardless of his self-accusations, questions about Connie kept springing up. What was she doing? How did she find things at home? Was she thinking of him? Was she missing him?

The memory of her felt like a ghost, ever so present, trying to be part of a world that had no real room for her.

Liddell closed his eyes. He remembered her laughter and her sighs. He saw her again in her blue dress, walking out of the opera. He remembered her violet barrette and the way she tucked her hair behind her ears with her long, delicate fingers. He remembered the light of her pale-blue eyes when she spoke, the contagious joy of her unrestrained smile, and her fast, eager pace when she walked. He recalled the smell of her soft skin, and the tension in her body when they kissed. He remembered the taste of her mouth and the sound of her breathless whispers while they made love. But what haunted him the most was the sound of her voice. Being deprived of it seemed the cruelest form of isolation. For some reason he kept feeling as if he was about to hear her voice again at any moment, but instead, it was always someone else's.

He opened his eyes, and stared at the empty white wall facing the dinner table.

He stood up, moved toward the boys, and watched them playing for a few seconds. He smiled. "I need your help, little men," he said.

"What is it, Dad?" Rutger asked.

"I want to hang an old painting of mine. I need you to hold it up in different parts of the house while I look at it and decide where I want it."

They went into his bedroom, and he showed the boys how to pick up the painting, holding it steadily from the sides.

They started at the narrow kitchen. Liddell immediately shook his head. "No." They went to his bedroom; the empty wall opposite the mattress seemed like a good place. "Nobody will see it here." He moved it to the corridor between the bedrooms. "Not enough light." Disgruntled and tired of carrying the heavy canvas around, the boys set it on the floor, leaning on the living-room wall.

"Have you made up your mind, Dad?" Rutger asked with impatience.

"Yes. It will go right there," Liddell said, pointing at the naked wall facing the dining-room table. He pulled a drill out of the otherwise empty pantry, and drilling a hole on the freshly painted brick wall, he secured a screw.

"Go on, boys. Pick up the painting and hang it from the screw. I will see from back here that it's properly leveled."

The kids did as they were told. They each stepped on a chair, lifted the painting, and hung its thin, rusty hanger wire on the new, plated screw. Liddell looked at the painting of himself and his mother. He closed his eyes briefly, thrust his memories away, and focused on the horizon line.

"Rutger, push your side up a bit. Klas, now you. That's it. Perfect."

He took a few steps back and stared at the canvas again. It looked level. Klas walked close to Liddell and put his small hands into his pants pockets.

"Dad," he said with a shy tone.

"Yes, Klas," said Liddell, still looking at the painting.

"Are you still my dad?" His voice was fragile, about to break.

Liddell closed his eyes, gathering his thoughts. Klas had been abandoned once and didn't need to be left behind for a second time. He loved the boy as intensely as he loved Rutger, and that was a thing at which he was not going to fail. He shifted around and bent toward him, facing Klas's innocent eyes. He carefully held the small-framed twelve-year-old by the shoulders.

"Klas, you will always be my son, and I will always be your father, regardless of whatever happens to us in life. I love you immensely, and I always will. Do you understand?" Liddell's eyes welled with tears.

"Yes, Dad."

"Look at the painting. Do you see the little boy under the tree? He will always be there. He is a part of the painting. He just can't go away. You and I will always be close to each other in our hearts because we're part of the same painting, the painting of our lives."

"Who is the boy on the painting?" Klas asked.

"It's me. And the woman sitting on the chair is my mother."

"Who painted it?"

"My grandmother, Johanne, did. She also taught me that beauty and love are everywhere, but it is up to us to notice them and to enjoy them. I was about your age, Klas, when she made this painting. I remember when she gave it to me. She said just what I have told you. We will always live together in the painting of our lives, deep in our hearts. When we love others, we are always with them in our hearts, because once they are painted into our canvas, they will stay there, no matter the circumstances."

"But Mum and you are not in love anymore," Rutger observed as he moved close to Liddell. "Does it mean that you erased her from your painting?"

"Not at all. I cannot erase her. She did what she thought was best for her and for both of you, and I respect her decision. She was an important part of my life." He paused and took the boys' hands. "The three of us are together now, but probably, later on, we'll be apart. You'll go off to university; maybe you'll marry and move far away, as I did when it was my turn to make a life. But that will not matter, because we love each other, and ultimately, love is what will keep us together in our hearts."

The boys nodded earnestly, trying to understand a concept that was maybe a little too difficult for them to grasp at that moment, but their eyes were fixed on his.

Liddell clasped his sons' hands, and as he did so, he could clearly see Connie, with her warm eyes, smiling at him.

# CHAPTER 7

# CONNIE

Connie asked for another glass of sparkling wine. She held the flute from the base and aimed the rim at the flight attendant.

"Are you sure, ma'am? You're making me nervous by holding the glass like that."

"It's okay." Connie looked at the young woman without sympathy. "You can pour."

"As you wish, ma'am...it's just that it looks so unsafe. I've never seen anybody holding a wineglass like that."

The flight attendant filled Connie's glass and kept walking along the first-class aisle, shaking her head. Connie looked at the screen in front of her: 9:00 a.m.

Her head was a whirlwind of thoughts and memories of the night before. A collage of mixed images of Liddell, as if flashing on a screen, with the random sound of the conversations they'd had during the last few days. She wanted to calm down and think things through, but she just couldn't focus.

She could still see him lying next to her: the solid muscles of his back, the bold sinews in his hands, the veins in his arms like thick lines drawn with soft bluish chalk. She still felt his arms tightly wrapped around her back and her waist, his fingers sinking in her warm flesh, their bodies raising and, in turn, subsiding with every breath they took, possessed by each other.

She sipped more wine.

The flight attendant moved from the back to the front, collecting the empty glasses before takeoff. "You scared me holding the glass like that. My goodness, it looked like you were gonna spill the thing all over. I'll take it, ma'am."

Connie didn't move. Physically and emotionally exhausted, she closed her eyes.

Her body bounced on her seat from side to side while they flew through some stormy clouds. She remembered that her father had sent her another one of her mother's poems the day before. Once the turbulence subsided, she opened her eyes, and with renewed energy, pulled out her computer from the overhead bin. According to Robert's e-mail, it was the last poem her mother ever wrote.

A world unseen,
and days of empty: talk,
thought, feeling, love.
I dug out from the vacuum
another missed opportunity.
Another sterile year.
No offspring.
I stare at the void. I'm with you there
In our own unseen world of unspoken words.
No witnesses, no passersby.
And the dead leaves of the past
roll along the lonely rhythm.
Of solitude.
Of your memory.

She was moved, but confused. Whose memory was her mother talking about? She couldn't think about it. The short burst of energy she'd felt quickly waned, and exhaustion took over once again. She put the computer away and fell asleep almost immediately.

⟫⟪

The two-hour layover in Detroit felt short. By the time she cleared immigration, customs, and security, she only had twenty minutes left before boarding her flight to Minneapolis. She ordered a double espresso at Starbucks, leaned on a table, and quietly watched the people passing by.

She saw a world on the move. A constant flow of families, businesspeople, and elderly travelers—men and women from all walks of life going somewhere. Regardless of their diversity, they all shared a certain sameness: the subtle rush as they walked through the terminal, and the slight sense of uncertainty while looking at the departure screens. They all shared a moment in time in a very crowded place that nobody belonged to. They were all in transit. They would all be gone in a matter of hours, maybe even minutes, and a new wave of people would replace them, restarting the ongoing cycle, over and over again, day after day.

A strong déjà vu surprised her. She was living this scene again, but something major, paramount, felt utterly different. "The viewer has changed," she whispered and sipped the unsweetened, dark-roast espresso.

Her cell phone vibrated on the table. Deb was calling.

"Hi, Connie. Welcome home!" Deb's vim always showed in her energetic tone.

"I still have one more flight ahead, but thank you. How did the kids do?"

"Oh, they were fine. I stopped by for a few minutes each day; they were okay. How was your trip?"

Connie hesitated. "It was…fine—great, actually. A lot going on, with all the museums and the flying…I'm exhausted."

The boarding of her flight to Minneapolis was announced over the speakers.

"Sorry, Deb, but I have to board now. Let's talk tomorrow, okay?"

"I leave for Colorado tomorrow. I booked a spa retreat for a few days, so I'll be off the radar. But don't worry, we'll talk when I get back."

"Perfect. Enjoy your holiday, Deb."

As Connie boarded the plane, she thought whether she wanted to tell her friend about what had really happened. She shook her head. *I need to understand it better myself before I can talk about it.*

Nick was waiting at the baggage claim, leaning against a wall. One hand was in his jeans pocket, and he held his cell phone with the other. Connie looked at him as she walked closer. Nick's eyes were fixed on the little colored screen, and he didn't notice her coming until she was a few yards away. He put his phone in his back pocket and smiled.

"Hey. Welcome home."

"Hi, Nick."

"Let me take your bag. How was your flight?"

"It was fine."

"Yeah...well, you are back. That's all that matters."

Connie remained quiet as they walked to Nick's SUV. He tossed the bag in the trunk, and they got into the vehicle without looking at each other.

"I thought you'd bring the kids," she said.

"I was at Eric's place for a few pregame beers. I'll drop you off at home, and I'll be back just in time for the game." His eyes were set on the highway. "My parents are there with them now."

There was a rather long period of silence. They had nothing to say. Her gaze was on the passing landscape. As they got to familiar territory, Connie noticed the signs on the highway for the first time in years. They looked new and bright.

She looked at a big group of trees, and although they formed a tight grove, she could discern a beautiful oak, a few birch trees, one lonely plane tree, and a pair of weeping willows. Then she looked at the sky—pale cottony clouds were moving fast, escaping from the dusk that approached at a hurried pace.

Bryan ran into Connie's arms as soon as he saw her coming through the front door. Connie felt her eyes welling with emotion. Stacey and Amanda rushed down the stairs from their rooms to greet their mother, uttering oohs and aahs as they hugged her. Pam and Joe stood a few steps behind the kids, smiling at the warm scene. Nick, meanwhile, dumped her bag in the garage and jumped back in the SUV. Connie noticed the taillights disappearing down the street.

"How was your flight home, my dear?" Pam asked, giving Connie a hug.

"It was okay. So long, though! I'm exhausted…"

"Nick told us how you got a call for a last-minute job. How did it go?" Joe asked. His wide smile looked just like Nick's.

"It went well. I visited a few museums. Now I need to put the article together." She relaxed as she sat on one of the dining-room chairs.

Pam and Joe stayed for another forty-five minutes. Joe, self-referential as always, told her a few stories from when he had been stationed in the Dreux-Louvilliers Air Base in France, back in the fifties.

Before leaving, Joe dragged Connie's bag from the garage and took it up to her bedroom. Minutes later, they were gone, and Connie and the kids walked together up the stairs.

Bryan wanted his gifts. Connie unzipped her bag and handed him two Asterix comics that she had bought at a bookstore in London during her morning walk. The twelve-year-old grinned when she also gave him a small Eiffel Tower statuette.

"How is it over there, Mom?" Stacey asked. She and Amanda were lying on Connie's bed, while Bryan was turning the pages of one of the comics.

"It's nice, very nice…and different. I mean, everything is different…the people, the languages, the buildings, the food. There is so much historical stuff that you could spend a lifetime there and not even see a fraction of it."

"It sounds awesome. I want to go!" Amanda cried.

"I don't know about that," Stacey added. "I'd rather go backpacking in the Rocky Mountains."

"You're talking about two completely different things," Amanda replied with an air of authority. "There's no point in comparing the Rocky Mountains and Europe. You could go backpacking in Ireland too. I hear it's gorgeous there."

Stacey shook her head, dismissing Amanda's suggestion. "Mom, the girls are planning a trip to Lake Tahoe for next summer. Katy's parents will chaperone. Can I go? Say yes, please, please!" Stacey clasped her hands together.

"I don't know, Stacey. We have to ask your dad."

A cell phone made a beeping sound from the distance, and Amanda rushed back to her room. Stacey kept talking about the upcoming trip to Lake Tahoe, but after a few minutes, she was back in her room, too. Bryan soon put the comics down and resumed playing video games in the family room. Connie slowly unpacked.

She carried her laundry bag, full from the trip, down to the basement, and headed to the washer. She stopped short, met by pile after pile of dirty clothes on the floor and even more welling up from the large hamper beside the machines. She dropped her bag on the floor and walked away.

The kitchen floor was covered with dust and breadcrumbs, the marble countertop looked like it had not been cleaned since she left, and the stains of spilled liquids had dried all over it. She opened the fridge to find it packed with leftovers in take-out boxes. *Unbelievable.*

She went to the garage to get the mop, looked around, and couldn't find it. Something smelled putrid. Two stinking half-full trash bags sat by the overflowing trashcan. She grimaced, turning her head, and discovered the mop's loose strings buried behind a few dozen empty beer cans and bottles. *My goodness. This is enough.*

She ran upstairs and stormed into Amanda's room. "What's all this mess downstairs?"

"Hold on, I'll call you back. Bye," she said. "What's going on? I was in the middle of something."

"The house is filthy. You didn't even clean the countertop or sweep the floor. There's laundry everywhere in the basement, and the garage is a mess—the garbage is overflowing."

"But you were coming home tonight. We thought you would—"

"Would what? Clean up all the mess you left? Is this how you welcome me back? You better go to the basement and start doing some laundry, girl. Stacey!" Connie yelled. "Stop what you're doing. Go vacuum the dining room. Now! Do you hear me?"

The girls sulked as they went down the stairs. Bryan looked at his muttering sisters with wide-open eyes. Connie followed the girls down to the kitchen. Amanda loaded the dishwasher, then put some rubber gloves on, and started mopping the floor. Stacey turned on the vacuum cleaner and pushed it across the dining room. Connie scrubbed the countertops, threw away all the leftovers from the fridge, sponged the grease spots off the microwave, and wiped down the cabinet doors.

She cleaned the dining-room table and brushed the crumbs off the chairs. She then went to the family room and asked Bryan to pick up the toys that were scattered all over the floor along with empty soda cans and half-empty packs of chips. She told Stacey to vacuum the carpet in there and went up to Bryan's room. The bed was unmade, and it looked as if it had never been properly tended since she left. She went through his backpack and found undone homework, pencils with broken points, pens without caps, and a half-eaten candy bar that had melted under the school folders, staining them with chocolate. She dropped the bag on the floor, shook her head, and moved into Amanda's bedroom. The same scene of disorder was repeated there and then again in Stacey's room. She entered her own bedroom again and found seven socks lying on the floor near Nick's side of the bed, and two pairs of underwear and three empty beer bottles under the bed.

The next hour passed by with more cleaning, arranging, putting garbage in bags, and sulking by her children. By the time they finished, Connie felt out of breath, disappointed, and jet-lagged.

She went to the bathroom, opened the bathtub faucets all the way, and put the stopper in. She threw in a generous amount of lavender salts, slowly undressed, and tossed her clothes in a corner. She stepped into the tub and slowly slid under the lavender bubbles. With eyes closed, her thoughts rushed to Liddell, seeking refuge in memories of him.

She saw his face again. It was as clear as if it were in front of her—she rejoiced in the memory of his dimples when he smiled, the wrinkles on the side of his eyes, and how he slowly blinked when he listened to her. *I wonder what he's doing. Probably having a nice, civilized dinner and good conversation with Sigrid. She probably waited for him at the airport, and they walked back to her car with renewed love, holding hands. He's moved on.*

She pictured him playing with his sons, helping them do their homework, and riding bicycles around their quaint small town. She felt permanently excluded from his world. But still, she couldn't stop thinking about him, remembering his voice, his green eyes, the shape of his hands, his unaffected yet elegant gait. She remembered some of their conversations, but she craved more. She wanted to remember it all, live it all over again and again; she dug deep in her memory and pulled out snippets of their time together. She wanted to see him, to call him. She yearned for anything from him...news, a text, a letter.

Nick's steps echoed as he stomped up the stairs. Her eyes opened wide—she suddenly felt exposed and vulnerable, in the wrong, like a child caught stealing candy. Nick stood by the door; she could sense it. Two knocks reverberated in the bathroom. Her hand rapidly muffled a sob, but a tear sneaked through her now tightly closed eyes.

"You okay in there?" he asked.

"Yes." Her voice had just enough strength to mask her distress.

"All right. I'll be downstairs."

Her throat choked. She let her torso slide forward, submerging her head under the hot, bubbly water.

She tossed and turned away from the light that broke through the Venetian blinds; the night had passed like a thick gray cloud. She opened her eyes and turned around to see the clock: Friday, 7:00 a.m. Hand to her forehead, she exhaled a profound sigh. Nick had gotten up and left the bedroom door open. She could hear his voice, and the girls' as well, down in the kitchen. She crawled out of bed and walked to the shower. She let the hot water rain down on her and then turned it cooler. After a few more minutes, she walked out, renewed.

Nick had made breakfast: scrambled eggs, pancakes with maple syrup, and coffee. When she came down the stairs, dressed for her run, Amanda set her coffee cup on the table, walked to her, and hugged her tightly. Connie felt her daughter's head on her shoulder. Her mood immediately improved.

"Good morning," Nick said, upbeat.

"Hi…you made all this?" Connie timidly asked.

"Well, I found out that you weren't happy with the way we took care of the house while you were gone, so…here it is, for you."

"And you think this will make up for the mess you made?"

"Why not?"

"I am still upset, Nick. How could you be so…so…uncaring?"

"Stop it—right there. Who left a whole family just to fool around visiting museums in Europe?" His voice grew louder with every word.

"Okay, so now it's my fault that you can't keep the house clean for three days."

"Hey, it wasn't me who left."

"Nick…you—you are impossible!"

"You started all this, Connie. Just calm down, okay?"

"No, Nick, I'm not calming down. Who do you think I am? One of your employees? I have a life too, and I won't be bossed around and keep my head down just because you made breakfast for once in your life. I will not take this anymore! Do you hear me?" She realized she was yelling when she saw Amanda, Stacey, and Bryan staring at her. Her face flushed with shame and anger; they had never argued in front of the kids before. Her lips quivered, and her knees trembled; she nervously tucked her hair behind her ears and rushed out of the house.

She stepped off the sidewalk onto the street, moving at a rapid pace. She scuttled away from the house, trying to calm down and put her thoughts in order. *It has all gotten out of hand. Why did this happen to me? Why did I have to meet you, Liddell? What am I going to do? Run away from my family? From my life? What was I thinking? I set myself up for a fall and betrayed my husband. And I thought I could dream with love…I'm so stupid.*

A light drizzle fell, the air got cooler, and gusts of wind brought in dark clouds that quickly filled the pale sky. Her walk became a jog.

Twenty minutes had passed when the drizzle turned into heavier raindrops, and thunder roared from the horizon in front of her. *I'd better go back.* By the time she got to her garage, the pouring rain was steady. The house was quiet. The kids were off to school, and Nick was at work. She went up to her room, took her damp clothes off, and had a long hot shower.

Connie put on a robe, took her computer and travel notebook, and sat at the dining-room table. She had a job to do. She sent Brenda a long e-mail, telling her about the success of the trip, thanking her for having chosen her, and asking a few questions about the final word count and overall article format; she finally mentioned that Liddell had taken wonderful photos—not that she had seen them—but just to mention his name and hope that Brenda would reply with news about him.

Then she started typing her notes into the computer and continued doggedly for the rest of the day. Once back from school, Amanda brought her a sandwich and a glass of white wine for lunch, and Bryan sat next to her and read one of the Asterix comics. Stacey brought her a cup of tea around four. Connie didn't take a break until around nine o'clock, when she was done with the manuscript. But she had failed to bury her feelings with work and had only recalled more intensely the time spent with Liddell, who by now was present in every thought.

Brenda's reply came in on Monday morning. Connie's questions had been clearly and politely answered, but the impersonal, somewhat uninvolved way in which Brenda replied made her think that there was something else going on. On Wednesday morning she got another e-mail from Brenda informing her that she had left the publishing company. The reasons she gave were professional exhaustion and personal issues—Connie recalled that Brenda's marriage had just broken up—but she assured Connie that the museum project, as they had come to call it, was unaffected by her resignation. She would be handing it over to the new manager, she said, a young and dynamic former art consultant who had become editor in chief for the magazine on both sides of the Atlantic. At the end of the e-mail, Brenda asked Connie to send her the draft, as well, because she wanted to read it for pleasure.

Connie worked even harder—she wanted to give this new editor a great impression. Finally, the opportunity had arrived to showcase her writing skills and maybe get offered a full-time job at the magazine. That morning she went to the library and picked up a couple dozen art books to do further research on what she had seen: she looked at pictures of the pieces of art from different angles, and she studied different interpretations by different authors. She watched *Madama Butterfly* again on DVD. For the rest of the week, she was up by six every morning and went to bed late at night, exhausted but utterly fulfilled. Like back in her college days, she was surrounded by volumes of beautiful art, but this time it was for real, she thought.

Friday afternoon finally came around. The week had passed, and the article was ready to be sent out. Nick had been busy but nevertheless had helped around the house, giving Connie the time she needed to focus.

She felt proud of her work. She had laid out the comments on the four pieces of art as four days of a single trip, almost as it had happened, adding tidbits of road experience and curiosities about each city. She read the article dozens—hundreds—of times, looking for typos, errors, and better ways to word each sentence. By Friday night she felt it was ready. She wrote an introductory letter to the editor in chief, attached the Word document, and pressed Send.

It felt like a release, but at the same time ethereal and unreal. She had written her longest article ever, and had put all her skill and dedication into making it the best possible work: her hopes were high.

The popping of the cork relaxed her, but even more so did the young Argentine Malbec. *Calm, a tender caress, a beautiful linger.* The wine was quite balanced for its age. She smiled, hands on her cheeks, and daydreamed about a career in writing, or even better, in art appreciation. This rediscovered passion for the aesthetics fueled in her a will to carry on living around beauty, with passion and expression. For a strange reason she felt closer to Liddell, as if by keeping her mind occupied with the thing that had brought them together she could stay close to him at all times. When she heard Nick coming toward her, she turned around and watched him getting closer.

"Are you still mad at me?" he asked with a smile that looked more like a wince.

"No."

"Good. Let's leave all this nonsense behind."

"What nonsense?" she asked with a steady look.

"All this trip BS, you leaving, the mess we made...let's just forget all about it. We were fine before all this happened. Let's go back to that, okay?"

Her thoughts went back to Deb and what she had said to Connie on the phone. *There's no way Nick will be on the same page that you are on now.*

"Okay," she whispered.

"Good. I knew we'd work it out." He nodded once and headed to the family room. He let himself collapse onto the couch and turned the TV on. Connie turned back to her computer.

A little over an hour later, a new e-mail popped up in her in-box. The editor had replied. She froze. She was possibly sitting in front of a world of opportunity. Maybe a contract—a life-changing contract. She imagined living in a world of written words and art appreciation, of refined thoughts and delicate feelings. She brought her hand to her mouth, nervous about opening the e-mail, taking just a little more time to savor all the things that it could mean. She saw herself walking around museums, taking notes, sitting at a café putting together thoughts and ideas, maybe traveling abroad, maybe going to Europe again. Who knew? It all was so close, just a click away. Her hand slowly moved over to her mouse; the cursor on the screen hovered over the new message. *Click.*

Dear Mrs. Stewart,
I trust you are doing well.
I received your article, written and delivered under the terms we had agreed upon. I have skipped through it, and I must say that you have done a good job mixing the views of an amateur museumgoer and the ideas that may, in the best of cases, spring from the mind of a person who has read a book or two. And as much as I see value in the views of independent, outsider participants, who are, more often than not, ignorant of the standards of professional art appreciation, I, as the new editor in chief of *Life with Style*, intend to redesign the profile of the magazine and raise its art section toward the upper echelons of contemporary art, making it a beacon amid the mediocrity of written material that abounds in the publishing industry at this time.

That being said, the article you produced will not be published.

A new series of professional interpretations will replace it, but this time, instead of the widely known pieces of art that became a cliché of Western art, I will personally review the more exciting works of young, unconventional, and challenging contemporary artists, many of whom I count among my personal friends. You have to understand that art, today, means immediacy, shock, and performance. Modern art shatters the conventions of our society and opens paths to untested ideas. We need to wipe out the old concepts of what art is and inform our readers about the new.

Needless to say, you will receive the compensation that was agreed on by the previous editor before my arrival at the magazine.

Best regards,

Trevor High-Stain III, Ph.D. CEO - CFO

Connie could barely breathe. The dream world she had imagined weakened at each word she read, finally tumbling down as quickly as a house of cards. She read the e-mail again and again, trying to find a spark of hope among the ruins, but she couldn't find any. The words were brutally clear.

She slowly closed her computer and walked in silence to her room. She closed the door, lay down on the bed, and cried. She washed all her broken hopes with long-held tears: the love that she had found and lost, the shattered dream of becoming an art writer, and a reality that had been—for too long now—dull and gray. She cried for the life that she had once dreamed of but never achieved. She cried for the vibrant girl she once had been, full of vim and joy, but who seemed so long gone now. She cried for the wasted years, ordinarily lived, pursuing a false sense of security, that couldn't save her from feeling disappointment. Was life this, after all? Where was the world of possibility she used to feel all around her? She wanted to go back in time and do things differently. She wished she had known better, that somebody had told her about the futility of a life lived without passion, without a real, tangible love.

But then her tears stopped welling, her sobs dwindled, and her agitated breath normalized. She fixed a wide, empty gaze on the white ceiling. She thought of him. She said his name out loud. "Liddell."

A knock on the door brought her back to reality. She quickly wiped her tears with the pillowcase.

"Who is it?" She tried to gain a few seconds.

"Mom, Grandpa's on the phone. He wants to talk to you," Amanda said as she entered the room. They looked into each other's eyes. Connie saw a mixture of confusion and tenderness in her daughter's surprised expression. Amanda gave her the phone and stood by the bed, looking down at her.

Connie smiled, shy, vulnerable. She patted the mattress signaling Amanda to sit next to her as she picked up the phone. "Hi, Dad."

"Hello, my dear traveler. How was it? I want to know all about it, from beginning to end!"

"We'll need a few hours. There's a lot to talk about."

"Visit me tomorrow. Come in the morning. I also have a couple of things to tell you."

She wanted to ask him what was it about, but she lacked the energy. "Okay, see you tomorrow, around ten."

"Sounds good."

"Bye, Dad." Connie put the phone down.

"You've been crying. Why?" Amanda asked.

There was an element of purity in Amanda's calm voice, an innocent curiosity that Connie also recognized in herself.

Connie sighed. "One cries for many reasons. Some can be explained and others just can't. But I feel better, now that you asked."

Amanda hugged her. Connie laid her head on her daughter's shoulder, embraced her, and stayed still. She realized that Amanda was crying too, but she kept her eyes closed, feeling nurtured and healed by the pure love of her daughter.

⇌ ⇌

"I hope you don't have anything else to do today because we have a lot to talk about," Robert said as he opened the front door to Connie.

"You're intriguing me, Dad. What's this all about?" She took her sunglasses off and kissed him on both cheeks.

"Your trip! The trip of your life! I want to know everything about it."

It was the first time that she would actually talk about the trip, because neither Nick nor the kids had asked her about the details. She felt anxious about what could accidentally leak out of her narration; she knew that Robert could read people quite well. *Let's see how this goes.*

Connie sat at the kitchen table. Robert poured two cups of fresh-brewed coffee, sat next to her, and started asking questions. They talked about the museums she visited, the artwork she had seen, and the impressions that she wrote down for the article.

Hours passed by as they discussed details about Michelangelo's work as a sculptor, painter, and poet, and whether Bernini was the first real art entrepreneur that the world had ever known. Robert argued that Rodin's rejection by the academy to enter the Paris Salon of 1864 with his *Man with the Broken Nose* was the catalyst to his artistic genius. When they got to Monet, Robert asked about Connie's feelings when she entered the Musée de l'Orangerie. Did it feel like a three-dimensional experience? But he was also hungry for mementos, the small stuff: How did the croissants taste in Paris? Were the English really as well-spoken as they appeared on TV? Was everybody dressed up at the opera? What about Italy? How did it feel to be standing in the "holy land of Western art"?

197

He smiled, in awe, like a little kid who was being told about how it would be when he grew up. Then the inevitable came.

"What about him?" he asked nonchalantly and sipped some coffee.

"Who?"

"Lenny."

"You mean Liddell."

"Yes, Liddell," he corrected himself.

"He...he is a well-traveled, cultured man, a wonderful companion, and I think he was a great fit for this trip."

"And—"

"And what?"

"Well, there has to be something else to say about him. You spent three days together."

"Yes, you're right. There is more to say about him." She cleared her throat and looked out the front window, picturing the face that had been etched in her mind since the moment they'd parted ways. "He is an extraordinary man. There is a pretty hard, formal shell around him, but he is extremely sensitive. I sensed a suppressed, muted joy that would suddenly spring to life and show his inner self. And although I don't know what it was that triggered it, it did come alive quite wonderfully. His level of attention to the people around him was refreshing. He made me feel looked after, cared for...almost...important." She looked at her father. "He's a really good man, and I wish him the best."

Robert's eyes had that inquisitive expression that Connie knew so well. He smiled and then reached out to hold her hand.

"Do you want to see her letters?"

"Absolutely!" She didn't need to ask whom he meant.

They went to his bedroom. Robert opened the closet and pointed to a large white box. There was a thick blue folder sitting on top. "The letters are in the box; the folder has all the translations.

Take your time looking at them. I'll be in the kitchen," he said and walked away.

Connie dragged the box from the closet and carefully pulled the lid off. Picking one of the letters at random, she realized she hadn't seen her mother's handwriting in years. It looked delicate, due to the fine fountain-pen nib she liked to use, and very slanted, with extended beginning and ending strokes. The letter *m* looked like a three-peaked *u*, and the capital *T* had a beautiful, round arabesque on the bottom. Having something in front of her that was so close to her mother as her handwriting made Connie feel comforted.

Then one particular memory came to her—Gagolin's letter. She grew nervous and started pulling the rest of the packets from the box.

Connie sat cross-legged on the floor; the thick white carpet of her parents' bedroom looked like a collage of letters and envelopes. She kept untying the bias tape that held the many packets of letters together, one after another. Her mother had been a neat person. The letters were ordered by date, and each year's packet was wrapped separately: 1965, 1966, 1967, and so on. However, the final years were grouped, 1982 to 1991, and 1992 to 2000. Her mother had not written anything in the year that she passed away, 2001.

"Nine years already," Connie whispered.

Connie felt a natural curiosity and wanted to read all the letters, but she put the feeling aside—there would be plenty of time later. Her eyes and hands were searching for that particular letter she had hand-delivered to her mother exactly twenty-eight years ago, when she returned from her trip to France. It had not surfaced yet, but she remembered exactly how it looked: a beige, square envelope, not bigger than a Christmas card.

"Connie, I've made fresh coffee," her father said behind her, from the bedroom's doorway.

"Yes, just one minute, Dad." She didn't turn around; she still had dozens of letters to go through.

As Robert's steps faded out on his way back to the kitchen, she gasped when she got to the end of the 1981 packet, immediately recognizing the elegant sweep of the cursive handwriting and the pale-black ink reading, "Aimée Lucien," her mother's maiden name, written in the center of the envelope.

With trembling hands, she pulled the yellowish paper out and read it to herself.

My beloved Aimée, dearest to my heart, akin to my soul,

Many years have passed since our last kiss good-bye, but however long this time is, it cannot dry your tears from my lips. Not yet. I still see your hands when I look at mine. I see your long and delicate fingers that have never aged, mingling with my now old and weathered ones; the thin silver ring that you wore on your right hand still flickers in my eyes. Why did you have to go? Why did life have to set us apart? I still ask those naïve questions, silly me. But to be shown how fulfilling and mesmerizing love can be, and once surrendered to its delights be deprived of it altogether...Oh! What cruel whims fortune imposes on us, its sheeplike subjects!

Every now and then, a bittersweet blend of feelings takes over me when I imagine the life together that we could not have, and the days of laughter and the nights of conversation that we cannot share anymore. I long for your caresses and sighs; I have thirst for your words of love. I recall the smell of your hair, mixed with lavender and sage; a starry night, dead leaves to lie on; the way you hummed Rachmaninov's "Vocalise" in my ear; your exhausted breath and sparkling eyes after we made love...the cream-colored roses you loved so much...and that I still collect.

I still read poems out loud, as you wanted me to, and I keep trying my hand at some, with the same mixed results; I still see your warm smile and rosy cheeks approving the palatable verses and your tender look and immobile head when the output was, as often, on the mediocre side.

Our small village hasn't changed much; you would still find your way around it quite easily. Those who were old have died, and their old ways are gone with them. The ones who were young have grown up and carved their own ways and views over the old. Nothing new. The roads still turn in the same directions and lead to the same familiar places, but nothing is the same since you left.

This is the only letter I will have sent you since your wedding (although I have written and kept hundreds by now), but you are still part of my everyday life. I still talk with you when am alone, I still see you in my dreams, and I still feel your presence. Our good friend and neighbor, Monsieur Quiqui, says that I live with the ghost of you; I agree with him.

I finally accepted that I will not see you ever again, that existence will pass on, for us both, in separation, and that our fate will not change a jot for our grievances, deserved or not. But this high-handed Fortune doesn't know that we still have each other in our hearts, and as we promised before we parted, we will meet at our will, in that place where hope becomes thought, wishes become true in the intimacy of solitude, sighs soothe our troubled souls, and longing subsides to warm memories. That place that is unknown to all others—our wordless, secret place where silence and memories dwell.

As always, I will see you there, my darling Aimée.

Adieu, ma chérie. Let's be as happy as we can be without each other and raise our glasses to the unyielding memory of the light in our eyes.

Forever yours,

GG

PS: Your daughter is a reflection of you; she already sees more than her mind can yet understand. I am glad for her and for you.

"So they had been…lovers," Connie said quietly, her eyes still fixed on the letter.

Gagolin had been her mother's first love, and the one she could neither forget nor talk about.

As Connie was putting the letter down, she saw a folded piece of white paper inside the same envelope, with her mother's handwriting saying, "My reply."

Monsieur,

How beautiful your soul is; how sweet your words are! Your tender smile and the soft expression in your eyes still fill my soul with light and overflow my heart with love. The fresh smell of those fragrant spring mornings, that so many times discovered us together, still fills my lungs each time I think of you.

You're etched in my heart because love, unlike our bodies, never grows old when it dwells in the province of the mind, when it resides in a poem, visits us in a wish, embraces us in a sigh. Because our hearts beat at the same rhythm and our thoughts travel together, because we'll find each other in the wind on the plane trees, on the flight of a seagull, in the joy of a glass of wine.

Your hands, trembling with passion, still discover my body night after night; your eager eyes still search in the

depths of mine, looking for that undefined but paramount spark, as you liked to say, that is only yours and
mine. Your lips still caress that dimple on the side of my
mouth, and the miracle of love, like a phoenix, is born
again and again.

Be assured, my dearest monsieur, that our love finds no
boundaries, and the senses are just a poor imitation of our
feelings. You there, me here, separated by a sea of space
and circumstances. But the time we had together lives on
and on. Like a fresh brook renewing itself every spring, I
see you every morning, I talk to you in the afternoon, we
stroll holding hands in the evenings, and your voice whispers words of love in my ears, soothing my sleepy heart
when I am in bed.

Don't you worry, my beloved, and be as happy as you
can be without me, for life asks no questions, and we can't
provide any answers.

Live the best that you can, my dear Gérard, knowing
that your beloved Aimée will always have a prompt smile at
your memory, a glass of wine ready to toast to our tears, and
the soft but eternal glow of love in her heart.

To the unyielding memory of the light in our eyes.
Adieu,
AG

*I can't believe you wrote this, Mom…but why did you sign as AG?* Connie
blushed as her own memories of Liddell mixed with memories of
her mother.

The letters brought her back to Monsieur Gagolin's vineyard,
and she understood why his fiery look turned into such a tender,
gentle gaze every time he looked at her.

Nick's brother, Chuck, and his family—his wife, the twins and a younger son—arrived on Sunday morning. They had driven all the way from Washington, DC, a day-and-a-half journey that they made every year, in early October. They always lodged at a nearby hotel but spent most of the day at Connie's house.

Connie greeted them at the driveway as they came out of the minivan, and they all walked together through the garage door. Nick stopped flipping burgers and hotdogs at the grill, came inside, and joined the lively party. Stacey and Amanda came down from their rooms, and Bryan tossed away the remote control of his video console and ran to his cousins.

"Connie! It's so good to see you! How you've been?"

"So busy, Rachel, you wouldn't believe it." Connie could recognize her sister-in-law's high-pitched voice even in a crowded football stadium. Rachel slowly pronounced every syllable as if she always had something really important to say. *Or as if she's talking to a two-year-old.*

"I heard you just came back from Europe. How exciting! Which places did you go?"

"I was in Rome, London, and Par—"

Rachel didn't let her finish. "Paris! Did you go to the Eiffel Tower at night? I love the way the whole thing lights up, with all the different colors, and then it blinks all white and then changes again. Do you remember, honey?" she asked her husband, who was talking with Nick.

"Remember what, honey?" Chuck answered eagerly, joining his wife and Connie.

"I was telling Connie about the Eiffel Tower at night. Do you remember when we watched it light up? It was after we had dinner at that really nice restaurant, Chez…Chez something…"

"Oh, yeah, it's awesome! And did you go to Versailles?" Nick's brother added.

Rachel interjected before Connie could even respond. "Oh, my goodness, that place is unbelievable! And it's just a half-hour ride from downtown."

"Well, I haven't been to either of those two. I left them for my next trip." Connie smiled to herself for speaking Liddell's advice to her out loud.

"Okay, everybody, let's eat!" Nick interjected.

They sat on the patio to enjoy the Indian summer that had visited Minneapolis after a cold-started fall. Connie had laid a long table with paper cups and paper plates, but real silverware, to make it feel somewhat proper. She had scattered three vases with flowers, and four glass water bottles; a crystal wineglass was at her place on the table and a couple more were in the center, for whoever wanted to drink wine, but they usually stayed untouched. She had made four different salads, which she interspersed with baskets of bread. Coolers with beer and soda were on the floor by the table, and Connie's bottle of Côtes du Rhône red was next to her plate.

The afternoon passed by quickly: Rachel talked constantly, monopolizing the conversations, as usual; Amanda and Stacey gossiped with their twin cousins, a boy and a girl of Stacey's age; and Nick and his brother talked loudly about football, beers in hand, ignoring everybody else. Bryan and his cousin, a boy just one year older than him, had grabbed burgers and promptly left the table to play video games.

As Rachel's words seemed to turn into smoke and disappear before reaching her ears, Connie quietly watched the familiar scene, one that everybody seemed to enjoy repeating year after year. Everybody except for her.

Amanda poured cranberry juice into her plastic cup and grimaced when she tasted it. "Yuk! This is warm."

"I'll get some ice. Excuse me, Rachel." Connie rushed inside—she would not miss this opportunity to get away from her yacking sister-in-law. She went down to the basement, where their second freezer was stocked up with ice. She took an ice bucket from the cabinet next to her wine cellar, filled it, and as she turned to head back upstairs, a white capsule from one of the bottles caught her eye.

"I'll go check on Mom." Amanda said. Rachel shrugged and sipped her beer. Amanda went through the double doors into the kitchen and stopped short when she saw her mother sitting by the kitchen island, alone. There was an open bottle of red Bandol on the countertop, she was swirling the wine in her glass, and her eyes were fixed on the window over the sink. She looked absent.

"Mom, are you okay?" Amanda asked in a whisper.

Connie slowly turned her head toward Amanda, and observed her vibrant, energetic daughter, who looked so much like her when she was that age. She saw the light of opportunity shining brightly in Amanda's eyes, still unstrained by the passing of time. The young girl looked radiant and fresh—free of regrets and empty of sad memories. Connie quietly contemplated the masterpiece of the human experience renewed, once again.

"Yes, I'm okay. I'm just taking a break," she said with a soft voice.

The week together had finally ended. On Saturday morning the two families strolled lazily across the driveway, headed to the guests' minivan. They had visited parks, gone to movies and restaurants, and had made as many cookouts as they could before the temperature finally dropped.

"You gotta come visit us next time," Chuck said to Nick, who had a beer in his hand.

"You know I hate driving." Nick winked and patted his brother on the shoulder.

Connie and Nick waved as their guests pulled out and disappeared on the winding road. Connie sighed, relieved.

She went back inside the house and opened her laptop; she was interested in an Impressionist exhibition that was about to take place at the Minneapolis Institute of Art. As she browsed the Institute's web page, a new e-mail chimed.

*Brenda? What is it now?*

Hello Connie,

I am working for the *Cleveland Arts Journal,* a nonprofit e-zine. After reading your impressive article, I wondered if you'd like to join us. We are hiring part-time writers, and there's a huge variety of subjects that you can pick from. The pay is about the same as in *Girls Now,* and I don't see a reason why you couldn't write for both.

Please check out the careers link on our web page for details, and let me know if you are interested.

Brenda

She quickly visited the *Journal*'s web page. It was just what she had been dreaming of—a database containing reviews of myriad works of art, from ancient to modern, treated in a colloquial manner, without any pretense and completely accessible to everyone. She immediately replied to Brenda, thanking her for the offer and asking her details about the articles' submission format. She smiled. *I'm back!*

# CHAPTER 8
# THURSDAY, OCTOBER 11, 2015

"Are you coming for dinner next Saturday?" Connie asked Stacey over the car speakerphone. "Your sister is coming from Atlanta; she'll stay over the weekend."

"Yeah, sure. Can I bring Allan with me? He hasn't met her yet."

"Of course, honey. How is your new job?"

"It's going great. By the end of the year I'll have eleven credits and so much experience. I get home exhausted, but it's worth the pain." Stacey sounded tired.

"That's my girl! You'll be a doctor before you know it."

"That still seems too far ahead! Hey, Mom, can I call you back? Allan's calling."

"Okay, honey. Later!"

Connie had a sudden flashback of Liddell. Ever since the trip, now five years past, she had recurring images of him, some more vivid than others, that did not seem to be predictable or softening with time. She could see him gazing at her, with his almost unnoticeable smile. "I can tell when you're smiling," she heard herself saying out loud.

She slowly shook her head. A lot had happened in the last five years. Amanda got her degree in finance with flying colors, and left for a job at a big bank in Atlanta. Stacey, now nineteen, just moved out with a friend after getting a part-time job in a nearby hospital; she was studying medicine and also managed to find time for a boyfriend. Bryan, who'd just turned seventeen, was a high school senior and had been accepted—with a full scholarship—at a college in Wisconsin.

She parked the car in the driveway, left the windows rolled down, and headed for the front door. She stopped by the flower-bed and pulled out some weeds; she noticed that the brown bricks surrounding the flowerbeds were badly weathered, and three of them were already cracked. She made a mental note to have the landscape company replace them. As she reached for the door-knob, she realized that its brass glossing had faded, and the knob itself was somewhat loose. *This needs to be replaced too.*

Inside, she headed to the kitchen, opened the fridge, and poured herself a glass of Torrontés white wine. The house was empty, silent, like every weekday morning. Nick was at work, and Bryan was still at school. She leaned back against the countertop and sipped the pale-yellow wine. *Flowers. Peaches. Sun.*

She had developed a routine that she quite enjoyed: she would visit the downtown museums daily until some work of art caught her attention. Once that happened, she would take pictures of it, look it up on the Internet, do as much research in the library as she could, and after taking it all in for a whole week, she would write a piece on the artist, the work, its context, and her reactions to it. The formula seemed to be working, and she had been deliver-ing a constant flow of content to Brenda and earning a modest but steady income that she had been saving.

Connie had stopped writing for *Girls Now* when Stacey finished high school. She realized that she had no idea what teenage girls were interested in anymore; neither did she care to find out.

Currently, the Minneapolis Institute of Art had a special ex-hibit on Mayan artifacts. After visiting it a few times that week, she had finally decided to write her next article about their ceremonial vases.

The morning sun washed the kitchen with a fresh, white light. Connie sat on her favorite stool and sipped the subtle wine. Then she opened her computer and browsed her local library catalog for titles on the Mayas. She had only scrolled through one page when, as usual, Liddell came to her mind. She sighed. *There hasn't been a day without you. Do you still remember me? Do you still think of me?*

She took another sip of wine and looked around the house. *We haven't changed the furniture in twenty years, at least.* The carpet in the family room needed a change too. Years of use had loosened up the dining-room chairs, and they appeared slightly crooked. The appliances looked old. *We have to renovate the house. Everything is worn-out, tired.*

She thought of the ironic parallel with her life with Nick. The thought of leaving him and moving out alone had been growing stronger since she came back from Europe, like a weed that had crept up through the mulch of their jaded life together. She had decided not to extirpate it but instead let grow and gain force. "Once the kids are old enough," or "The right time has to come," had been her usual responses to the strong feeling of starting a new life.

She got a text from Bryan. He was going to sleep over at a friend's house. She knew the family very well. *They are great people.* The doorbell rang. Connie looked at her watch instinctively. Eleven thirty. She wasn't expecting anybody.

"Mrs. Connie Stewart?" the postman asked.

"That's me."

"Sign here, please," he said, and handed her a legal-sized white envelope. "Have a nice day, ma'am."

She closed the door and went back to the kitchen, moved her computer aside, and placed the envelope on the island. The return label read Arges & Tilkian, Notaires—Marseilles, Lyon, Paris.

She tore the envelope open and pulled out two items: one was a computer-printed letter, both in French and English; and the other was a letter-sized brown envelope. She read the letter first.

Dear Madame,

I am in possession of the will of Monsieur Gérard Gagolin, who passed away last year without having any known heirs. As is common in these cases, all property belonging to the deceased passed on to the municipality of his town. But in this particular case, while the property was being cleaned out and inventoried, the clerks found a box containing a great number of letters. After a meticulous study of these documents, a letter was found that proves that you are a descendant of this man, and thus his rightful heir. I have attached that letter, along with its translation into English.

I look forward to hearing from you about completing the probate process.

Yours truly,

M. E. Tilkian, avocat

Connie put the piece of paper down and remained still for a few seconds. She then raised the brown envelope and slightly caressed it. *Monsieur Gagolin.* She turned it around to open it when her cell phone rang. *Not now.* She looked at the screen, put the envelope down, and answered the phone.

"Deb!"

"Hi there. What are you up to?"

"I'm in the middle of something. Can I call you back?"

"Are you writing?"

"No, I'm opening the mail."

"Uh, okay…and what's on sale at Costco this week?"

"Deb, this is important mail. I'll call you back!"

"Fine. I just wanted have some coffee with you."

"Give me a few minutes, okay?"

"Now I really want to know. What's going on?"

"Bye." Connie almost threw the phone across the counter and picked up the envelope.

She delicately pulled out about a dozen pieces of paper, most of them handwritten in French, while others were the computer-generated English translations. She put the handwritten letters aside and read the translation.

My dear Connie,

I am sure you don't understand why you are getting a letter from me, but if you are reading this, it means that somebody found it, and this somebody has sent it to you. I hope this is the case.

Certainly, I am aware that you don't know who I really am, and that is precisely the reason why I am writing to you on this rainy Sunday afternoon.

Your mother, Aimée, was the love of my life.

We met when we were born, literally speaking, and we became inseparable. Our love knew no limits: we went to school together, we played together, we read together, we grew up together, and we discovered love together. We couldn't stay away from each other; we were two souls destined to become one. We spent our lives living for each other.

Oh, what lovely conversations we used to have! Your mother had the most beautiful grin in the world, have you noticed? She knew it very well, but she rarely showed it; instead, she smiled shyly. She used to say that her grin was her gift to me. But those days are long gone, even though I still live them again and again in the solitude of my humble vineyard.

I would like to tell you some things that were kept hidden from you. To begin with, Pierre—your grandfather—and Guy—my father—were brothers. Yes, Connie, you are a Gagolin, and I am (well, I was) your second uncle.

Pierre and Guy grew up in the family vineyard—which has been in Gagolin hands since 1842—and took full control of it in the year 1946, when their father died. They quickly divided their duties: Guy tended the vines, and Pierre made the wine. Either of them could have done both, but Guy was an innate farmer, and Pierre, with his exceptional palate, wanted to focus on making and selling the wine. They were a perfect team, achieving moderate financial success despite the dismal postwar economy. The domaine grew in reputation but not necessarily in production; the small plot of land and the farming techniques tailored to obtain quality prevented any increase in quantity.

We all lived under the same roof, and we all worked very hard. My father and I invariably at the vines: tending, pruning, tying, plowing the tracks, organizing the harvest, etc. Pierre and your mother were usually in the cellar, working with our wines but also bottling the wines that they would purchase from other vignerons. Pierre taught your mother everything he knew about wine, hoping that the then male-dominated wine aristocracy would eventually give way to women. But that never happened in their lifetime.

We also entertained the wine buyers, who came many times a year, from all over: Paris, London, America. My mother and your grandmother were exquisite cooks, and always managed to prepare feasts with the game that I supplied and the seasonal ingredients from the well-stocked vegetable garden that they tended.

In the midst of it all, Aimée and I were unknowingly living the time of our lives. We had decided to keep our love secret because our families were quite Catholic, and we didn't know how they would react. I heard marriage between first cousins is more accepted nowadays.

It was when the 1954 vintage had just been bottled and was ready to sell that our little world started to crumble. The '54 was what we would call a "humble vintage," which is to say a bad year, but we still needed to sell the wine. Some vignerons did better than others, as is always the case, but our plot was battered with late thunderstorms. Much fruit was damaged, and there was talk about hail coming soon, so the harvest had to be rushed while the vines were still wet. The wine, and the sales, were not good. The wine from 1955 wasn't any better, but this time Pierre and Guy had started to argue. Pierre second-guessed Guy about the harvest day he had chosen, bluntly saying that he was making the same "mistake" as the prior year. Guy, in turn, questioned Pierre about his doings in the cellar, arguing that he was spending too much time with other people's wine and not enough attending their own. Aimée and I knew that there was no one to blame but the weather and tried to intercede, bringing some sense to their heated tempers, but they just wouldn't listen. Debt started to pile up.

When the 1956 wine, from the worst growing year we ever had, was bottled and we tasted it, there was not much we could do to keep them from accusing each other bitterly. And that was also the year when Pierre was offered a job in the American company. At first, he didn't tell Guy, but I found out through Aimée. He would be the head buyer for the whole South of France at a big wine importer there, in Minnesota. What a long title! It certainly wooed Pierre, who without hiding his contempt for his brother, packed up everything and announced that they were leaving, swearing that he would never again set foot in the domaine.

What a strange morning that one was. Bitter silence, few words, tears of anger, tears of heartbreak. I watched them get in the Citroën Avant that the Americans had sent to pick them up. The driver tossed their two bags in the trunk and shut it with a thump, and then they got into the car and drove away. Just like that. Aimée turned to look at me through the back windshield. She waved; I waved back.

Hard times followed, and my father was devastated. He worked himself flat-out at the vineyard. My mother took a laundry job to help pay the debt, and I took over the cellar. Too much to do for just the three of us. Mother had a stroke and passed away two years later. I barely wondered why— exhaustion? Disappointment?

But then the vintages got better, consistently, year after year. The year 1962 was truly exceptional. With its proceeds we paid off the debt and settled into a quiet and humble lifestyle.

We never heard from Pierre again, but your mother and I wrote regularly. She was lost for words when Pierre decided to change their last name to "Lucien."

I never married, not because I couldn't, but because the love I knew had no comparison with any other love and never would have. I remained alone. Alone with Aimée's memories. Alone with the thoughts of her.

Pierre was quite a stubborn man. He wanted Aimée to settle in America, get married, and have a family. He didn't even allow any talking about their past. He wanted to make sure that their life in France was completely forgotten.

Right after Aimée met Robert, she stopped writing. It hurt when I read her last letter, but I was happy for her. She had moved on. I'm sure Robert turned out to be a loving husband and a good father.

Aimée and I never saw each other again, but we promised to be happy, as happy as we could be without each other. She did her part, and I think I did mine: my vines became my love.

So, my dear niece, this is it. This is the truth that finally came to light. As with most cases like this, the truth is known only after everyone who was involved has died. Which is fine by me. As I am dead, too, you are the heir of Domaine Gagolin, a small but proud bastion of winemaking traditions, and one of the oldest vineyards in the whole of Bandol. I hope you can keep it and continue the history of the Gagolin family.

Farewell, my dear niece. Have a beautiful life, and I wish you just one thing: that you get to know what real love is before your time on earth ends. Everything else is an affectation.

Gérard Gagolin

Connie felt her whole body turn to stone. Then something cracked inside. Tears ran down her cheeks while it all came back to her with renewed strength: memories of her mother, of Monsieur Gagolin, and of Liddell blended together in a surreal collage of sounds, images, and suppressed wishes. She pushed the letters aside and wept for a few minutes, without even trying to attenuate the surge of emotion that welled from inside her.

When the tears and the sobs naturally dried out, she looked around her. The glass of wine, the kitchen, the appliances, the dining room and its furniture, the house—it all seemed foreign, inadequate. She felt inadequate. Her cell phone rang again.

"Are you done with the mail?" Deb said with a relaxed voice, as if she were polishing her nails or watching TV.

"Come see me, please," Connie said with a sob.

"Oh, my goodness! What happened?" Deb cried out.

"Nothing. Just come. Would you?"

An hour later they were facing each other at the kitchen island. Deb had opened a bottle of Bandol rouge, and they sipped the wine while they looked at Gagolin's letter.

"What are you going to do?" Deb asked.

"I wish I knew."

"Well, you have property there now. You have to take possession of it. You have to talk to these attorneys; you'll probably have to go there and see what's left of it."

"Yeah, I guess."

"Do you want me to go with you?"

"Would you come? I'd love you to," Connie said with a relieved smile.

"Of course. To Bandol? Yeah…"

Connie held Deb's hands firmly. "Thank you."

⋙ ⋘

Nick got home past midnight. During the last five years, a beer after work had morphed into solid nights of drinking. He left the car in the driveway and stumbled through the garage door. Dimmed, soft-yellow lights kept him from colliding with the furniture as he walked across the entrance hall and into the kitchen. He yanked the fridge door open and pulled out an imported beer. He opened a drawer and immediately slammed it closed.

"Where the fuck is the opener?"

He opened another drawer, and beer in hand, he shuffled the silverware, making a loud clinking sound. He uttered a curse, left the bottle on the countertop, and searched the drawer contents with both hands. He pulled out a bottle opener, but right before popping the cap, he raised his head and saw Connie sitting in the dining room, staring at him.

"Wow!" he barked. "You scared me. What you doing there?"

"Waiting for you. I got some news."

"What is it now?" He opened the bottle and sucked the beer foam.

"I inherited a vineyard in France."

"What?"

Connie stood up and walked to the kitchen. She handed him the letter from the attorney, but he refused it, waving his hand. "Just tell me about it. Can't read now. Don't have my glasses."

"You can't read because you're drunk," she automatically replied.

"What are you talking about? I'm not drunk, for fuck's sake."

"Your language."

"My language?"

He got close to her. His breath smelled like cheap liquor and cigarettes.

"Now you smoke?" Her eyes pierced his.

"Whoa, whoa! I fucking apologize. You're so fucking sophisti- cated." He slowly pronounced each word without taking his eyes from hers. Then he gulped more beer.

Nick's half-open blue eyes looked small and mean, but his defi- ant smile didn't scare her. His furrowed sweaty forehead and the deep lines around his mouth made him look much older. Connie saw a resentful, defeated, petty man—time had slowly demoted her husband to a coarser version of who he once was. And somehow it was precisely what she needed to see to finally make up her mind.

"I'm done with you, Nick. *Done.*"

She hastened up to her room, locked the door behind her, and sat on the floor, her back against the bed. The feeling of being out of place was too strong. She heard Nick's heavy steps going into the guest room, a rumble and curse as he tripped over some furniture, and the slamming of the door. Her dry eyes stared at the wall in front of her, resolute.

Friday morning was quiet. They met in the kitchen, the only place in the house that they seemed to share, just for brief periods of time.

"Hi," Nick said casually.

Connie minimized the screen listing houses for rent in the neighborhood just before he walked past her. She closed her laptop computer and put it to the side.

Nick's hair was damp: he had showered and seemed to have forgotten or was just ignoring what had happened the night before. With a composed smile, he pulled a cup from the top cabinet and poured some coffee for her.

Connie took the cup. "I got a letter from an attorney yesterday. Apparently I had a relative whom I didn't know about who passed away, leaving a small vineyard for me."

"How much can you get from it?"

"I have…no idea."

"The word's probably gotten around. Let them fight over it first, and then close a deal."

"I don't know if I want to sell it."

"What're you gonna do? Spend the summers in France? With the peanuts that Brenda pays you for your articles?" He tut-tutted and took a bite of his toaster waffles. "Besides, by the time they give you the tax bill, you'll have to sell it just to pay what you owe," he added with his mouth still full.

She had a feeling that Nick was probably right. "I'll see what the deal—"

"Hey," he interrupted, "just get whatever you can and put it in your retirement fund. You probably have less than five hundred bucks in it."

"Don't tell me what to do with my property," she fired back, holding his gaze.

Nick swung his bag around his shoulder, picked up his travel coffee mug, and without saying another word, stormed out of the kitchen.

Leaving Nick had become a certainty in her mind—just a matter of time. Connie opened her laptop and kept scanning the list of two-bedroom houses that were available for rent in the area. Regardless of what might happen with that vineyard—which could well be nothing of consequence at all—after five years of writing, she had enough savings to make the down payment on a small place. But first she would rent something nearby until she decided where exactly she wanted to live. She scrolled up the list and saved the information on a quaint two-story little house—her first candidate—that was conveniently close to her dad's. Then she jotted down the phone numbers of two other realtors. She would make a first visit that same afternoon.

Connie launched Skype and called the French attorney.

Monsieur Tilkian was fluent in English. He had a deep, grave voice with a heavy French accent, and talked very slowly. He told her that she needed to go there in person, to sign the inheritance papers. Once that was done, she could go back to America and organize the sale from there. He briefly described the property, which Connie vaguely remembered, but stressed that the buildings were very old and had not been well maintained; however, the hundred-year-old Mourvèdre vines were in excellent condition.

"One more thing, Monsieur Tilkian. Do you have any idea of its market value?"

"The vineyard is located in a prime area of the Bandol *appellation*; it is very sought-after. We are talking about a value of almost a million US dollars. This is the sale price before taxes, of course, but I'd prefer to speak to you in person about it. There are certain caveats involved, and there may not be much left once we finish with the inheritance process. When could you be here? Next week, maybe?"

She closed her eyes. "Yes. I'll be there next week."

"*Magnifique!* You have my office location and my phone numbers. Please let me know your arrival date as soon as you have it."

"Will do. Thank you, *Monsieur.*"

＝＋＋＝

Nick came home even later that Friday night. He and the rest of the management team had left the office earlier and gone golfing—a team-building activity, they liked to say—which really meant that they had been drinking all day. Connie was already in bed by the time he arrived; she heard him going straight into the guest room.

She had turned the lights off, but her eyes were wide open. She couldn't fall asleep, and she knew she wouldn't. Too many things were spinning in her head: the determination to leave her husband, the rental houses she had visited that afternoon, this unexpected trip to France, the vineyard—and hovering above it all, the memory of Liddell. A part of her wanted to write to him, to talk to him, to tell him all about it. The other part had given up. *I can't just turn up out of the blue, after five years, and pretend that he'll still be willing to see me. He's probably busy with his family and his work.*

She tried to focus on the vineyard just to stop thinking of Liddell, but he kept coming back, along with dozens of small memories of their time together. Suddenly, he had stepped out from the background of her mind and occupied all her thoughts.

＝＋＋＝

On Saturday morning she visited Robert. He was working in the garden, as usual.

"Connie, my dear!" He said with an open smile. They slowly walked inside; her father's mental condition had improved greatly, but his body was frail. He had been using a cane lately, and he gently leaned on Connie.

"How's the sciatica, Dad?"

"It could be worse. It can always be worse." He washed his hands at the kitchen sink, and they sat at the table.

"I have some news. Take a look at this," she said, handing over the letters.

Robert put his glasses on and carefully read them. Then he read them again, sighed, and gave the letters back to Connie. "She was torn between two worlds."

"But she loved you." Connie knew that her father had read the last letters between Amy and Gagolin.

Robert looked pensive. His eyes, gazing slightly upward, seemed lost in thought. A relaxed smile appeared on his face. "Your mother stayed with us throughout her whole life, and that is true commitment. She could have left me anytime, but instead she decided to leave her past behind, and although it certainly kept creeping up on her, she kept it in line, away from her relationship with me." He took Connie's hand. "Yes, she probably still loved Gérard, but I also believe that she loved me. A person's heart is far more complex than we like to think. It is uncharted territory, just for each of us to explore—and on the inside, no rules from the outside world apply."

"I'm happy to hear you saying that, Dad."

"She was the love of my life—and my love for her never wavered."

Connie hugged her father, relieved by his words.

Back at home, Connie looked up flights and hotels and then called Deb—they agreed they would fly on Wednesday. She went back online and purchased both plane tickets, and although Deb would give her the money back for hers, what they charged her credit card seemed an astronomical number. *And those were the cheapest seats. I'd better get a bargain hotel.* She made reservations in a hotel located in the outskirts of Marseille that had a few good reviews, and the photos looked decent. She was staring at the computer screen when Bryan walked through the garage door.

"Hi, Mom."

"Hi, honey. How are you?"

"Good." He kissed her and peeked at the screen; Connie had the airline receipt window open. "Wow, that's expensive!"

"I hope to get it back somehow."

"Why don't you and Dad retire there?"

"I don't think it'd work."

"Of course not. I was kidding."

"Oh, yes…of course," she said. *I guess it's that evident.*

"I found a job opportunity at the college, during the summer. I will apply for it. Nothing wrong with a little extra money before the school year starts. What do you think?"

"When would you leave?"

"In two weeks." He made himself a sandwich, and grabbed a bag of chips from the pantry and a can of soda from the fridge.

"Two weeks. That's so soon."

"Yep." He took a mouthful of chips.

"Well, it looks like you already made up your mind. Talk to your Dad. If he's okay with it, I don't see why not."

"Already texted him; he's fine. I'll go pick up Ken; we have some homework to do." He stood up and headed back to the garage door. "We'll stay up late; we have to finish the science project tonight." The voice of the seventeen-year-old young man vanished into the garage.

*That will be it. Bryan will be gone, too. I should be proud. He's going to college, like Stacey and Amanda.* She looked at the screen. She felt carried away by an unexpected whim, something stronger than her own will. Her fingers frenetically typed sentences with the same speed as they deleted them.

She wanted the e-mail to look casual and disguise the fact that she wanted to see Liddell so badly. She read what she had written.

*That won't work.* She deleted it. She wrote another message with a more serious tone. *This won't work either.* After writing and deleting five more times, she finally wrote one single line:

Hi, Liddell. I'll be in Marseille on Thursday.

She added her cell phone number and the hotel information at the bottom. Without giving herself time to think twice, she pressed Send.

⟞⟝ ⟞⟝

Connie sat in the middle seat and watched Deb shoving her carry-on into the overhead compartment and then ease into the aisle seat next to her. Deb's white-gold earrings matched her elegant station necklace and left-hand ring. The subtle makeup, her stylish, casual-looking hair, and her perfectly manicured nails showed a well-off, pampered woman in her fifties.

"How much are we talking about?" Deb asked.

"The attorney said around a million. We'll see."

The flight attendants started the safety announcements over the loud PA. Deb covered her ears with her hands and closed her eyes. Soon after, they were airborne—headed to New York and then to Paris. After a brief layover at Charles De Gaulle Airport, they boarded a regional flight to Marseille. By the time they landed, it was three in the afternoon on Thursday.

Exhausted after their long journey, they dragged their bags through the baggage claim and took a taxi to the small hotel where they would stay for the next two nights. They remained silent throughout the taxi ride.

The neighborhood around the hotel was not reassuring, the desk clerk spoke little English, and the room was minuscule. Two beds were pushed up against two of the empty walls, and a tiny nightstand stood between them. A small lamp with a low-watt yellow bulb barely illuminated the room.

"This is really cheap," Deb said, frowning up at the stained ceiling.

"I know, but the last-minute flights were too expensive. I didn't have any budget left for the hotel." Connie shrugged. "It's only two nights. We'll survive."

"Connie," Deb said with a sweet tone, "let's get out of here. We deserve better. I'll pay for a good hotel."

The modern hotel at the Old Port was much nicer. Deb arranged a roomy apartment suite with two bedrooms that included a small kitchen.

Connie checked her e-mails—no word from Liddell. She e-mailed him the new hotel information and remained quiet, staring at the screen.

"What are you doing with that computer?" Deb asked. "Let's go eat!"

Connie closed the lid of her laptop before Deb could get any closer. "Just looked up a restaurant a few blocks from here. It seems nice."

They sat outside. The restaurant had a back patio with a few gas heaters scattered among the rectangular tables. Once the food arrived, they ate quietly; they wanted to go back to the hotel and get some rest.

On their stroll back, Connie had an uneasy feeling in the pit of her stomach. She'd never told Deb about what had happened between her and Liddell, and she thought about what she would tell her if he actually showed up. Deb would probably be mad at her for not telling her before, and she would be right. If anybody could understand Connie's situation now, it was Deb.

"I owe you the story of what really happened on that writing trip to Europe, Deb."

"You had an affair with the guy?" Deb said and fixed her gaze on Connie.

"How did you…" Connie stared at her friend, mouth open.

"I wouldn't blame you if you did. You know what I think about your husband."

"It wasn't *just* an affair. Knowing him—and in those circumstances—was a wake-up call. It changed…it just changed everything. And I'm still in love with him."

"Is he coming to see you?"

"He hasn't replied to my e-mail yet." Connie looked ahead. They had arrived at the hotel.

The next morning, they went down the main street toward a patisserie just a block away from the hotel. It was a magnificent day—the blue sky seemed bursting with color, and everything looked bright and possible under the Provençal sun and its potent energy.

After coffee and a croissant, they walked the few blocks to the attorney's office.

Monsieur Tilkian was waiting for them outside, standing by the door of his stucco office building in a nineteenth-century commercial row. He welcomed them in French and in English; his handshake was firm, and his manners seemed naturally elegant. A tall, stocky man in his late sixties, he had strong facial features and a perfectly combed full head of black hair.

After brief introductions, he said, "Let's see the domaine first, and we'll talk about what to do with it later. My car is parked around the corner—follow me." He spoke fast and gesticulated with both hands. The women increased their pace to keep up with him.

"Why all this rush?" Deb whispered to Connie, shaking her head.

"He probably has more important things to do today than showing a run-down farm to a couple of foreigners."

It took them some time to go through the crowded, narrow streets of Marseille. They seemed doomed to stop at every corner as the traffic lights turned invariably red as soon as they reached them. Monsieur Tilkian didn't seem bothered by it. Connie was getting anxious. Surprisingly, once they got on the highway heading east, the traffic disappeared.

The rolling hills along the way, scattered with shrubs and evergreen trees, had patches of uncovered earth here and there, where the hard and rocky soil that lay underneath could be seen with the naked eye.

"See that?" Monsieur Tilkian said, pointing to the hills. "Those dry rocks have been responsible for centuries of hard labor at the vines—since Roman times."

Connie remembered what Monsieur Gagolin had once told her about the landscape. The winemakers of Bandol had been digging the rocks and planting the vines for hundreds of generations—climbing every day to tend them and making terraces to keep the soil from washing away, working in excruciating heat and resisting the implacable and forever-wild Provençal wind: the mistral. As a reward for overcoming those impossible hurdles, the grapes, since time immemorial, had been turning into wines with such a unique and strong character that it made all that effort worthwhile.

They exited the highway and took several turns on the winding back roads that crossed the hills, running alongside vineyards and stone houses, until they got to a dirt road, no wider than a car. Connie and Deb sighed in recognition. Until that moment, the landscape had not been particularly familiar, but a couple hundred yards along the dirt road it all came back to them.

"I remember all this," Deb said, pointing at a line of massive plane trees on their right side. There was a patch of vines behind the grove, and a larger plot could be seen across the road, on their left side, next to a large and run-down stone building that dominated the setting, increasing its size as they approached the end of the road.

"Look!" Connie exclaimed to Deb, pointing to a small stone table surrounded by curved stone benches. "I can't believe it's still in the same place. Do you remember when we sat there and had that chilled, delicious rosé with Gérard?" Overcome by a mixture of surprise and excitement, she covered her mouth with her hand. "In all these years, it hasn't changed...not a bit," she whispered.

Monsieur Tilkian parked his silver Citroën a few yards away from the farmhouse's main entrance, and they slowly got out of the car, turning their heads in every direction. As Connie and Deb ambled along the path leading to the main door, memories flooded back from a distant time that somehow had stayed unchanged through all those years.

The attorney pushed the heavy handle down and bumped the wooden door with his hefty shoulder. The door opened, and a cool, musty breeze came out of the house; the hinges made a high-pitched squeak, and a rusty dust came off them, dancing through the sunbeam that crossed the air. The inside lights didn't work, and the house smelled like old mold. They quickly opened the wooden shades that hung on the windows like brown leaves clinging to the trees in autumn. A crashing noise came from the back of the main hall when a windowpane fell to the brick floor when Deb forced it open.

Once the sunlight streamed through the open windows, they saw the work that the municipal clerks had done in the old house. Gérard's belongings had been put in boxes, which were neatly piled across the long reception room and were labeled with a black marker.

Monsieur Tilkian cleared his throat. "The building is in relatively good live-in condition, according to traditional country standards, of course. The property is located in the best of the Bandol *appellation,* and the resale value could reach interesting heights."

"This needs a lot of work," Deb said, looking at the ceiling. The old oak beams looked dried out.

"The farmhouse has one hundred and eighty square meters, four bedrooms, three fireplaces, a relatively large kitchen, and a couple of odd, or shall we say, multipurpose rooms. Built, rebuilt, modified, and expanded through the last five hundred years, it possesses the perfect orientation—receiving the summer breeze that keeps it cool during the hot months, and facing the southern sun to keep it warm during the winter. The water comes from the well behind the kitchen; there is a bathroom inside and another outside the premises, using a septic system, and it would appear that one of the windows now needs a new pane." Tilkian had recited his description in one long blow, barely stopping for breath. "The real value of the property obviously lies on the Mourvèdre vines, which are over a hundred years old and in prime condition."

"If Gagolin died a year ago, who's been taking care of the vines?" Deb asked.

"It was Monsieur Gagolin's next-door neighbor, Monsieur Quiqui."

"Can we go to Gagolin's private cellar?" Connie asked.

"Certainly. Please beware of the spiders, Mesdames."

Connie now remembered her way around the house. She walked across the main hall, took the narrow corridor to the right, and opened a small, almost hidden cast-iron door that seemed etched on the left-hand wall. Monsieur Tilkian, who had followed, gave her a tiny flashlight and then returned to the hall. When she and Deb first arrived at the B and B, Monsieur Gagolin had showed them the house and taken them down to the cellar. Now, after so many years, a dreamlike feeling overwhelmed her as she went down the spiral stairwell. Her right hand firmly clasped the rusty handrail while her left hand shifted the flashlight up and down. Gagolin had a tremendous amount of wine in his cavernous underground cellar. Stacked in zigzagging lines, piled up in corners, and stashed in holes made in the rock foundation, the old dusty bottles were everywhere.

"There is so much wine in here...no wonder he sold so little of it—he kept it all for himself!" she said and looked up at Deb, who was now standing by the cellar door.

"Bring a couple of bottles!" Deb said with a loud laugh.

Connie climbed the narrow staircase back to the hall and moved farther down the corridor. Helped by the sunlight that flooded in from the main hall, she quickly inspected the empty rooms, poking her head in as she walked toward the end of the hallway.

Monsieur Gagolin's bedroom was spacious but minimally furnished: a small bed, a dresser, and a large chest looked lost inside the large, high-ceilinged chamber. Next to the bed was a stack of three cardboard boxes, labeled *Lettres*. Connie tore the packing tape off the top box, opened it, and picked up a handful of letters. The letters weren't inside envelopes, but just folded in twos or threes. She looked at them closely. They were relatively new—they must have been some of the last ones he wrote. The writing was clumsy, more like unreadable symbols written in a rush. Connie caressed the thick papers with her fingers. "Monsieur Gagolin..." she whispered. He had been writing to himself—just as her mother had done—as if someday Amy would read them.

She heard a soft and familiar French male voice coming from the main parlor. *Somebody else is here. I'd better go back.* She put the loose letters into her purse and closed the cardboard box the best she could. As she scuttled back, she heard Monsieur Tilkian speaking in French and the melodious, yet unrecognized, voice replying.

"Ah!" Monsieur Tilkian stopped what he was saying when he saw Connie entering the room. "This is Monsieur Quiqui, the good neighbor!" he announced with a sonorous voice.

"I remember you, monsieur," Connie said in French. "We met thirty-three years ago, when my friend Deb and I spent a few days here in the house. You joined us for dinner one night." Connie stretched her hand toward him.

"Ah...*oui, oui,*" Monsieur Quiqui replied with a wide, warm smile and softly shook Connie's hand.

Quiqui was in his late seventies; short and wide, his tanned face was completely covered by wrinkles, which somehow drew the attention to his shiny blue eyes. His bald head was pale and round, and a halo of white hair surrounded his crown.

"Monsieur Quiqui was Monsieur Gagolin's good friend. He saw the cars outside and decided to pay a visit," Tilkian explained. "He is also one of the people I told you were interested in buying."

"Oh, that's good to know," Connie said, nodding at him with a smile.

"If madame is so kind," Monsieur Quiqui said, "I would like to continue working the Gagolin's land. Their family—your family, madame—and mine have always followed the same winemaking philosophy and shared the same love for the soil of Bandol."

"It would be an honor for me, monsieur."

"I am very old, my three sons do all the work now, but please be assured that the tradition and quality of the wines will continue for many years."

"Well, it looks like we are making progress here," Tilkian added, "that is fantastic news. Now please, we have to finish this visit."

After a glance at the commercial cellar and buildings, Tilkian started closing the doors and windows and suggested they take a walk to see the vineyard before heading back to Marseille.

"What are you going to do?" Deb asked Connie while they crossed the yard once again, this time heading to the larger portion of the vineyard.

"I'd love to keep it," Connie said, "but I know I'll have to sell. I can't afford to maintain it." She looked at her friend in the eye. "But at least we saw it one last time, right, Deb?"

The vines were colored with many shades of orange and brown. The grapes had been harvested the month before, and now the plants looked tired, the weight of a whole season removed from their branches.

Connie and Deb stood silently at the edge of the plot for a few minutes, their eyes lost on the quiet mass of sleeping vines.

"I'm leaving Nick," Connie said quietly, with eyes lost on the horizon.

"It's about time. You two always looked so unpaired..."

"You noticed?"

"Since the first time I saw you together."

"Well, I guess it took me this long to figure it out..." Connie said, as she looked at Deb.

Deb's eyes were wet. Connie saw a lonely woman, and although her appearance was spotless, there was a hue of missed chances that imbued her whole person. Deb had kept herself locked up, waiting for that someone that never came, or maybe that she never cared to search for. Connie also saw longing in her friend's eyes, and as Deb shyly smiled, the light of opportunity shone timidly within her.

"I am happy for you. I mean, you have this wonderful guy; I'm sure he's waiting for you," Deb said in a broken voice.

Connie held Deb's hand. She'd never seen her friend so vulnerable before. "Deb, it's not too late—it wasn't too late for me—you can still find love if you are willing to. There's still beauty to be found out there."

Deb nodded, and her mouth quivered.

They heard two short honks, and turning around, they saw Monsieur Tilkian's car pulling back, getting ready to leave. He waved from inside the car, signaling them to get in.

"We'd better go," Connie said. "This guy is in a real hurry."

Connie got into the car and noticed Monsieur Quiqui standing by the farmhouse door. He lifted his hand and slowly waved good-bye. Connie waved back, and for some reason she felt sure that she would see him again.

They were back in Marseille in thirty minutes. Monsieur Tilkian managed to park right in front of his office and reminded them to take all their belongings before leaving the car. They followed the attorney as he opened one of the narrow double doors and then walked up the shiny wooden stairs to the second floor. His small office was decorated with old portraits, heavy canvases with pastoral subjects, and three or four marble busts. Connie and Deb sat on the two Louis XV chairs by his heavy mahogany desk while Monsieur Tilkian spread a large map in front of them. After briefly looking at it, he circled a small area with an ivory pointer.

"This is where the two plots of vines are. One hectare of prime location in total."

Connie slowly nodded. "How many acres is that?"

"Two point five. Do you have six hundred thousand dollars?" he asked, looking at Connie and Deb over his black-framed glasses.

"What? Of course not," Connie immediately replied.

The attorney took his glasses off. "Then it will have to go on the market. The domaine is worth around eighth hundred thousand American dollars—maybe nine hundred if we waited to find a buyer that would pay that much—out of which sixty percent will go to pay French inheritance tax. This is because you are not a direct heir, say, his daughter, so the rates are quite high. Then some twenty years of overdue property taxes will be deducted, which your beloved uncle failed to pay, and after all legal fees and charges are covered, what's left will be yours."

"What if I sold just the vineyard? Could I keep the house and the other buildings?"

Monsieur Tilkian put his glasses back on, pulled a calculator from a drawer, and typed some additions, percentages, and deductions. He wrote down some figures, checked some values on the property's folder, and finally said, "This is just an estimate, but if you sold the vineyard and kept the farmhouse and the other buildings, after all taxes and fees, you would end up with a modest sum, maybe twenty or thirty thousand US dollars, at best." He took his glasses off yet again. "A mixed blessing, as you say in America. What do you think?"

Connie nodded.

"I'll have the exact figures by the end of next week. If everything goes as planned, you can take possession of the farmhouse in around three months."

"Sell the vineyard to Quiqui," Connie said, rushing the words.

"Wise choice, madame. He is willing to pay a bit more than the others. And he doesn't care about the house; he already has one!"

Connie rose from her seat, turned around, and hugged Deb. Then she closed her eyes firmly and hugged her best friend harder.

By the time they left Monsieur Tilkian's office, it was five thirty. The afternoon felt warm and soft, almost tired. As they headed back to their hotel in silence, she wondered if Liddell had answered her e-mail.

Before she could check, her cell phone rang.

Connie halted and looked at the phone's screen. It wasn't a number she recognized. More so, it wasn't even an American number. *Could it be him? Just like this? Oh my God.* The phone rang one, two more times. Connie closed her eyes and took the call.

"Hello, this is Connie." Her voice trembled.

"Hello."

The sound of Liddell's voice brought him winging back to her, full throttle. She felt his hands on her body, the taste of his lips on her mouth, the scent of his skin all over her.

"I...I just saw your e-mail," he continued. "I was camping out in the woods, with no phone signal. How are you?"

Connie pressed the phone against her ear and blocked the other with her free hand. Her heart pounded, her hands and cheeks felt hot, and her knees were weak. She turned around and shifted a few steps away from Deb, who was watching her every move, a look of surprise on her face.

She leaned against the wall of an abandoned shop, opened her eyes, and took a deep breath. "I wasn't expecting your call. How... how you've been?" She smiled, like a child with a treat.

His voice deepened. "I've never stopped thinking about you. Not a single day, not a single hour, not a single moment."

"I know—me too," she confessed in a whisper.

"How long are you staying in France?"

"I'm leaving tomorrow morning. Where are you?"

"Still in Stockholm. Sigrid and I got divorced."

*Divorced.* The word felt so heavy. A single word, meaning so many things—ending, change, beginning.

"I can take a plane to Paris tonight and meet you at Charles De Gaulle. How long is your layover?"

"I won't have time. I'll only be there for a couple of hours."

"I'll go anyway. If only to see you once again, just for a few minutes."

That cliff feeling again...but this time it felt too real. She fantasized of finally leaving behind a life of loneliness and unfulfilled wishes, a life tarnished by the dream of what might have been, and embracing a life with Liddell. It would be an ideal life—a new beginning—forever close to the only man she realized she ever truly loved, and they would be happy ever after.

Blood rushed through her temples and caused a pulse to beat wildly in her throat.

"I need to think about this." Fear took over. *What am I doing?* She closed her eyes. "Okay. I will see you there."

⇥ ⇤

"Connie, wake up," Deb gently rubbed her shoulder. We're close to landing in Paris."

"Landing?" Connie cleared her throat. "Did I sleep all the way?"

"You did. You were obviously exhausted. And me too. We stayed up pretty late last night—but what a story. I mean, I'm happy that you met a man like him." Deb pulled out a pocket mirror and put on some lipstick. She pressed her lips together after she painted them. "You need a hairbrush," she said.

Connie rested her head on Deb's shoulder and closed her eyes as she recalled what had happened in the last twenty-four hours.

"You own property in Bandol. Isn't that just amazing!" Deb said. "Now you have somewhere to come to during the winter."

Connie slowly opened her eyes. The flight attendant's voice came over the speakers.

"Please fasten your seat belts; we have started our descent to Paris. It is now time to turn off all your electronic devices."

Deb puckered and expanded her lips as she retouched them with lipstick. "By the way, it's seven o'clock. That huge delay in Marseille, because of the strike, messed it all up. Now we'll have to run, or we'll miss our connection home."

Connie remained silent. Her head ached, and her ankles felt swollen. She moved away from Deb, and she let her head fall back on her headrest. Liddell had called. It had not been a dream. *I wish it had been one, though. I wish he hadn't gotten divorced. I wish he had forgotten me instead, and that all that remained of me in his life was a subtle, sweet memory. I wish I had been strong and not told him that I was coming to France. But why am I feeling anxious? Didn't I long to see him all these years?*

237

The plane touched down with a strong swerving sensation. The pilot seemed to be fighting the wind that buffeted the plane from side to side on the runway.

*I'm weak. And seeing him one more time could mean…It doesn't matter now. It's not going to happen; there's no time.*

As soon as the flight attendant opened the plane's door, Connie and Deb sprang up out of their seats. Repeating "excuse me" and "pardon me," they firmly elbowed their way out. They ran through the terminal with their purses and carry-on bags, zigzagging through the crowds until they reached the gate for their flight to Minneapolis.

The flight attendants had been holding the plane for them. Deb quickly pulled her boarding pass, and after handing it to the gate agent, she zipped onto the jet bridge. Connie stood still, a couple of yards away from the increasingly puzzled agent, who stretched her hand toward Connie's boarding pass.

"Please board the plane, ma'am. The passengers are waiting." The agent was American, with a slight southern accent.

Deb turned around and came back from the jet bridge. "Connie, come on! What's going on?"

Connie remained quiet. A deep serenity that she hadn't felt in years suffused her. She looked at her boarding pass and remembered Liddell's face. *Possibility.*

She folded the boarding pass and gently slid it in her pocket. The bewildered agent stared at her with a blank expression.

A single look between Connie and Deb was enough for them to understand each other. Deb nodded, and her lips widened into an open smile.

Connie took a deep breath and felt the fresh, light air of possibility entering her lungs. She smiled. "Come visit me in Bandol, Deb. Have a nice trip home."

Connie walked to baggage claim and waited for her bag to come up on the carrousel. The gate agent had made a few calls on her radio, and Connie's bag had not been loaded into the plane to America.

She pulled her blue bag and checked in at the Sheraton Hotel inside the airport. Once in her room, she e-mailed Liddell and waited. She tried to calm down, to relax, to lie down, but it was just not possible. *A shower will help.* She had a hot shower, and slid under the white sheets of the king-size bed. She gazed at the clock on the nightstand. *He shouldn't take long.* She closed her eyes, expectant.

Two knocks on the door pulled her out of the bed in a rush. She threw a bathrobe around her shoulders and slowly swung the door open.

There he was.

They stood still, looking at each other in silence. Liddell had not changed much, but his gaze seemed worn-out, tired. A certain sadness filled the bottom of his eyes, but as the seconds passed, his lips opened up in a shy smile, and his eyes recovered the tender serenity that Connie had always remembered. She moved to one side and signaled him to come in. Liddell mumbled awkwardly, but after the first step forward, he took her in his arms and kissed her passionately.

Connie sighed loudly, and wrapping her hands around his head, she pulled him inside the room, the door closing behind them. They kissed as they had not kissed anyone else since they parted, five years before, while a sense of timeless immediacy washed over them both.

He hurriedly undid his belt and pulled his pants down as Connie nervously unbuttoned his shirt. Then she let her bathrobe fall on the floor, and hugging him, they both lay on the bed.

In a continuous kiss that deepened more and more, they loved each other. This was it: real life, real touch, real love.

"What are you going to do with the manor house in Bandol?" Liddell asked, his fingers tickling up and down Connie's waist.

"I will move in there," she said and smiled.

"Just like that? What about your family?"

"Bryan has a scholarship, and Stacey is using a college fund that Nick and I started when she was born. They're old enough."

"Does your husband know?"

"No. But I'm not worried about it."

Liddell turned over to his side. "I couldn't move to Bandol; I have a full-time position at a major company in Stockholm now." His eyes scanned hers. "Come with me. We'll live in my apartment, by the water. It's a gorgeous place, and you can write from there; we'll finally be together and—"

Connie wrapped his face with both hands and kissed him before he could finish the sentence. She kissed him tenderly, savoring his lips and kissing his dimples.

"I'm sorry, my love. But no."

"No? Why?" Liddell looked puzzled. "Now that we can finally be together..."

"Have you ever thought that we don't really know each other? We only spent three days together—three days."

Liddell rose from the bed and held her hands. "I don't need to spend more time with you to know that I'm completely in love. This feeling is so strong—unwavering. Our time together has been magic, pure magic. Do you have any doubts?"

"I don't. Not a single one. During those three days we unknowingly became the artists of our own lives. Just like Michelangelo, Bernini, Rodin, and Monet, we captured a moment in time, the certainty of love—the most intangible truth—and carved it in our own selves. We didn't use eternal Carrara marble, large canvases, or a ton of bronze—the medium was each of our soft and still beautiful hearts. Now this work of art will stay with us forever, unstained, unmatched, forever polished, forever powerful, in the depths of ourselves."

"But why not expand on that work of art, making it a million times more beautiful? Why don't we build a life together on it? We were meant for each other; we both know it. Why keep this wonderful future together locked away?"

"It wouldn't work, Liddell. A masterpiece can't be reproduced or improved, but only the opposite. I love you immensely, and you occupy all of my thoughts and dreams, and precisely because of that, I don't want to risk tarnishing our love with everyday life. Our love became that pure and sacred thing in my life that I realized I lacked and so much needed, but it has to stay still to remain sacred. Our love has to live inside of us if we want to preserve it. At least that's the way I see it—we're not naïve teenagers anymore. We both know how this could end up if we lived together: a thought not shared, a kiss not meant, a small distance growing between us, and then…what do you think will happen?"

Liddell looked down.

Connie continued. "I was never sure of what I really wanted in life, and somehow got carried away by it. And I don't totally regret it, because it gave me three kids whom I adore, and memories that I will always treasure—watching them grow, make their own decisions, and become their own selves." She sighed.

"But after my experience with Nick and the passing of time, I realized that I prefer the ideal to the real. I consciously opt for the unchangeable truth that lies within us to the declining reality that surrounds us. I am so sorry, my love, if you imagined a life together, but I can't be anybody's woman anymore. I just can't."

Liddell kissed her hands tenderly. "I love you—deeply, immensely, beyond words."

Connie drew closer to him; their breaths became one, and their skin rubbed each other's with renewed hunger.

He sighed, with eyes closed, as tears rolled down his cheeks. Connie cried in utter fulfillment. Their hands locked firmly, and she let her body fall, and rest, on his.

# EPILOGUE

Connie pushed her straw hat back and squatted to pull the weeds from the fully bloomed cream rosebushes that dressed the stone front of the house. The handyman whom Monsieur Quiqui had recommended had just finished upgrading the electrical wiring at the house, and the plumbers had finally left the bathroom fully functional after four long months of procrastination, excuses, and snail-paced work.

The satellite Internet connection worked unbelievably well, and Connie had been submitting her articles to Brenda regularly and uninterruptedly since she'd moved in, almost a year before. Her savings and the money from the vineyard sale had paid for the repair work and left some, and her modest income was enough for her lifestyle. She didn't have to worry about wine—Quiqui gave her more cases of the new harvest wine than she could ever drink, and Gagolin's cellar could provide her with old vintages for centuries to come.

After he got the divorce letter, Nick had been looking for loopholes in the legal system to hide their assets and give her the least possible amount of money that he could, which did not surprise her.

Bryan had visited her at the beginning of the summer, and Stacey and Amanda were planning on doing the same sometime during the fall. Deb had also come once and even brought Robert along with her.

Connie heard a distant bell sound. She rose, turned around, and watched the postman getting closer. His battered old bicycle looked small under the massive line of full-leaved plane trees that lined up on the side of the dirt road leading to the house. As he got closer to her, the young man swung his mailbag forward, stopped beside her, and pulled out an envelope.

"*Bonjour, Madame,*" he greeted her and gave her the letter.

"*Merci, Alain.*"

It was a letter from Liddell, the first in a month. Sometimes they wrote more often, always longhand, and they relied on the mail service for the deliveries.

He never visited. Connie preferred it that way. Of all the people she ever knew, Liddell was the only one who could fully understand her. And he did.

She caressed the envelope while looking at the neat cursive handwriting on the front: *Constance Gagolin.* Then she plucked a cream rose, and as she walked into the house, she smelled its sweet scent. *Freedom.*

# AUTHOR BIOGRAPHY

Cyrano Cayla has always been entranced by art, literature, travel, and wine. After two decades of experiences in those fields, he has combined these interests in his first novel, which is also a reflection of the close relationship between the aesthetics and our emotions.

In addition to the works of the great painters and sculptors of all ages, an extensive collection of literature that runs across different eras and countries serve as inspiration for Cayla.

He lives in Cleveland, Ohio.

To find out more, please visit:

www.cyranocayla.com

Made in the USA
Charleston, SC
11 March 2017